KILLING
TIME

By Marcus Dalrymple

Marcus Dalrymple was born in Buenos Aires, Argentina in 1966. He was educated in Mexico and at boarding school in England. Marcus trained as a journalist before moving into teaching. '**Viva Mexico!** – a year in the Sierra Madre,' was published in December 2011. '**Killing Time!**' is his first venture into fiction.

KILLING TIME

Black Cat Publications

bCb

Originally published in Great Britain by Black Cat Books an imprint of Black Cat Publications

Copyright © Marcus Dalrymple 2012

ISBN-10: 1477428534

EAN-13: 9781477428535

Front Cover design: Copyright © Marcus Dalrymple 2012 – The Road to Oaxaca

Black Cat Publications

**Printed and bound in the U.S.A
By Create Space**

Although the events and the characters in this novel are all fictitious, they are based on real incidents in recent Mexican history, where abductions, murder, casual (and gratuitous) cruelties, drug and human trafficking are endemic in some parts of the country.

CONTENTS

CHAPTER 1

*In 2003, 402 individuals were kidnapped in Mexico.
268 of them never returned home.*

✝

A fly buzzed around the room and then came to an abrupt halt on the whitewashed wall. The room was small and cramped with a rusty fan revolving dissolutely from its housing in the ceiling. There was a single, dirty green mattress on the terracotta tiled floor and an old table with a broken drawer and a simple wooden chair. Through the shuttered, half open window wafted the stench of carrion from the still, silent swamp. He heard a dog barking in the distance and a donkey braying in a neighbour's yard and then all was quiet. He watched the fly; the tiny movements of its legs - and then it was airborne again, flying frantically.

The day had begun with a walk from his hotel to the local supermarket to buy a bottle of water and some fruit. The Hotel *Paraiso* was a dingy *pension* in the centre of town with 10 rooms and communal showers but it was cheap and a stone's throw away from the beach. The owner was an unsmiling man called

Alberto. He was in his early fifties with a dark, scarred face and a week's black stubble on his chin. He wore a grubby vest, tucked into tight denims and suede cowboy boots with steel toe caps and he sat all day in the hotel's dimly lit lobby watching television, a thin stick of sugar cane in the corner of his mouth. Occasionally he would look up to shout obscenities at his two obese teenage sons who lay indolently in hammocks out on the cracked patio. His wife, *Concepcion* was a tragic looking woman who rarely spoke. She had been pretty once; with the high cheek bones of an *indigena*, but her split lips, broken teeth and permanent black eye, bore witness to 16 violent years spent living with *Alberto.*

He had been an easy target – a conspicuous *gringo*: slim and blonde with money to spend on a foreign holiday. Not many *guerros* came to *Puerto Sal*, preferring the livelier, more bustling resorts of *Puerto Escondido* and *Huatulco* further up the coast. In contrast, *Puerto Sal* was a quiet fishing village with two *casas de huespedes*, a shabby *cantina* and general store.

The *gringo*, dressed in a Chumbawumba concert T-shirt, shorts and flip-flops, had just paid for a bottle of water and a bag of oranges when they came for him. A shiny, black Chevrolet Suburban with tinted windows, looking incongruously new and clean on the streets of *Puerto Sal*, pulled up on the pavement alongside him as he turned towards the hotel. Two men holding sawn-off-shotguns stepped out in front and behind blocking his path and gestured to him to get into the vehicle. They both wore black vests, (their dark biceps covered in gang tattoos) black jeans and snake-skin boots and expensive, aviator sun glasses. One of them had what looked like a huge burn mark on the side of his face. He had a goatee beard and a sweaty bald head and was about six foot three inches tall. The other was smaller and stocky and wore a black bandana tied around his head and a wispy moustache. The young *gringo* noticed a prominent gold tooth in the front of his mouth. Neither spoke. The *gringo*'s eyes darted from right to left and then he instinctively dropped his bag of shopping and tried running around the hood of the car and across the street but his way was blocked by a third man who opened the passenger door and waving a nickel plated revolver in his face, said in English, 'We don't want to hurt you *amigo*, just get in the car.' He was smaller than the other two goons and dressed like a business man.

Bundled into the back, he was hooded with a rough piece of sackcloth before being pushed down onto the floor of the vehicle. He felt the heel of a boot come to rest on his shoulder and another just above his knee cap but paralysed by shock, his mind went blank and he could think of nothing but the words of a UB40 song, that his mother particularly liked, playing over and over in his mind like a stuck record: 'Red, red wine..' it went.

'*Vamonos cabron!*' he heard the suited man shout from the front of the car and then, '*Apurate!*' and he felt the car swerving away from the curb, the screeching of tyres and smelt burning rubber. 'Red, red wine, stay close to me,' played on as he subconsciously tried blocking everything else out, as if negating the terrifying ordeal would somehow make it go away.

The fly was buzzing in the room again, though he couldn't work out where. The thick air stank of stagnant water and rotting rubbish and for the first time he noticed his bedding. The green mattress was filthy. There were old urine stains all over it and it smelt of sweat and alcohol. A coarse, brown blanket was folded at the foot of the bed and the striped pillow that his head had been resting on, was covered in saliva watermarks that he knew were not his own. He looked up at the badly painted pale, blue ceiling and noticed the fan again, revolving slowly, circulating the humid air.

Moments later, the wooden door opened on rusty, squeaky hinges and two men entered unceremoniously. The first was young; no more than a boy, clad in scruffy jeans and a short-sleeved white shirt and straw hat. He was dark, with the beginnings of an adolescent's moustache. His eyes were black and deep-set, his mouth unsmiling. He was holding a shotgun in both hands and pointing it into the room. The second was the man who had waved the pistol at him earlier in the day. He introduced himself as *Cesar*. The *gringo* recalled his crumpled, brown suit and white shirt, and his shiny black hair combed to the side in a parting. He took the chair from underneath the table, swivelled it around and sat down to face the *gringo*. He was chewing bubble-gum.

'I have come to apologise,' he said, smiling. 'I hope you were not hurt when we came to pick you up this morning. Some of my men are stupid imbeciles with no culture,' he said continuing in English with a thick Mexican accent. 'Believe me when I tell you that you will be well looked after. We have nothing against you personally; but you must try to understand that you are useful to our cause.' He removed the piece of gum from his mouth and stuck it under the table before taking a crushed packet of Marlboro's and a silver lighter from his shirt pocket. He put a cigarette in his mouth, flicked open the lighter and lit up and after inhaling deeply, blew the smoke out in silver circles into the centre of the room. 'When we get what we want,' he resumed, 'you can go back to your family.'

James had not spoken a word to anyone in almost six hours. A doctor would probably have said he was suffering from mild catatonic shock. He was

22 years old and after graduating from university had been travelling with a friend through the southern states of the U.S. He had always wanted to cross the *Rio Grande* and see Mexico and when his friend Toby, had returned home urgently to attend to some family business, James had jumped on a greyhound bus in *San Antonio*, Texas and headed for the border. He spent a night in a cheap hostel in *Ciudad Juarez* to the sound of *Mariachi* music and then headed south by bus exploring *San Miguel Allende, Guanajuato* and *Morelia* before moving on to Mexico City where he spent a few days in the faded grandeur of the Hotel Montecarlo, in *Calle Uruguay*, near the city's central square. From his guidebook, he learnt that the 19th century German explorer Humboldt had once resided there and that D.H. Lawrence had stayed in the hotel less than half a century before. His room overlooked the street. It was plainly decorated and clean and the bedding was cool and crisp and he soon discovered that the city had more than its fair share of delights. In spite of its choking smog and heaving, chaotic traffic, he found it a vital, vibrant place throbbing with pace and life. There was nothing sterile or tidy about the Federal District. It sprawled for miles towards a rim of snow-capped volcanoes, one of which, *Popocatepetl* smoked majestically on the horizon. He travelled everywhere by bus, joining commuters in the morning as they set out to work, sharing cramped spaces with

people carrying bags of fruit and vegetables, pirate CD's and DVD's and on one – some live chickens. These mini buses drove at breakneck speeds, often with their concertina doors still wide open, dodging in and out of the traffic like vehicles in an episode of 'Whacky Races.' He spent a morning out at *Teotihuacan* visiting the pyramids of the Sun and Moon and walked around the city's anthropological museum. He idled through leafy *Coyoacan* and being a student of art, made the obligatory pilgrimage to Frida Kahlo's house where peacocks wandered about the gardens and the blue walls were festooned with self-obsessed portraits of (arguably) Mexico's most celebrated modern artist. He spent a day on the capital's network of green canals at *Xochimilco* and wandered around markets thronging with stalls selling rugs, bark paintings, colourful glassware and leather goods where he bought a couple of friendship bracelets and an embroidered wall hanging for his mother. Returning to his hotel room one evening, exhausted but full of hunger to see more of the country, he resolved to stay on. He sensed there was something surreal, almost fantastical about Mexico, with its mixture of sights and sounds, smells and tastes and its clash of cultures; new and old, rich and poor. Now into his third week in Mexico he decided to journey further south over the *Sierra Madre Occidental* to the indigenous capital of the country – *Oaxaca*. It was June 30th 2003, he had recently left

7

college with a first class degree and he had the rest of his life to look forward to.

Less than a month before, James had completed his fourth and final year at St Andrews University. He was a softly spoken young man, popular among the other students in his department and with the members of the water-polo club, an alternative sport which he played with a passion. But his gentle sensibilities belied some very tough genes. Major Alexander Cooper-Brown, his great grandfather, was one of only a few soldiers serving with the Royal Engineers to have survived the Battle of the Somme. He had been awarded the Victoria Cross for diffusing an unexploded shell which saved the lives of many in his platoon only to have both his legs blown off by a grenade as he retreated to his trench. James' grandfather, Colonel Crispin Cooper-Brown, had fought with Montgomery's Eighth Army in the deserts of North Africa during The Second World War, and he too was a highly decorated soldier having been awarded the Distinguished Service Order for single handedly taking out a German machine gun post on the approach to El Alamein. And then there was Lieutenant Colonel Piers Cooper-Brown, James' father, who had fought at Goose Green during the Falklands War with the Parachute Regiment and later, with the Special Air Service in Kuwait during the First Gulf War under General Peter de-la-Billierre. James however, had no desire to enter the armed forces. He had inherited his mother's gentle manners and artistic bent. Virginia Cooper-Brown was from an established Devonshire family and had been brought up on a farm on the edge of Dartmoor. She was a theatre critic and divided her time between London (where the Cooper-Brown's had a small flat in Chelsea) and the family home in Mosscombe, just outside Lambourn in Berkshire. James was proud of his family's military past, but was honest enough to recognise that he didn't possess the inclination or the courage to follow in his father's footsteps, a decision that had disappointed his old man.

During his final week at university he had split up with his girlfriend Charlotte, with whom he had been together since their days in the sixth form at Wellington College. She had met a handsome rugby and cricket blue called Julian at a summer ball she had attended with James and a week later had dumped him. Her sudden rejection of him and her very public desertion had hurt James deeply. She had been his one and only girlfriend, and his decision, to join his best friend Toby, on a driving tour of the southern states of America, was partly fuelled by a desire to get over Charlotte. It had seemed like the perfect antidote for a bruised ego and a broken heart. They rented a car in Raleigh, North Carolina and visited Nashville,

Graceland, Memphis and Charleston and ended up in 'The Big Easy' – New Orleans, where they took a riverboat tour of the Mississippi on an old steamer called The Jefferson Davis and tried to fit in by drinking Southern Comfort and attending jazz sessions. James enjoyed the slow pace of life in the south and took numerous photographs of the antebellum architecture and the once grand, former cotton plantations of the Confederate States. And then out of the blue, Toby received an email recalling him home.

0057 DAYS

CHAPTER 2

218 bodies were discovered in a mass grave outside
Guadalajara.
All victims had been murdered in
drug related crime.

✝

In the evening *Cesar* and the dark youth returned. The air was thick with mosquitoes and the pink rays of dusk shone through the shuttered slats in shards of delicate light.

'I hope you have been treated well?' asked *Cesar*. '*Manolito* here,' he said turning to the dark youth, 'tells me you ate a *sopa de fideo* and some *tortillas* and that you have had a *café de olla*. This is good,' he said. 'It is important for everyone that you remain fit and healthy. Now we would like you to do something for us.' He produced a thin, black digital camera from a shoulder bag and then from his inside jacket pocket, removed a piece of folded typed foolscap. 'We would like to video you whilst you read out this statement,' he said unfolding the piece of paper and handing it to James. 'First, please read it over to yourself. When you feel ready we will start. This is the first stage of getting what we need; and hopefully for you, the beginning of your journey home.'

*J*avier Ernesto Madrigal, was born in 1952 in the *barrio* of *San Francisco, Oaxaca*. In the context of Latin America, the story of his childhood and adolescent years was not an unfamiliar one. The son of a *Zapotec* fruit seller, who peddled watermelons from a decrepit trolley on the city's streets, he started life with every disadvantage. Small and slight in stature, with a harelip, he was one of five brothers and three sisters. His mother had died in childbirth in a filthy hovel at the age of 26 when *Javier* was only five years old. Bullied and teased at the local school due to his hideous deformity and tardiness to speak, he had learned early that life owed him no favours. His eldest brother *Leon,* had left *Oaxaca* for the big lights of Mexico City when *Javier* was 13, leaving the young *Madrigal* and his drunken father as the only breadwinners. Mexico in the early 1960's, was enjoying its first tourist boom, with young Americans flocking across the border to experience the delights of its unspoilt beaches and the charms of its colourful, colonial towns and cities. Property was cheap and marijuana was easily available to a whole new generation of hippies eager for an endless summer of love. Thieves and pickpockets soon discovered that there were rich pickings to be had among the naïve and unsuspecting *gringos* that now thronged the streets, squares and pre-Hispanic monuments of the state of *Oaxaca*. *Madrigal* quickly learned that crime was much more lucrative than either begging or selling slices of watermelon and it wasn't long before he had gained an unrivalled reputation as the most astute and nimble fingered *delincuente* of them all. From the outset, driven by poverty, insecurity and an almost atavistic will to survive, he was utterly ruthless. On hearing (aged 12) that a rival gang had taken over his patch during *La fiesta de los muertos,* popular with foreign tourists and therefore fertile ground for young thieves, he sought out the gang's leader, a violent adolescent named *Chico* who was then aged 15, and stabbed him to death with a kitchen knife, in an alley off the main *Zocalo*. He soon learned that in order to make a name for himself in the squalid shanties and *barrios* of the city, his actions had to be unequivocal. Defending oneself could never be enough. He had to root out all opposition without fear of retribution.

B y the age of 15, *Madrigal*, who was now known to both his associates and enemies alike as E*l Alacran* – 'The Scorpion,' had moved on from pick pocketing and mugging to selling marijuana and narcotics to westerners and wealthy middle class Mexicans. It was 1967 and business was good south of the border. Less than 10 years later, *El Alacran* enjoyed a complete monopoly of the southern Mexican marijuana trade and was beginning to corner the market in Columbian cocaine coming through Central America via Panama and across the Guatemalan border. *Madrigal* became notorious. He punished those who betrayed him with breath-taking brutality. He knew that fear was a potent tool and he instilled it without impunity. If someone let him down, decided to go with a rival supplier or tried to muscle in on his market, his assassins not only killed the perpetrator but wiped out his family too and threatened his friends and community. But he was also a philanthropist and his acts of charity won him admiration and support, especially in his heartland, the poor *barrios* where he had grown up. He became an advocate for the dispossessed, the homeless and unemployed who loved and adored him with the affection usually devoted to saints. He was to many a saviour, funding the building of schools, medical centres and work co-operatives for women and by the mid 1980's the CIA (based in their headquarters in Langley Virginia) were beginning to take note of his activities with increasing alarm. He wasn't quite *Pablo Escobar* yet; but he and his powerful cartel were a hornet's nest on their southern border that they could do without. Analysts were predicting that within 10 years, the Columbian problem (as they termed it) would be eclipsed by a far more dangerous one: a Mexican issue right on their doorstep.

James was asked to sit on the chair and face the camera which *Cesar* held steadily in his hands. The message he had been handed was typed on one side of the paper. He recognised the font and point size: Times New Roman, type size 10, single line spacing. In the dim light, it was almost too small to read.

'It is important that you read it slowly and carefully,' advised *Cesar*. 'The sooner this video is broadcast, the sooner you will be set free. We must try to work together on this. You understand?' James did not respond.

'My name is James Cooper-Brown. I am English. I am being held by members of the *Madrigal* Cartel in retaliation for joint U.S. and European action against the innocent people of Mexico, but particularly the poor and dispossessed *campesinos* of *Oaxaca*, *Chiapas* and *Tabasco* states, who have been robbed of land and rights by western imperialist countries acting through international corporations. These agents have stripped the land of its forests and enslaved its people. They have taken the natural resources and drained the oil wells, leaving the *indigenas* of Mexico in abject poverty. Now they have had enough. The *Madrigal* Cartel will use any and all weapons at its disposal to fight against these new imperialist forces, even selling weapons to their enemies and kidnapping their sons and daughters.

The cartel is asking for $5,000,000 in return for my freedom. This ransom must be paid in full within one month of this broadcast. Failure to comply with these demands will result in my execution.

I am being treated well. The *Madrigal*'s fight is not against me personally but against the governments of George Bush and his ally Tony Blair.'

'Thank you James,' said *Cesar* smiling. 'Think of this as the start of your journey to freedom,' and he and *Manolito* left the room.

James felt suddenly exhausted. He pushed the chair aside and collapsed onto the filthy mattress and buried his head in the stinking pillow and wept uncontrollably, his whole body shaking as the gravity of his situation dawned on him for the first time.

An hour later, *Cesar* returned. This time he was alone.

'CNN should receive the video by morning.'

By now James had composed himself. He was determined that none of his captors would see him in an emotional state. He sat up, leaning on one elbow and for the first time in over 36 hours, he addressed *Cesar*.

'You might as well kill me now. The British government will never pay a ransom. It's their policy not to negotiate or make deals with drug traffickers or terrorists, and contrary to any information you might have gathered, my family would never be able to raise five million dollars.'

Cesar walked over to him and patted him on the shoulder: 'Time will tell my friend, time will tell. We all agree that family is the most important thing in the world. If your family love you James, they will find a way to pay,' and he turned and left the room, locking the door behind him.

It was only then that he really noticed the window. All this time it had been there, open. He got up and pushed the shutters back. The evening light flooded into the room in a wave of pink that washed over the dirty cell and into the corners. Below the window, the ground gave way to a steep *barranco* falling 50 feet into a muddy brown river. On the opposite banks he could see banana trees and fields of maize and sugar cane. The house, it seemed, stood alone. He could vaguely make out the tiled roof of another building with a satellite dish, to the west, about a mile away but apart from that, he couldn't see any road or village. He leant out of the window as far as he could and looked up. A further two or three metres of brown adobe wall rose to some plastic guttering and above, he glimpsed the edge of the roof which was lined with bits of broken glass and barbed wire . He looked down again, at the murky waters of the river as they meandered by. If he was ever going to escape; that was the way out. He half closed the shutters again, repelled by the wafts of stagnant air coming off the river and sat at the small table. That's when the thought occurred to him: how did *Cesar* know his name? It wasn't as if he were famous or well known. Since arriving in *Puerto Sal* less than 48 hours before, he had barely spoken to anyone. He had bought a coconut on the beach from some fishermen and a few provisions at the small supermarket but on neither occasion had he introduced himself or had to produce his passport. *Cesar* could only have got his name from the miserable owner of the Hotel *Paraiso*. The night he had checked in, he had written his name and passport number in the hotel's tatty register. Had *Cesar* and his gangsters put pressure on the hotel's owner to reveal his details? Or maybe the grubby little man in the dirty white vest had been in on the kidnapping from the beginning?

He felt lonely again and full of loathing and self-pity. Why hadn't he returned home to the U.K with Toby? Or left Mexico City after his sight-seeing trip? He thought about Charlotte again and pictured her making love to that bastard Julian. Feelings of homesickness that he had not felt since his first days at prep school aged eight, swept over him. He desperately wanted his parents to know about his predicament. He wanted them to do something about it; to get him out. Like a small boy running to his mother with a grazed knee and wanting a plaster and a kiss, he needed someone else to take him away from this hell hole. He thought of his great grandfather, his grandfather and his own father:

all those brave Cooper-Browns stretching back through the generations. How would they have reacted? He suddenly felt ashamed. He recalled watching his father observing him as a small boy and had wanted to know what this grave, often unsmiling man had been thinking. Was he disappointed that his boy was not made of sterner stuff? He had not been a natural team player at school, preferring swimming and rock climbing. He avoided fights and confrontation and hated rugby until he and others realised how fast he could run and he was stuck out on the wing where the occasional ball came his way and without any effort he would score a try. He knew that being picked for the Wellington First XV had made his father proud. He remembered the way the old man had smiled when he had seen the team list at the beginning of the Michaelmas term in the school's undercroft. And there was his name: James Cooper-Brown: left wing. But James had been much happier with his artistic achievements; the theatre sets he'd help make, his pen and ink drawings of the college on display on exhibition day, and his role as Banquo in the school's production of 'Macbeth,' which had been widely praised.

Virginia Cooper-Brown had been regarded as something of a beauty in her student days at London's King's College and had often been compared to the actress Julie Christie. Even at 48, she was still a lovely woman. She had shoulder length ash blonde hair, high cheek bones and deep green eyes. She had never worn makeup and only now, thin lines had begun to appear at the corners of her brilliant eyes and around her delicate mouth. In her youth she had shunned the balls and parties that many of her contemporaries attended and had even turned down an invitation to model for one of the capital's top agencies, preferring the quiet company of her close friends and family. A student of literature, she was an ardent theatre goer, spending almost all her allowance on trips to the West End and some of the more experimental theatres in Islington and Hackney. During the holidays she returned to the family home on Dartmoor where she pursued her passion for riding; rising early, saddling one of the farm's horses and setting out into the cold, iron grey dawn. She loved these silent times, when only the curlews' shrill calls could be heard high above and windhovers darted between desolate trees and her horse's breath hung like tortured statues in the brisk chilly air.

She met Piers Cooper-Brown in 1978 when she was 21. He was engaged to an old school friend of hers called Amanda Briggs (the daughter of a baronet) and one May evening the three had met for drinks at Harvey's on Sloane Street. Piers was at Sandhurst at the time, with the prospect of a commission in the Parachute Regiment and was four years her senior. Many years later, Virginia had confessed to James and his younger sister Eleanor, that it had been 'love at first sight,' but worried that the acrimonious falling out with Amanda, that her affair with Piers had inevitably caused, would later come back to haunt her. Her parents disapproved of the relationship, not because they disliked Piers, but because they felt that life as the wife of an ambitious army officer would be a lonely one. Shortly after this first meeting, Piers broke off his engagement to Amanda and began seeing Virginia regularly. The rift with his former fiancée caused a minor society scandal with Piers being labelled as a 'rake' and Virginia 'a hussy' by a columnist for the Tatler. 'All that's wrong and odious about modern youth,' was how the couple had been described. Ten months later, however, they were married at Kensington's registry office. There were no guests or family present, just Piers' closest friend, Matthew, who had also been at Sandhurst, and Virginia's older sister, Lucy. They spent their honeymoon touring the Western Isles of Scotland in Piers' Triumph Herald and leaving the car on Mull, had ended up on Iona for a week, before Piers was recalled to his regiment and the first of two tours to Northern Ireland.

0056 DAYS

CHAPTER 3

20,000 weapons belonging to drug cartels were recently seized by the Mexican authorities.
87% of them were smuggled in from the U.S

After two days, a routine was established. At seven o'clock, James, was woken up   with a *café de olla* and plate of scrambled eggs mixed with onion, tomatoes and chilli: *huevos a la Mexicana, Manolito* called it. It was not an unpleasant meal, but as the days passed, James looked forward to the ritual less and less. At half past seven, the door was unlocked and after putting a hood on, he would be taken to the bathroom down the corridor. It was squalid and dirty and the first time he had needed to use it, he almost vomited at the smell that greeted him as he closed the door. The basin and toilet had not been cleaned in months and the latter was stained with faeces. There was no toilet roll and the tiled floor and stained mirror were cracked. After that James insisted on cleaning it himself. He requested a cloth and spent his 15 minute shower time scrubbing the place down. *Manolito* provided him with a small towel, new toothbrush and toothpaste and after showering in tepid brown water, James would put on the same set of clothes: the T-shirt, faded shorts and flip-flops and knock on the door to be released. This routine was repeated at half past seven in the evening though at night time he was only allowed 10 minutes to wash. He was never alone, at least not for the first three weeks of his captivity. There was a guards' rota. *Manolito* would be on for a week followed by two other young men, one called *Pepe*, the other *Carlos*. They too were locked in the room with James like captives themselves and would have to radio out if they needed to relieve themselves or when their duty ended. These young men were always armed with either a shotgun or an ancient looking Russian made AK47 which they would leave nonchalantly leaning against the door. To begin with none of the guards spoke to James. They would sit, flipping through car, gun and pornographic magazines of various kinds, dozing, listening to music through headphones (wired into old Sony Walkman's) or texting furiously. James meanwhile, would lie for hours on the faded green mattress, his face to the wall, sweating in the humid, airless room, his mind wrapped up in thoughts of regret, Charlotte, his days at university and home. Images played through his head like a slide show over which he had no control. He tried to blot some memories out, fearing that they would eventually drive him mad but even this he was unable to do. From being an independent young man with dreams and ambitions he had lost everything – even control over his own thoughts, feelings and emotions.

Virginia Cooper-Brown was gardening when the local police knocked on the door. The Cooper-Browns lived in a converted tythe barn with two acres of land. She loved spending time in her garden. To her it was the antithesis of how she spent the rest of her week: frantically trying to meet various editors' deadlines for the different publications she wrote for, and rushing about London from one theatre production to another. She loved her work, but the four days she spent up in Berkshire often felt like a haven in a storm. Now with both children away from home (James recently graduated from university and Eleanor, away at boarding school) the house had been quiet for months. The Cooper-Browns had often thought of downsizing, and buying something smaller in Newbury or Henley, but had never got around to it. It was five o'clock on a hazy summer's afternoon and the scent of mint wafted across the immaculately mown lawns and rhododendron bushes. Piers was still at work. He owned a small security firm called Risk Factor which he ran with Matthew Waterman, his closest school friend and a former fellow officer with the Parachute Regiment. They had both passed the arduous selection process for the SAS and been stationed at Hereford together for several weeks. The company offered close personal protection to VIP's and celebrities and businessmen travelling to volatile regions of the world and advised NGO's on how best to protect vulnerable personnel working in far flung places like Kabul and Mogadishu. Piers and Matthew (who held a 25% stake in the company) managed the business from their small Lambourn office, leaving the leg work for younger employees recently out of the armed forces and hitting civi-street for the first time. Nonetheless, the two remained in peak physical form. Both now aged 52, they entered adventure races together competing with men often half their ages, ran marathons and enjoyed weekends away climbing in Snowdonia (and when time allowed) Skye's remote and rugged Cuillins. They also regularly practised their shooting skills at an army range in Warminster and were still expert marksmen. Although the firm was small in comparison to some of the larger multi-national corporations, they enjoyed an unrivalled reputation for never having lost a client in the field and for recruiting the very best former Special Forces operatives. Piers and Matthew spent a lot of time travelling to international conferences and trade shows which suited the Cooper-Brown's somewhat unconventional marriage. Piers and Virginia were fiercely independent individuals who loved their respective, chosen careers and their arrangements, in between raising a family, had had no adverse effects on their relationship over the years. Virginia often told her closest friends that spending time away from Piers made their time together more intimate and valuable. They never took each other for granted. Whilst all around her it seemed, their mutual friends and acquaintances were getting divorced or separated, the Cooper-Browns remained blissfully married. They were a fine example of a romantic, middle aged couple growing gracefully older together.

Virginia dropped her pruning shears on the grass and her gardening gloves in a bucket and walked around the garden to the side gate where she found a police constable and a young woman on the door step.

'Mrs Cooper-Brown?' asked the tall constable. He had a mild Geordie accent.

'Yes,' she replied. 'Is something wrong?'

'I wonder if we could come in for a moment?' said the pretty, dark haired woman. 'I am afraid we have got some bad news.'

'Is it Piers?' asked Virginia, alarm beginning to register in her voice. 'Has he had a fall or something?'

'May we come inside?' repeated the young woman.

'Yes of course, I do apologise.'

They walked back through the side gate and into the sitting room through the open French windows where Virginia invited them to sit down on the floral patterned three piece suite.

'I'm PC Brian Sanderson, Madam, and this is Jacky Moss, the family liaison officer. It's your son James; he's been kidnapped in Mexico.'

'Kidnapped? Mexico?' Virginia replied incredously. 'But he's in the States; we are expecting him home any day now!'

'The Foreign and Commonwealth Office received a video through its embassy in Mexico from CNN late yesterday purporting to be from a group known as the *Madrigal* Cartel. They claim to have kidnapped James.'

Virginia sat back on the sofa, and wrung her hands together and looked down at the carpet; her face was pale with shock.

'I am sorry,' she said, 'I should have offered you both a cup of tea.'

'This is going to be painful for you madam, but we would like to ask you to confirm that the young man addressing the camera in the video is indeed your son. Is Mr Cooper-Brown not around?' he said handing her the small laptop.

'No,' she answered, regaining her composure, 'but he should be here any minute now.'

PC Sanderson clicked on the play button of the computer's media player and almost at once James came into view, sitting on a wooden chair. He was dressed in a dirty T-shirt and shorts. His blonde hair was matted, there were dark semi circles under his eyes and he looked drained and exhausted. He was holding a piece of paper. There was silence for a moment and then he looked up at the camera and began to read the statement before him. Virginia stifled a cry, but the tears had already begun to gather in the corners of her green eyes. She watched the two minute clip which ended when the screen went black and placed the laptop back on the coffee table.

'Why don't I put the kettle on?' offered Jacky, getting up and walking towards the kitchen.

'Thank you,' replied Virginia, 'that would be very kind. The tea is in a tin above the sink.'

'I am afraid there's more bad news,' continued Brian Sanderson. 'The group are asking for a ransom of $5 million and the release of various members of the cartel, extradited to the U.S. last year, in exchange for James' freedom.'

There was the crunch of a heavy vehicle driving on gravel and moments later the sound of a car door closing and then they heard the front door opening.

'Ginny?' called the voice of a man from the hall. 'What the devil are the police doing here? It's not that damn business of the hedge again I hope?'

A middle aged man dressed smartly in a crisp white shirt, dark grey trousers and a pale blue silk tie entered the room carrying a briefcase in one hand and his suit jacket in the other. He was about five feet eight inches tall and dark with flashes of grey hair above his ears. He was tanned and clean shaven with light green eyes and heavy eyebrows. He was handsome, in a rugged way with a livid scar above his right eye.

Virginia, stood up and walked over to her husband and hugging him tightly she began to sob.

'James has been kidnapped in Mexico,'

Jacky appeared from the kitchen carrying a tray with a pot of tea, three mugs, a bowl of sugar and a small jug of milk.

Virginia let go of Piers and slumped back onto the sofa dabbing her moist eyes with a white handkerchief she'd taken from her blouse sleeve.

'Sir, can I get you a cup of tea?' Jacky asked the man who had just entered the house. She presumed he was Virginia's husband.

Piers put his briefcase down next to the sofa and dropped his jacket over the side of an armchair and sat down. 'Thank you,' he replied. 'That would be very nice.'

PC Sanderson stood up and introduced himself.

'Yes, it would appear that your son has been kid-napped somewhere in Southern Mexico. The Mexican police are still not sure whether he was specifically targeted or whether his kidnapping was random and opportunistic. All they have at the moment is this video footage taken of James sometime in the last 48 hours which was then sent to CNN's offices in Mexico City. They are asking for a ransom of $5 million.'

Piers suddenly looked drained of colour. He leant forward in his chair and clasped his hands together.

For a man who had faced death on many occasions during his distinguished army career, he looked crushed and diminished by the shocking news. Jacky placed a mug of tea on the coffee table in front of him, and he looked briefly up to thank her.

'We are terribly sorry that this has happened to you and your family, but it looks like we will be into a bit of a waiting game until we hear again from the *Madrigal* Cartel. You will be contacted early tomorrow morning by a representative from the Foreign Office. We will pop around again in the afternoon. There are one or two questions we would like to ask about James in general, if that's all right?'

'Do you have any other children?' asked Jacky rising from the sofa.

'Yes,' replied Virginia. 'James has a younger sister, Eleanor. She's away at school and has just finished her A-levels. I fear she is going to take this news very badly.'

0055 DAYS

CHAPTER 4

Mexican drug trafficking organizations were estimated to generate between $1 billion and $2 billion annually from exporting marijuana to the U.S in 2003.

✟

On the fifth evening of his captivity, the two thugs who had kidnapped him outside the supermarket in *Puerto Sal* opened the door to his room, and the larger of the two, with the burn on the side of his face, gestured with his finger for James to get up and follow him. Both wore sunglasses, even though night was approaching. James wondered if there was guilt or shame behind these masks. He had read somewhere that the eyes were the portals to the soul. Or perhaps there was nothing, just the dark look of men used to killing.

'We are taking you to another place,' he said in English. 'A safer place for everyone.'

In the dying light of day, the scar on his face looked like melted wax; it was ribbed and shiny and raised; almost reptilian.

The second thug stood outside in the dimly lit corridor. He was wearing the same clothes and he reeked of *mescal*. James noticed his gold tooth again as he smiled menacingly.

He threw James a black hood. 'Put this on!' he barked.

James' hands were shackled roughly behind his back with thin plastic ties that dug into his wrists and he was pushed down the corridor. Deprived of sight and without his hands to feel his way, he stumbled forward. He heard a door opening ahead and the banging of a fly screen and then the two men guided him down some steps onto gravelly ground. The river's stench filled his nostrils. The air felt clammy; as if it was about to rain and he could hear frogs croaking in the long grass by the water's edge. He was bundled into the back of a car. He couldn't figure out if it was the Suburban though it smelt the same: the leather seats, the odour of cheap air freshener mixed with the men's sweaty bodies. Again he was thrust down onto the floor of the car before he heard the doors closing and moments later the sound of wheels crunching over rocky ground. He felt claustrophobic with panic rising up from his stomach. He tried to move his head to one side to breathe easier. The car sped off bumping up and down on the uneven surface of what James surmised was a track. It dipped in and out of pot holes and then skidded out onto a black topped highway where the vehicle picked up speed and the ride became instantly smoother. He felt sick and took deliberate deep breaths to prevent the panic from constricting his airway further. He was terrified that if he vomited he would choke. He wondered if indeed they were taking him to another safe house or whether the two goons had been brought in to kill him and dump his body somewhere. He could hear muffled conversation and then someone turned on the radio and jacked up the volume and the car vibrated and throbbed with the sound of *ranchero* music. He tried breathing evenly until the panic and nausea eased before edging himself into a more comfortable position.

For more than an hour they headed higher into the mountains. James could feel the car twisting and turning into tight hair pin bends as the driver changed up and down the gears. There was the hot smell of diesel and then as they rose steadily higher he could feel cool air coming through the car's windows and the scent of pine woods. He knew they must be driving inland, away from the coast and into the *Sierra Madre Occidental* - perhaps closer to *Oaxaca*, but certainly somewhere remote. After a further 30 minutes the car slowed and the road became rutted and bumpy again. His body was slammed against the bottom of the vehicle as it negotiated huge bumps and ditches in the track. They drove on for another hour before they finally stopped. He heard the car door opening and then he was lifted out and once again guided across a patch of muddy wet ground to some steps. A door creaked and he felt a smooth floor beneath his flip-flopped feet and heard another door opening before he was thrust forward into a room where his hood was removed.

This new cell was pink and windowless, with a single light bulb hanging from the ceiling on a twisted black cable. There was a wooden bed in the corner made up with pale green sheets but they looked clean and the pillow was covered. He had never seen pink quite like it. It wasn't what he would have called 'girly pink' – there was in fact nothing feminine about it. It was a deep, vibrant colour that pulsated with life and vigour and as he took it in he wondered if he would be able to relax in such intense surroundings. Maybe the choice of décor had been deliberate: a subtle way to break him down further. There was no other furniture in the room but despite the absence of a window or even a fan for that matter, it felt surprisingly cool. Perhaps it had no external walls for the hot Mexican sun to bake or adobe to absorb the sapping humidity of the tropical nights. James flicked off his flip-flops and sat on the bed. Moments later, the door opened and *Manolito* came in, the AK47 in his hand. It was three o'clock in the morning. Without a word, *Manolito*, sat down with his back to the wall, dropped his straw hat over his sunglasses and nose and promptly fell asleep. James waited for five minutes before turning off the light. He felt utterly drained but unable to sleep after the day's events which had left him tense, worrying about his uncertain future. He took off his shorts and

T-shirt and with only his boxers on, lay on his back on the soft springy bed. He could hear *Manolito* snoring. He heard a mosquito droning and footsteps moving about the house on creaking floorboards.

When he awoke it was seven o'clock in the morning and the light was on. *Manolito* had gone and in his stead, *Pepe* sat in the corner, his eyes closed, a pair of headphones in his ears, his lips mouthing the words of a song.

'Good morning,' James said sleepily. *Pepe* opened his eyes and smiled for the first time.

'I was about to wake you up for breakfast,' he said grinning. These were the first words James had heard him utter. He was thin and effeminate with almond shaped eyes, shoulder length shiny black hair and smooth olive skin. He wore orange Lycra shorts, a pair of open sandals and a baggy white, sleeve-less T-shirt and his slim arms were encircled with numerous bracelets. Piled next to him on the floor were several fashion magazines, one of which had a sultry picture of Salma Hayek gracing its front cover.

Manolito despised *Pepe*, describing him as a '*pinche maricon*' – a flaming homosexual.

'If it was up to me I would put him down like a dog,' he had said in disgust. 'He is a disgrace to his family and his community – he's an aberration of nature.' But James soon began to like *Pepe* and he looked forward to the days when he was on duty. Contrary to his first impression, *Pepe* loved to talk.

'When I was 16 years old, I tried to kill myself,' he told James without any prompting as they sat in the room after breakfast. He spoke English interspersed with Spanish but James could make out the gist of what he was saying. 'I went down to the *rio* and slit my wrists with my father's razor and lay down in the cool muddy waters and waited to die. I was so ashamed. I didn't want to be like the other boys in the *barrio*, kicking footballs and fighting. I wanted to be like the beautiful women from *Tehuantepec* I used to see at the *fiestas*, with their hair piled up and decorated with roses and their colourful petticoats. I was tired of the daily abuse and beatings I endured from my neighbours. My father and brothers disowned me. How could I be a *Chavez* and a *puton*? They would say to me. Then one night my drunken father threw me out into the streets like a dog. I could hear my mother screaming at him and then I heard my father slap her as I stood in the rain, her cries drowned out by the thunderous night. I spent days on the street until the nuns at *El Convento de Santa Ana* took me in, and allowed me to sleep in an outbuilding for the night. But still I wanted to die. In the morning I broke into the house through the bathroom window and stole a razor and went down to the river. I lay there and watched my blood warming the waters around me. I just wanted to disappear and then a *cabron* of a fisherman down river spotted me and dragged me out. At the hospital they told me had I not been rescued, I would have bled to death within minutes. Later that week, when the doctors had patched me up, I was wandering the streets, when I bumped into the fisherman outside the *cantina*. He said: 'If I had known you were *Chavez'* homosexual son, I would have left you to die,' and he spat on me. The next day, one of the women at the flower shop gave me some money and I took the bus to *Veracruz*. I didn't care anymore. I became a prostitute and later a heroin addict. And then I took an overdose. One of the old *putas* in the *barrio* took me to the *clinica* and days later I woke up to find that she had taken me in. She was a wreck of a human being – 30 years on the game, she was dying of HIV but never have I met a person with such a heart of gold and she loved me as if I were her own child. Less than six months later I watched her die in agony. That's when I decided to live again: to honour her memory and the sacrifices she had made so that I would survive. I got a job working in a fish restaurant in the old port. That's where I first heard the name *Madrigal*. *Juan* was one of his agents down in *Veracruz* overseeing the shipment of drugs and he took a shine to me. He told me that he would take me back to *Oaxaca* and that he would look after me. He was always kind. He never abused me but the relationship was short lived. He was killed one night in a knife fight. They say his throat was cut from ear to ear.

When they discovered his body, down an alley, it had been there for two weeks. Rats had eaten out his eyes, his ears and all his extremities – even his genitals. The only way they could identify him was from an old black tattoo of a scorpion on his right arm. But *Madrigal* had heard about me and said I could be useful as a messenger, so that's why I am here. I am not a bad person, *Jaime* – believe me; I know how much your family must love you and how much you desire to return to them. I know that I have fallen from God's grace, but I have been given a second chance.'

0054 DAYS

CHAPTER 5

*2,119 people were murdered in drug related crimes
in Mexico in 2003*

✟

No one would have suspected that Monica *Gonzalez* was anything other than the pretty, dark haired doctor from Donna, Texas, who had been working for the *Los Ninos* foundation in the *Lacondon* region of *Chiapas* for 18 months. Although Monica was born in the U.S. and was therefore a citizen of the United States, her parents had been wetbacks. Her mother and father and their four children made the perilous crossing of the *Rio Bravo* from *Tamaulipas* into Texas in 1976. *Luis Gonzalez* found illegal work harvesting fruit whilst *Lupita*, his wife, was hired as a maid by a wealthy middle class couple and they lived along with two other Mexican families in a trailer park where Monica and her younger sister were born. She had attended the local high school and excelled both academically and on the sports-field and after graduating she went on to study medicine at John Hopkins University in Baltimore.

What none of her colleagues at *Los Ninos* were aware of however was that Monica *Gonzalez* was also a CIA field agent, working deep undercover monitoring the traffic of narcotics coming across the Guatemalan border. She had graduated from the Company two years before and specialised in advanced communications systems. She was also an expert shot and highly competent in unarmed combat, skills she had hitherto not been required to use. Although they were Mexican, Monica's parents had raised her and her siblings with a deep sense of patriotism and national pride in their adopted country. They had sacrificed everything to forge a new life in the United States and they were determined that none of their children should experience the poverty and privations that they had endured. Life north of the border had not been easy, but as *Luis* and *Lupita Gonzalez* watched their six children growing up, they were extremely proud of their achievements. All of them had gone to college and in addition to a doctor; the *Gonzalez* family boasted a state trooper, an attorney at law, a primary school teacher and a high school baseball coach. The journey from Mexico all those years before had cost them their life savings. They had paid a courier $2,000 for green cards and a safe passage across the *Rio Bravo*, only to be robbed of their money and possessions and abandoned with 15 other Mexicans in the dead of night in the desert, moments before they were due to make the crossing. Three of their relatives had drowned, swept away by hidden currents as they attempted to traverse the swollen river in the early hours of that dreadful morning and the *Gonzalez'* had begun their new life in the U.S with a hatred of corruption. Monica's parents had taught her that much of the poverty and misery in Mexico was fuelled by the drug trade and men like those who had betrayed them. So when she was approached by the CIA in her final year at medical school with the offer of a stipend and training in return for covert work combating the trade in narcotics, it seemed like the perfect way to combine working with the disadvantaged and doing her bit for the 'War on Drugs.' She was young, passionate and idealistic.

Monica was based in a clinic in the remote village of *San Juan Bautista.* Every morning she would drive her battered white Dodge Ram from *San Cristobal de las Casas,* where she lived, along a 20 mile stretch of dirt track deep into the jungle. She was devoted to her work and the families and children who attended the clinic, many of whom walked considerable distances to get there and were suffering from diseases and conditions such as rickets, tuberculosis and typhoid, long since eradicated in the United States.

On the evening of July 5th, Monica and her colleague, fellow paediatrician, *Tarcisio Uribe,* were enjoying a *Corona* beer and a DVD in her apartment and had ordered pizza from a local restaurant. There was nothing romantic about their relationship, it was purely platonic. The two young doctors worked closely together and over the months they had become good friends and enjoyed each other's company. Monica's apartment was tastefully furnished with Mexican rugs on the waxed wooden floors, a comfortable rattan sofa and armchairs. There were framed *Tamayo* prints on the walls and textiles and the place was airy and clean. The film 'Heat' starring Robert De Niro and Al Pacino had just started when there was a knock on the door. *Tarcisio* looked out of the window and spotted the restaurant's delivery motorcycle parked on the curb. Three flights of stairs below, on the ground floor, lay the body of the pizza delivery boy. Just 16 years old and fresh out of school, he had been shot at point blank range in the head with two hollow tipped, silenced, 9mm bullets fired from an Italian made Beretta. His two assailants had concealed themselves in the stairwell moments before, when he had pulled up outside the building. They were carrying a nine foot roll of carpet. The larger of the two men *Sergio*, had a hideous scar caused by a burn on his face. His associate, *Diego,* was short and stocky with a gold tooth in the front of his mouth. They had parked their inauspicious white van on the opposite side of the road. Both men were armed with handguns and flick knives, the preferred weapon of street fighters the world over. *Tarcisio's* limp body hit the floor seconds after he opened the door. The power of the 9mm parabellum blew him back three metres before gravity took over and he fell slumped against a pine console table. He had been shot between the eyes. Monica reacted instantly. Picking up a heavy glass ashtray in her left hand she moved swiftly towards the door. As *Diego* entered the apartment, his right arm extended in front of his body with the pistol, his left hand steadying his aim, Monica grabbed his wrist from the side, forcing it down whilst bringing her right leg up and kicking him hard in the groin. As he fell forwards towards the floor, she brought her knee up into his face and dealt him a huge blow to the back of his head with the heavy ashtray. He collapsed, groaning in agony to the floor where he lay curled up in the foetal position. A split second later, *Sergio* entered the room. He was at least a foot taller than Monica and built like a wall. He was brandishing his flick knife, the Beretta tucked into the back of his trousers, and he was grinning.

'Don't worry bitch,' he said, 'we are not going to kill you; at least not yet, so why don't you come and give your big daddy a kiss?'

Monica grabbed a table lamp and ripping it out of its socket she threw it at the giant but it glanced off his shoulder, hit the wall and shattered. There was about two metres of floor space between them. As he inched towards her she tried to jump kick his right knee but the rug she was standing on slipped beneath her and she fell to the floor. As she was getting up *Sergio* delivered a crushing punch to the middle of her face that smashed her nose and fractured her right eye socket whereupon she collapsed to the floor like a rag doll.

'Hey, asshole, get up!' said *Sergio* kicking *Diego* in the stomach as he lay writhing on the floor. 'We need to get this whore out of here *pronto*.'

Diego managed to stagger up still clutching his crushed testicles, blood running down his back from a gash on his head. The two killers brought in the rolled up length of carpet from the hallway, untied it and after throwing Monica into the middle of it, trussed her up like an *enchilada*. Minutes later the white van was heading south out of *San Cristobal de las Casas* towards the *Usumacinta River*.

0053 DAYS

CHAPTER 6

*Mexicans are fed up with the United States of America:
"Their multimillion-dollar market for drug consumption,
their banks and businesses that launder money in
complicity with ours, their arms industry—more lethal
than drugs, for being so evident and expansionist—
whose weapons come into our country, not only
strengthen criminal groups, but also provide
them with an immense capacity for carnage,"
wrote one angry journalist.*

✠

The day after receiving the devastating news that
their son had been kidnapped was Saturday July
6th. Piers and Virginia had been up until the small
hours of the morning when anxiety and exhaustion had
taken their toll and they had collapsed onto the king-
sized double bed and fallen asleep fully clothed. They
were awoken at half past nine by the phone ringing.
Piers picked up the receiver on the third ring and a man
at the end introduced himself as Edward Hutchinson
from the Foreign and Commonwealth Office's Latin
American Desk. He sounded young and asked tenta-
tively if he was speaking to Piers Cooper-Brown. He

began by saying how sorry he was to hear about their son's plight but was quick to reassure the Cooper-Browns that everything possible was being done politically to secure James' release.

'As we speak,' he said 'our embassy and consular services in Mexico City are in contact with the Mexican authorities to ascertain exactly what happened to James. The Mexican Interior minister has vowed to take a personal interest in this case and has promised that he will bring to bear all the necessary resources in order to free your son. He feels a particular affinity with your situation having served as the Mexican ambassador to the United Kingdom five years ago,' and then there was a pause. 'It is my duty, Mr Cooper-Brown,' he then went on, 'to inform you that it is not the policy of Her Majesty's government to deal directly or negotiate with terrorist or criminal organisations or to sanction the payment of any ransom in exchange for your son's release,' he was about to continue when Piers politely interrupted him.

'Yes, thank you I am well aware of the Government's policy in this regard.' By now Virginia was at her husband's side, still dressed in the crumpled clothes she had worn the previous day. But the telephone conversation was not over.

'Naturally,' continued Edward Hutchinson nervously, 'in circumstances such as these, one of the first things we do is to make some preliminary enquiries into the hostage's personal circumstances and family background. It helps us to build a profile of the captive and to predict how he or she might respond both physically and psychologically to their new surroundings and situation. It did not take us long Sir, to discover that you served with HM's armed forces in the Parachute Regiment and also with the Special Air Service.'

'Yes,' replied Piers.

'Please excuse me for sounding patronising,' continued Edward superciliously, 'but can I also counsel against attempting to take this matter in any way into your own hands,' and he chuckled uncomfortably. 'It could only complicate matters further, not only for yourselves, certainly for James, but could damage any political or diplomatic means being taken by the government to secure your son's release and would contravene international law.'

L ater in the afternoon, PC Sanderson and Jacky Moss called by to see how the Cooper-Browns were bearing up. Virginia made tea and after exchanging pleasantries, PC Sanderson leant forward on the sofa and said, 'All the national and local media are now well aware of what has happened to James. We are expecting you to be mobbed by the press tomorrow morning. Of course we will do what we can to protect you from the worst abuses of journalists and photographers, but this is likely to be a big story at least for a few days.

Are you prepared to make a brief statement?' he asked diplomatically. 'It might be a good idea to do so immediately. When the press realises that there isn't much more to be said at this stage, they will lose interest and move on like vultures. Do you have a recent photograph of James?'

It was during his second night in the hills that James fell ill. He heard his stomach rumbling twice like a deep volcano within him, before his bowels exploded violently. Fortunately it was whilst he was taking his morning shower that it happened and he managed to make it to the rank toilet in time. Days of constipation, stress, dehydration, lack of hygiene and sleep had finally taken their revenge. He struggled back to his cell, though later he could not recall how, and fell onto the bed where he lost consciousness. The following days passed in a haze of fractured thoughts and memories. A local doctor, on the *Madrigal* payroll, who was a dissipated alcoholic by the name of *Chiro*, diagnosed amoebic dysentery. He connected James to an IV line and a bag of saline solution to counter the dehydration and prescribed a dose of antibiotics. James lay for two days sweating deliriously on the bed. His mind was a blaze of sunlight one moment, filled with songs and tunes he had not heard for years; and then there were images of vibrant English summers spent at the family home. Familiar voices echoed through his head;

he could hear Charlotte calling him until his internal screams blocked out the pain. When he awoke, 48 hours later, *Pepe* was at his side, dabbing a damp cloth to his humid brow.

'We thought you were dying,' he said gently. 'I was very worried about you. The others,' he continued, 'they thought they would never get their monies,' and he laughed.

After breakfast, the two friends chatted for several hours. 'James, do you believe in *el mal de ojo*– the evil eye?' *Pepe* asked him.

'I am afraid I have never heard of it: it sounds ghoulish!' he said laughing.

'I do not believe in it either, but my mother who was very superstitious believed in *el mal de ojo*. She believed you could curse someone by summoning up evil spirits or asking a *curandero*, a witch doctor, to impose it on a person. She said she knew of people who had died from it, like my cousin *Josue*. She once told me that a former girlfriend put the evil eye on him and after two weeks he was dead.

'What? Do you mean he just dropped dead two weeks later?' James asked incredously.

'No, it did not happen like that. One morning he woke up with a fever and a rash to his face. My aunt took him to the doctor who prescribed some antibiotics and ointment to put on the spots. But my cousin refused to take the medicine. He said he knew who had caused it. His jealous girlfriend had told him she had cursed him. Only a *curandero* could lift it. So one day a witch doctor came to the house. He stripped *Josue* naked and laid the skeleton of a rattle snake on his belly and sprinkled chicken blood over the bed and covered my cousin with honeysuckle and lit candles and incense. But still his condition did not improve. The *curandero* told my aunt he needed more potent ingredients like scorpion venom but obtaining enough of it would cost a lot of money. Soon my uncle had sold his mule to pay for the medicines, but within two weeks *Josue* was dead. The doctor who signed his death certificate said he had died from blood poisoning. If he had taken the prescribed medication he would still be alive!'

'But that's rubbish!' exclaimed James. 'He didn't die because of a curse; he died because he didn't take the antibiotics.'

'I know that too,' *Pepe* replied, 'but many people just think that modern doctors are *curanderos* in white coats with fancy equipment and diplomas. They think that modern cures have been around for centuries. Everything comes from nature they say, only now these medicines come in little glass bottles with labels and students have to study to become doctors. In the old days certain people were born with skills, gifts and abilities that we have lost.'

The following day *Pepe* was replaced by *Carlos*. He had a fleshy pocked marked face and hardly any teeth and his hands and arms were festooned with tattoos of skulls and deathly figures. He seldom spoke except when he was drunk. Then he would sit with his back to the wall, his sunglasses covering his dark dead eyes and regale James with tales of extreme violence and sexual perversion.

'Man, I once cut this *pendejo* open from nipple to navel. There was so much blood I could smell it on my hands a week later. The *idiota* deserved it; tried to cheat me out of 100 *pesos* in a game of dominoes,' and he went on.

James dreaded the times spent cooped up with *Carlos*. When he wasn't drunk and loud and bragging, he sat morosely slumped in a corner leafing through hardcore pornographic magazines or playing games with his flick knife. He would place his hand, palm down on the wooden floor, fingers splayed, and stab the floorboards between them as quickly as he could.

'You know *amigo*,' he said trying to interest James in a centrefold picture of a young blonde woman with her legs spread open. 'I had a *gringa* bitch like this one; a real sweet peach she was. Wanted it so badly she did, could not wait to be fucked by a big Mexican dick. Well, me and the boys gave her real treat..' he droned on. James tried blocking his ears. He didn't want to know, he didn't want images in his mind that he knew would be impossible to exorcise.

One night he awoke in the chilly hours of dawn to find *Carlos* sobbing and cursing loudly to himself in the corner, his head in his hands. He was rocking backwards and forwards.

'Curse the day I was born and my mother and father who brought me into this miserable hell.'

James sat up and leant his back against the cool, damp wall.

'What's the matter?' he asked softly.

'You will never understand!' replied *Carlos* in his broken English.

'You, with your money and education; you will never comprehend the things that I have done and seen and the places I have been. My grandmother, her little house was full of candles and shrines and the smell of incense and melting wax. She prayed to *La Virgen* all the time and spent her Sundays in church, confessing to that asshole Father *Dominguez*, but it's all a lie. There is no God out there, no Baby Jesus looking out for us. We live for a moment and then we die violently.'

James sat silently. He did not know what to say. He despised *Carlos*. He hated his violent stories and his endless bragging. He loathed his rotten breath and his skin that seemed to ooze with the smell of *mescal* and *tequila*. But here was a broken, vulnerable human being.

'I thought all Mexicans believed in God?' he said naively. 'You have to live with hope and faith,' he said trying to console him, 'otherwise life and death are meaningless.'

'*La Virgen* and Jesus are what you *gringos* brought to this land to subdue and enslave us. There is no God or salvation for people like me; only hell and damnation!' and he began banging his head against the wall.

'Do you know what we did tonight?' he said, suddenly rising to his feet and pacing around the cramped room.

'Do you know what I did tonight; me and the others? We drove out to this little *ranchito* owned by some pitiful *campesinos* with a few chickens, pigs and a field of maize. We were all drunk and high. *Cesar* told us to whack them all – wipe them all out, is what he said. They are traitors and cannot be trusted. So *Sergio*, *Diego* and I drove out there in the pick-up. We parked the car in the woods, killed the lights and the engine. It was two o'clock in the morning. We took cans of petrol and guns. *Sergio* doused the walls of the corral and the little house in gas, lit a cigarette and threw the lighted match down. The place went up like a furnace. You should have seen his face illuminated in the light of the flames. It was like looking at the devil himself. He was laughing. We could hear children and women screaming inside and then a man dressed only in his shorts ran out. *Diego* shot him as he stood in the doorway his hair on fire. And then the house collapsed and all we could hear were the pigs squealing and the smell of burning pork. Where was God tonight?' *Carlos* asked rhetorically.

'There was no God there tonight to protect that family from us. We killed women and children! Where was God the night my grandfather was shot by *gringos* when he tried to cross the border into *El Paso*? We killed those people tonight because *Cesar* said they had gone over to one of *Madrigal*'s enemies. They had to die; all of them, even the children. God abandoned this country long ago,' and he fell silent, his right hand still clutching a jar of *mescal* and minutes later, James could hear his heavy breathing as he slept slumped with his back to the door.

0052 DAYS

CHAPTER 7

*America's picture of Mexico is too often broad-brushed
as a vivid red bloodbath. Mexico is watched like
a summer blockbuster where drug cartels are the
shady characters and corruption is the narrative.
We have detached Mexico, and consequently fail
to accurately assess the truth next door.*

✟

Excruciating pain told Monica that she was conscious. Hanging two inches off the floor from a wooden beam in the ceiling, her body was bruised and battered. She was unable to open her eyes which looked like two puffy stewed prunes. She had lacerations on her wrists where the ropes cut into her and three broken ribs in addition to the wounds she had sustained in the attack the previous night. But she knew as yet that she had not been sexually assaulted; that would probably come later. Monica could not see *Sergio*, but she felt his presence, his pungent body odour and rank, sour breath. He came close up to her. She could feel his huge bulk pressed against her and the acrid scent of his cigarette.

'Tell us what we need to know, and I promise, you will die quickly,' he said menacingly. 'Otherwise, we have ways to keep you alive for weeks, even months. Then you will know what it is really like to live in hell.' He paused for a moment and she felt him move away.

'We need to know exactly what information you have been feeding the Americans and the *pinche policia*. What action is being planned by the Mexican military and your friends at the CIA?'

Monica said nothing. *Sergio* moved to a work bench where he picked up a cordless Black and Decker 240 volt drill. He switched it on. Monica could hear the bit's high pitched whirring as it revolved at 2500 revolutions per minute. She clenched her teeth but still said nothing. Two minutes later her piercing screams were drowned out by the sounds of the dense jungle that stretched for miles in every direction as the forest burst into a cacophony of bird and insect song and a flock of crimson-headed partridge took to the air, their wings flapping wildly.

On Monday 7th July, the sleepy village of Mosscombe in Berkshire became the centre of media frenzy. In addition to the BBC and ITN, there were journalists from all the major national broadsheets and tabloids as well as representatives from the local press. Everybody in the village seemed to profit, that is except the Cooper-Browns who were holed up in their converted Tudor barn behind curtained windows and locked gates – imprisoned by their own tortured thoughts and private, anxious fears. Local farmers made small fortunes renting out fallow fields to the convoys of media vans and vehicles that descended on the Saxon hamlet. The village pub, The Jolly Huntsman, had not seen it so good since the wedding of Prince Charles and Lady Diana back in 1981, and by the evening of July 8th, had run out of Strongbow cider and Barnes, the local ale. Taking the police's advice, Piers had prepared a brief statement to read to the army of journalists that was now practically camped out on the Cooper-Brown's front garden. At 11 o'clock in the morning, a sober faced Piers, dressed in a pair of dark grey suit trousers, shiny black shoes and an open necked pale blue shirt, opened the front door of the house and stepped out into the thrust of microphones, voice recorders and shorthand pads. He was accompanied by PC Sanderson, and his closest friend and colleague, Matthew Waterman who stood by his side. Virginia remained inside the house. She was too upset to face the crowd, even one that seemed genuinely to sympathise with her family's plight. Removing a page of typed A4 paper from his trouser pocket he unfolded it and began reading slowly and clearly.

'My wife and daughter and our family and friends have been truly shocked by the recent abduction of our son James in the southern Mexican state of *Oaxaca*. James had been travelling with a friend in the U.S when he decided to journey south. The Foreign and Commonwealth Office and the Mexican authorities believe he was kidnapped sometime towards the end of last week. The *Madrigal* Cartel, based somewhere in the *Sierra Madre* have claimed responsibility for the kidnapping and are demanding a ransom for his release. It is still early days and as yet no additional information about James' wellbeing has been forthcoming from his captors. We would like to thank the Mexican government and the Foreign Office for their continued efforts in trying to secure our son's release but would ask those who are holding him to free him as soon as possible and ensure his safe return. That is all we have to say for the moment.'

As he was finishing, a journalist from 'The News of the World,' pushed a microphone into his face and said:

'I understand Mr Cooper-Brown that you once served in the SAS. Do you not wish to exact revenge on those who have taken your son?'

Piers shoved the microphone away and replied.

'What my personal thoughts and feelings may or may not be at this moment in time, are my concern. I would be grateful if you would respect our privacy.'

The following morning the paper's headlines read: 'Former SAS soldier and father of kidnapped Brit, turns the other cheek.' By the evening of Tuesday July

8th, most of the media circus had left Mosscombe and the village was quiet once again.

Deep in the *Sierra Madre*, a new day was dawning. By seven o'clock, *Carlos* was back to his sullen self. He had dark bags under his eyes and his skin looked sallow – almost yellow. James wondered if he was suffering from jaundice.

'Forget my ranting last night,' he said when James returned from the bathroom. 'They were the feeble confessions of another person. Those *chingaderos* deserved to die. No one should turn their back on *Madrigal*, betray his trust or decline his hand of friendship.'

James had a sudden urge to be sick but he didn't wish to appear weak before *Carlos*. He took a deep breath and saying nothing he turned his face to the wall. An hour later, *Carlos* was relieved of his duty and *Pepe* returned. For the first time since being kidnapped, James actually smiled with relief. *Pepe* too, seemed pleased to see him and after the door was locked behind him, he produced an old radio cassette recorder from his rucksack and a handful of tapes.

'I am going to introduce you to the best of Mexican music,' he said smiling. 'First, I want you to hear the voice of the biggest *maricon* of them all – *Juan Gabriel*. He sounds like an angel and when he and *Rocio Durcal* sing together, it's like heaven itself has opened its gates,' and he loaded the cassette and pressed 'play.'

Ten days after the kidnapping, *El Alacran, Javier Ernesto Madrigal* hit back against the adverse publicity that was being directed at the cartel by both the Mexican and international press.

'Murderous criminals,' is what one national daily called him and his associates whilst another labelled him 'A parasite living off other peoples' misery.'

Madrigal was furious and quick to respond. *La Nacion*, the most liberal of Mexico's broadsheets, published his strong rebuke.

'It is true that I deal in drugs and guns,' he confessed. 'Politicians and great leaders throughout history have been opportunists. Did not our Yankee friends to the north fund their dirty war in Vietnam from the sale of heroin? They justified their actions claiming they were fighting an ideological war against communism, against the enemies of Christianity. They argued that any means justified their ends. We too are fighting an ideological war, against the forces of American and European neo-imperialism that seek to enslave us with crippling economic policies and words like 'democracy,' whilst the indigenous people of this country remain without dignity, education, health, housing or even food. Yes, I am fighting a dirty war. I kidnap innocent youths and kill my enemies and those who oppose me because we are fighting a war for survival. Americans talk about justice: I have delivered more justice for my people in two years than the Americans or Europeans could bring in a decade. I stand by my word. If my *compadres* who now sit in American jails (some of them on Death Row) are not released; if my demand for $5,000,000 is not met, I will execute the Englishman for the sake of my country. Not only will I kill him, I will target every policeman in *Oaxaca*, every newspaper editor that betrays my people with lies, every judge and lawyer who condemns our actions. These are the people who have sold out our nation – the legion of *Malinches* who would rather take the Yankee dollar than invest in the people of Mexico!'

It was a brilliant, calculated piece of self publicity: the tyrant portraying himself as his nation's saviour. But there was some truth in what he had to say and much of it resonated with many of Mexico's left wing intellectuals who were tired of the endless hypocrisy of the country's leading political parties, most notably the PRI, which had divorced itself years before from its *Zapatista*, quasi socialist ideals. Mexico had become a puppet of the United States.

0051 DAYS

CHAPTER 8

'The U.S. is a star player in the drugs war. However,
when it comes time to play an active role in ending
the game, the U.S. suddenly calls timeout. Time to
sit on the sidelines,' U.S senator Dwight Jacobs.

✝

*E*nrique Ramos, the administrator of the field hospital in *San Juan Bautista*, had been on the *Madrigal*
payroll for two years. A decade before he had been a
young idealistic doctor with a desire to work among the
poorest and dispossessed people of his country. He had
trained in Sacramento, California and on returning to
Mexico had found work with a national children's charitable trust called *'Los Ninos de Guadalupe'* that ran
schools, orphanages and hospitals in remote parts of
Oaxaca, Tabasco and *Chiapas*. His first position had
been head of a paediatrics unit in *Rio de la Selva* in
Tabasco. He had vision and was ambitious and when
the post of administrator in *San Juan Bautista* came
up, he applied successfully for the job. *Enrique* was
astute and intelligent and it was not long before he
became aware, that for a charitable foundation, *'Los
Ninos'* was never short of funding. His own position

was generously remunerated and all the staff from the cleaners to clinicians were well paid and enjoyed bonuses such as free medical insurance and annual check-ups. His requests for medicines and equipment were never declined and yet many of his doctor friends and former fellow students working in both the private and state sectors seemed to complain ceaselessly of the lack of funding, resources and the crippling bureaucracies. He began questioning why his position was so comfortable and relatively easy and his enquiries inevitably led him over a period of months to an uncomfortable discovery. The hospital in which he worked, the children's treatment, medicines and equipment were all being paid for by the *Madrigal* Cartel.

O n the morning of March 14th 2003, *Ramos* was sitting at his desk in his office, poring over an audit for a recent order of a new MRI scanner, when a black Range Rover Vogue with tinted windows rolled up and parked outside the hospital's main entrance. Moments later, two men entered his office and sat down on the brown leather sofa opposite him. Neither of them spoke for a minute or two. They were dressed in dark, grey Italian pinstriped suits, white shirts with button-down collars and black ties. Their shoes were shiny, save for a few specks of *Chiapan* mud and both men wore dark sunglasses masking their eyes. Their hair was cropped and they were tanned.

The taller of the two, aged about 38, removed his glasses and leant forward clasping his hands together. The distance between *Ramos*' desk and the sofa was about two metres and seemed to serve as a potent, menacing metaphor. 'We are here,' it said,

'and you are there!'

'Doctor *Ramos*, do you enjoy your work here in *San Juan Bautista*?' He asked quietly, even softly.

'We have heard reports that you are an excellent doctor and what you and your colleagues are doing here is nothing short of miraculous.' He paused for a response. His companion sat mute staring at the ceiling. Although he was a couple of inches shorter, he probably weighed 210 pounds. He was a suit filled with muscle, with not an inch of fat anywhere on his compact body. *Ramos*, who was still reeling from this surprise visit, sat speechless for a moment. He was not someone known for his timidity.

'Who the hell are you, walking into my office like this?' he asked angrily when he regained his composure. 'Do you have an appointment?'

'Let's cut the crap!' answered the first man.

'You know exactly who we are and we know exactly who you are.'

He removed a Blackberry from his pocket and began reading *Ramos*' curriculum vitae from his time at the *Los Pinos* primary School in *Tlacocalpan* to his present employment. No details were spared.

'Your father, *Juan Ramos*, was a history professor at UNAM University until his untimely death from a coronary at the age of 62, five years ago. Your Mother, *Teresa Ramos*, lives with your younger sister *Sofia*, (who is 21 and a law student) at the family home in *Calle Saratoga*, number 236, in *Lomas Hipodromo*,' and he went on.

By now, *Ramos* had dropped his pen on the desk and had slumped back in his chair. He heard the man reading but his thoughts were elsewhere. Everything he had worked for in his life, all the major details of his existence, the people he loved, his values, beliefs and dreams suddenly seemed like a sham, wiped out by one irrefutable fact: he was being paid by the most notorious criminal in Mexican history, and this one man now had complete control over his life. There was another pregnant silence. The muscle in the suit casually removed a black U.S made Walther PPK with a walnut handle from a shoulder holster. He took out the clip, blew into the barrel, replaced the clip and pushed the safety catch off before laying it carefully on the glass coffee table in front of him.

'Mr *Ramos*, I shall re-phrase my question,' said the first man ominously.

'Do you value your work here? Because if you do not, we can arrange for some really nasty *tipos* to pay that beautiful bitch of a sister of yours and that hag of a mother, a little visit. These people are not as nice as us. They have lived in some real hell holes. When they see your house, with its double garage and maid's room, its library and nice furnishing they are going to want to take everything. They are going to want to have a good time with Sofia too and maybe your mother as well. And they are going to leave a mess. But please do not think for a moment that they will leave your sister and your mother alive: that would be like to prison. No my friend, some fisherman in *Xochimilco* will find their bloated, mutilated bodies floating in the canal one morning,' and he smiled wolfishly.

Ramos closed his eyes. There was silence. Then the two men got up. The muscle replaced his gun in its holster and the taller of the two leant across *Ramos'* desk and whispered.

'Now you have a long think about our little chat today, won't you? And I would suggest you stop poking around in places you shouldn't be!' and they left closing the office door behind them. *Ramos* heard the purring of the diesel engine, the crunch of tyres on gravel and they were gone. That was the day that Doctor *Enrique Ramos* died inside. He remained dedicated to his work, he was affable to his colleagues but the light that had once shone in his bright, ambitious eyes faded.

Unwittingly, it was *Ramos'* actions that betrayed Monica *Gonzalez*. A month later a new pharmacist by the name of *Antonio Torres* began working at

San Juan Bautista. He was young and handsome and soon became popular especially with the female members of staff who flirted endlessly with him and vied for his attention. He had been placed in the hospital by the cartel to keep an eye on *Ramos* and to monitor the safe passage of narcotics coming into Mexico over the Guatemalan border. When Doctor Monica *Gonzalez* failed to respond to his manly charms, advances and his boyish sense of humour he was affronted. No woman had ever refused him. Monica, in his mind, was by far the most attractive woman in *San Cristobal*. She was educated, sophisticated and like him (he assumed) from a wealthy middle class family. He had bedded countless women, but there was something about Monica; perhaps it was because she was independent and seemed remote, that attracted him. When his male pride and sense of *machismo* took a blow, he became suspicious and began stalking her, believing that she secretly had a boyfriend. And that's when he ran into Mike Espinetti.

Mike was in his late forties. An experienced CIA handler, he had been living south of the border for almost 20 years. On the evening of April 20th 2003, Espinetti had arrived in *San Cristobal* for his monthly debriefing with Monica and parked his hired car outside her apartment. It was nine o'clock on a Wednesday night and the cobbled streets of the town were silent and still. He had just got out of the little white Chevy and was removing his black canvas holdall that contained his Toughbook, toiletries and change of clothing when a drunk *Antonio Torres*, who had been watching Monica's apartment, crossed the street clutching a half empty bottle of *Sol* beer.

'Hey asshole,' he said impertinently in English with a slight American accent, 'What the fuck is your business with the American chick?'

Mike bent down and placed his bag on the ground before turning to face *Antonio*.

'*Amigo*,' he replied, 'that's my business. Why? Are you her bodyguard or something?' he asked sarcastically.

A veteran CIA operator, Mike had come across many men like *Antonio* over the years. He was short, about five feet seven inches tall but wiry and extremely agile. He was also trained in various martial arts including Aikido and Jujitsu. *Antonio* was now standing less than a foot away and Mike could smell alcohol on his breath and cigarette smoke in his clothes. *Antonio* was dressed in a navy blue polo shirt, jeans and docksiders.

'Too right I am!' replied *Antonio*. 'She's also my girlfriend so you better back off punk!' and he went to push Mike. Espinetti however, anticipated the move and sidestepped quickly, smashing his left elbow hard into the side of *Antonio*'s head. As *Antonio* fell towards the wall, Mike stepped in front of him and grabbed him by the scruff of the neck, pinned him against the side of the building and punched him hard in the solar plexus knocking the wind out of the Mexican, who crumpled to the ground. Mike bent down beside him and yanked *Antonio*'s head back by his long, shoulder length black hair.

'Now you listen good, dick-brain! Monica doesn't have friends like you, so here's what you are going to do. You are going to go home like a good little boy and you are going to stay away from her. If I so much as get a whiff of you again my friend, I swear I will break every bone in your puny little body and you'll spend the rest of your miserable life in a wheel chair, sucking your food through a straw and shitting into a bag – *comprende?*' *Antonio* nodded in terror before collapsing into the street.

Unfortunately *Antonio* did not stay away from Monica. Now, more obsessed with her than ever and humiliated by his encounter with Mike, he wanted to know more about her and her friends and how she came to be working as a doctor in *San Juan Bautista*. Using his contacts in the cartel, it was not long before *Madrigal* and his associates came to the conclusion that there was a mole working within the foundation. Her days with *Los Ninos* were numbered.

0050 DAYS

CHAPTER 9

Extortion of migrants' families is common since the smuggling of so called 'wet backs' into the U.S has been taken over by organized crime in recent years.

✝

Back in Mosscombe, Berkshire, Virginia was directing her energy into ensuring that James would not be forgotten. She was all too aware that after a week or so, the national and local media would soon move on to other stories. No news was not news (as far as the press was concerned) and unless James were suddenly freed or executed, the media would inevitably focus on other matters.

Coming down for breakfast on Wednesday July 10th, Virginia found a stack of mail piled up against the front door. Piers had already left for work and Eleanor, James' younger sister, was still in bed having arrived the previous night from boarding school. Piers and Virginia had hardly spoken since the kidnapping. Each had become an island unto themselves; wrapped up in their own thoughts and feelings of guilt, loss and pain. They had not argued. Their relationship had always been close and affectionate, but James' sudden disappearance had left them unable to communicate or express their private anxieties, as if doing so would somehow make their worst fears come true: that they might in fact never see their son again. Not only had *Madrigal* taken James, he was tearing apart his family.

Virginia picked up the stack of letters and putting them on the kitchen table, she made herself a cup of tea and a slice of toast. The letters had been posted from all over the United Kingdom and almost all of them carried the same message of support and sympathy. Some offered prayers, a few even money and one or two were written by extremists and crackpots. There was a letter from the United Front that suggested targeting all Mexicans visiting or residing in the U.K. Another deranged individual wrote, 'If I were you, I'd kidnap the first Latino you see – give 'em a taste of their own medicine!' These rantings, Virginia binned without a second thought.

After spending an hour reading and sorting the post, she got a pad of paper and pen and began making notes. Already, and against the advice of the Foreign Office, Virginia was thinking of ways to raise the ransom money. She knew that Piers would never agree to this, and it worried her that going against his wishes would drive another wedge between them but she could not sit idly by waiting for James' release or the off chance that he might be rescued by a police or military operation. Only a week before, a Dutch aid worker had been killed in Afghanistan when a rescue attempt by local forces had gone disastrously wrong.

At the top of the list of people she wished to contact was Robert Swinton, her brother in law (and her sister's husband) who was a director of a big city firm. Under his name was the Lambourn MP followed by the editor of the Swindon Echo. She then wrote down the names of all their friends and acquaintances and a list of their own assets which included the barn, Piers' Range Rover, her brand new Audi, stocks and shares, their holiday house near Aldeburgh in Suffolk, one or two items of antique jewellery she had inherited and an old oil painting of 'The Charge of the Light Brigade' which had belonged to James' great, great grandfather. She decided to omit Risk Factor from the list. She consulted the Sunday Times' business pages and found the Dollar to Sterling exchange rate and calculated that $5 million was approximately £3 million. It was still a huge amount of money to raise, but it now seemed possible. If they re-mortgaged the house, sold the Range Rover, the Audi and their place in Suffolk surely that would generate at least half the ransom – the rest, she concluded, Robert could raise through his business contacts. She had never liked him much and always thought him patronising but Virginia felt that the nature of their awkward relationship would make asking him for assistance easier and by the end of the morning she felt surprisingly hopeful. By now, the kitchen table was littered with scraps of paper covered in jottings, contacts and telephone numbers including two estate agents whom she planned to call in the early afternoon to give her an estimate on the value the house. After tidying up the table she called her sister.

'I shall damn well make sure that Robert comes on board with this,' Lucy promised.

'He can raise this kind of cash over a dinner party with some of his banking cronies. Don't worry Virginia,' she said reassuringly, 'by the end of next week we will have the money.' Just before ringing off she added, 'Have you told Piers about this?'

'No,' replied Virginia. 'I only started really thinking about it over the last couple of days. We have barely spoken since the news,' and her voice suddenly sounded fragile as she pulled back the tears.

'Don't you think you ought to?' counselled Lucy. 'He's going to find out one way or another pretty soon, especially since you are planning to re-mortgage the house and sell his Range Rover.'

'I realise that,' said Virginia, 'only I know what his response will be and I don't want to hear it at the moment. He believes giving in to these people will just lead to more kidnapping. But I am James' mother, I don't want him held captive by these criminals one more day than is necessary.'

For no apparent reason the regime inside the house was suddenly relaxed from one day to the next. James remained locked up for 24 hours a day, but he was no longer hooded when he needed the bathroom and *Manolito* even brought him magazines and newspapers to read.

'We have *Carmela* looking after us now,' said *Pepe* gleefully, the next time he was on duty.

'No more *huevos a la Mexicana*. You can have a slice of papaya with lime juice and *huevos rancheros*! Do you know Don James what *huevos rancheros* are?'

James confessed that he did not.

'They are the taste of Mexico,' replied *Pepe*. 'Fried eggs, with re-fried beans, bacon and *tortillas* covered in chilli sauce. I will ask *Carmela* to cook them for us tomorrow morning.'

James wondered who *Carmela* was and why conditions in the house had all of a sudden improved.

Pepe continued. '*Cesar* says that *Carmela* can have all the ingredients she wants, maybe she will cook us *enchiladas suizas* or even a *molé*,' and he went on to describe in detail some of his favourite Mexican dishes.

'Did you know that *molé* and *tamales* were served at Aztec banquets and that *Oaxaca* boasts the best of both? You will have a chance, my friend to savour the kind of food once eaten by the great *Moctezuma* himself!'

James had asked *Pepe* on more than one occasion who *Cesar* was and who exactly was holding him, but *Pepe*'s answers had always been vague.

'*Cesar* is one of *Madrigal*'s lieutenants,' he would say, 'but apart from that I know nothing.'

'Who is this *Madrigal*?' James asked him one morning. 'I have heard his name before.'

'People say he is *Benito Juarez* or *Emiliano Zapata* re-born,' *Pepe* replied wistfully. 'He is our champion.'

'So why did he arrange to kidnap me?' James asked, anger beginning to register in his voice.

'In order to set us free,' *Pepe* replied, naively. 'But please do not worry *Jaime*, you will be going home soon, maybe this is why *Carmela* has come and we now have good food, maybe *Madrigal* and the others are celebrating,' and he promptly changed the subject. 'So what did you think of *Juan Gabriel* and *Rocio Durcal*? Don't they sing beautifully together? Now listen to this one,' he said and he inserted a cassette into the tape recorder and moments later the room was filled with the sound of *Lila Downs* singing *Llorona* in her smoky guttural voice.

0048 DAYS

CHAPTER 10

A 'Pax Mafioso,' is an example of corruption which
guarantees a politician votes in exchange for turning
a 'blind eye' towards a particular cartel. The practice
was commonplace in Mexico in 2003.

✝

*M*adrigal built the core of his billion dollar empire
in the late 1990's and had modelled himself on
the head of the *Medellin* Cartel in Columbia – one *Pablo*
Escobar. *Madrigal* had been a student of *Escobar*'s glit-
tering and stunning success not only as the leader of one
of the most wealthy crime syndicates on the planet but
also as a philanthropist and master of public relations.
Madrigal was quick to learn that violence was not the
only way of gaining power and influence. It could certainly be effective; but money, he soon discovered, could
be much more persuasive, and few could resist it. He
was often reminded of Aesop's fable of the Wind and
Sun. The Wind had tried blowing the poor traveller's
coat off, but it was the Sun's warm rays and seductive-
ness that had persuaded the man to remove it. Hence,
like *Escobar* and others before him, *Madrigal* adopted
a policy of *'oro or plomo'* – money or the bullet. If the

offer of money was not sufficient in bribing a judge, jury or politician – and it usually was, then the bullet would do the trick.

To begin with, he had significant enemies. The U.S. and Columbian governments had declared a war on drugs: 'This insidious enemy within our nation that is consuming and corrupting our youth,' they had claimed and Mexico's president, *Carlos Salinas de Gotari* followed suit. Whole police forces and army units were set up with the sole purpose of wiping out the narcotics trade. *Madrigal* responded with characteristic violence. When one of his chief accountants was arrested and charged with money laundering for the cartel; and blackmail and bribery had failed to persuade the police to drop the charges, *Madrigal's* assassins proceeded to eliminate the entire *Morelia* police department where the man had been arrested. A month later, all charges against the accountant were dropped for lack of evidence. *Madrigal* knew then that he had become almost untouchable. Soon he was buying football teams and stadia and funding various social projects and once he had bought and supported the Industrial Workers' Union, he became the most powerful man in the country, though in the daily life of the nation few would know it. His face did not adorn the *peso* bill, there were no statues of him and he still remained a fugitive; a name on a global list of 'Most Wanted.' Yet this did not stop him owning a fleet of aircraft (which he used to transport his product) and several luxurious *haciendas*. By the end of the 1990's, *Madrigal* had police departments, lawyers and judges, heads of industry and even well-known politicians on his payroll. The family home, a huge ranch in the foothills of the *Sierra Madre* on a cobbled road called *Juarez* Street above *Huatulco* Bay, boasted stables, a 20 metre swimming pool, a helipad, tennis court and a bowling alley. *Madrigal* was rarely there, but it was the principal residence of his partner *Lorenza Martinez* (a former Miss Mexico) and their two daughters, *Alondra* and *Paloma*. The eldest, *Alondra*, was a Princeton law graduate, and in a rare interview with a Mexican daily in 2003, shortly after James Cooper-Brown was kidnapped, still claimed her father was a saint, 'Yes a complicated man,' she admitted, 'but if sainthood is based on pure mathematics; an equation between good and evil, positives and negatives,' she argued, 'my father's charitable work and love of his land far outweigh his alleged crimes.' She was an articulate, extremely well educated and astute woman and by the end of the millennium was already being touted as a future candidate for the presidency.

'Look at me!' she once told a journalist for *La Nacion*, 'Am I not progress? My grandfather sold watermelons in *Oaxaca* market and yet within two generation his grand-daughter holds a degree in international law and could one day be Mexico's first female president!'

O n discovering the bodies of the pizza delivery boy and *Tarcisio Uribe* in *San Cristobal de las Casas*, a national manhunt had been launched to find the killers. For Mike Espinetti, the disappearance of Monica *Gonzalez* was both a personal and professional loss. She had been an excellent agent providing Langley with regular updates on drug trafficking across the border and the two had become friends. Mike did not immediately suspect that *Antonio Torres* had anything to do with either the murders or Monica's disappearance, but as her handler he felt responsible for what had happened to her and volunteered to head the team searching for her whereabouts. Their investigations revealed that *Torres* had been planted in the hospital to spy on his colleagues and report on their activities. It would not have taken long for the obsessive young pharmacist to discover that Monica *Gonzalez* was also a CIA agent.

T orres had been easy enough to find. Mike figured that on a Friday night, he would be out in female company in one the town's handful of bars frequented by tourists, middle class Mexicans and the trendy crowd. At half past 11, on July 10th, five days after Monica's disappearance, *El Girasol,* on *Calle de la Revolucion*, was full of young people eating and drinking and listening to a local band. It was the second bar that Espinetti had scouted and he spotted *Torres* through the window, with two young blonde women sitting at a table near the small stage. It was a cool evening, and already a month into the rainy season, and Espinetti was dressed in a brown leather jacket, black jeans, boots, a dark cotton polo-neck and baseball cap. He parked his rental, a black Jeep Cherokee, opposite the bar and waited. In his canvas bag he had a handful of nylon ties, two metres of climbing rope, a six inch, Cudeman bowie knife with a serrated blade and his CIA issue, snub-nosed, Sigg Sauer 9mm handgun. At half past one in morning, the band played its last song and minutes later, *Torres* and the two women stepped outside and turning north, headed towards his apartment on *San Sebastian* Street. Behind them, Mike followed slowly in the car. As *Torres* was fumbling for the keys to his apartment's entrance, Mike silently moved in behind him and stuck the pistol into the small of his back.

'You two, fuck off!' he said addressing the startled Danish women.

The girls stifled their screams and took off down the street back towards the bar.

'Remember me?' Said Mike quietly. 'Where's your ride?'

'It's the Toyota Hilux across the street,' answered *Torres* shaking. He looked terrified.

'Get in and move across to the driver's side!' he ordered. 'Try anything fancy and your brains will be all over this thing,' he continued. 'You and I are going to take a little trip.'

Ten days later, *Antonio Torres'* badly decomposed body was found in thick woods outside the village of *Chamula*. His hands were tied behind his back and he had been shot once in the head. His blooded feet were bare and bound and three of his toes had been amputated. The post-mortem carried out on his corpse, revealed he had been injected with a dose of sodium amytal, a powerful 'truth' serum. His pickup truck was found days later, torched and half submerged in the waters of the *Sumidero* Canyon. Mike was in Mexico City when he read the news of *Torres'* demise. He didn't feel any remorse. *Antonio* had been responsible for the murder of two innocent people and the kidnapping and torture of a valued friend and colleague who might now be dead. But *Torres* had been useful. He had confessed to alerting the cartel to his suspicions about Monica and he told Mike shortly before he died that she was being held in a remote disused coffee warehouse on the *Usumacinta* River, close to the Guatemalan border. Within 24 hours of receiving this information the CIA had already put together an extraction plan to rescue her.

0046 DAYS

CHAPTER 11

In 2003, 38 women from Honduras, El Salvador,
Guatemala and Nicaragua, covered 2,800 miles
and crossed 14 Mexican states to reach Reynosa
on the Texas border. Eighteen were kidnapped
by drug cartels for sex trafficking.

✝

James never slept well at night. Fear and anxiety were the overriding emotions that he felt especially during the early hours of morning when he longed for sleep. He was counting the days. As he lay on his bed unable to sleep, listening to *Carlos'* drunken snores, his thoughts wandered home. He pictured his parents and particularly his mother who he knew would be frantically worried about him. He felt for Eleanor who had just completed her A'levels and wondered how she was coping. He thought of Toby and his other friends and inevitably his mind drifted on to thinking about Charlotte. Months before, they had planned on holidaying in Turkey. They were going to start in Istanbul and then travel east, visiting Bodrum and Mamaris. He was sure that she was unaware that he had ended up in Mexico and had been kidnapped. She was probably

on a beach somewhere in Thailand with Julian. He got
to thinking about how his own parents had met. Had
not his father broken off his engagement to another
woman in order to be with his mother? Perhaps what
had happened to him were 'the sins of the fathers'
being passed on down. Less than a year before he had
become a Christian. His conversion had been un-dra-
matic; more the realisation over months that life was
meaningless without God and for him Christ was the
only advocate for humanity; that his salvation rested in
Jesus. He was not one to proselytise publicly. He preferred discussions and conversations with people who
genuinely wanted to know what he believed and why.
He really didn't believe in the Hindu notion of Karma –
that was tosh! You made your own good and bad luck
in life and then he thought of *Pepe*, a deeply damaged
person, someone who had been dealt a very raw deal
and yet this extremely confused young man had a deep
Christian faith.

'I have done terrible things in my life,' he told James
one night as they sat listening to music, 'and terrible
things have been done to me but I have accepted God's
grace without questioning. I have been forgiven,' he
said, 'I have accepted who I am!'

Occasionally James was entertained with the
thought of happy memories, mostly from his
childhood. He recalled the stories of derring-do that

his father would recount from his own personal experiences of war and his days in the army. His favourite, was one his father told of an encounter with a group of Hell's Angels in a pub outside Bristol.

'I had only recently passed the SAS selection,' his father would begin, 'and was with three friends returning from a training exercise on Exmoor. On the way home, we stopped at this pub in Clifton for a pint and a ploughman's lunch. It was a quaint kind of place just off the Bridge, with a lovely beer garden and walls covered in ivy. We were sipping our pints out in the garden overlooking the gorge when we heard this almighty roar of a dozen or so motorcycles from the car park and looked on as a group of overweight, leather-clad bikers dismounted from their shiny chromed Harley Davidson motorbikes and ambled en-masse into the pub. We ignored them and continued with our lunch but a few moments later we heard the sound of breaking glass and when Pete went to see what had happened, he informed us that one of the Angels had thrown a bar stool through the window and called the publican a 'wanker' because he didn't have a particular ale on tap that they wanted. The landlord was about to call the police when the leader of the gang stepped forward and offered to pay for the damage but warned the man that if he reported the incident they would be back to 'really trash the place.'

All was quiet for 15 minutes and then we heard a woman shriek and so we put down our drinks and went to see what the fuss was about. Apparently one of the bikers had slapped the publican's teenage daughter on the backside and now he wanted them out.

"I've had enough of this lot," said Pete who was a paratrooper and built like a rugby prop. He was dark with green eyes and a nose like a boxer's.

"I say we take these arseholes on and teach them a lesson," he continued.

I tried to reason with him pointing out that there were only four of us and about ten of them but Pete was already half way across the room and heading for the leader of the gang who was propped up at the bar shouting more obscenities at the poor publican. He was a lardy looking man, with a great big fat bald head that was so white you could see his bulging blue veins. He wore sunglasses and had a big handlebar moustache and tattoos of naked women on his chubby white arms.

Pete deliberately put on this really posh accent and approaching the biker said, "I was wondering, my good man, do you know what a headache is by any chance?" The biker looked at him with utter contempt and replied.

"Who the fuck are you? You old ponce!"

To which Pete responded, "Well you will now!" and head butted the man full on in the centre of his fleshy pink face, flattening his nose with a sickening crunch. The biker screamed with pain and instinctively raised both his hands to his bloodied head whereupon Pete kicked him hard in the groin and pushed him over into a table and chairs before he collapsed to the floor in agony.

That's when all hell broke loose. The remaining bikers piled forward towards Pete who had picked up a chair by its legs and was about to use it as a shield.

"We need to get out of here quick!" I shouted at him as Andy and Chris headed out of the door towards the Landrover. Just as the Angels were about to pile onto Pete, he threw the chair at them and legged it out with me. Andy had got the Defender started and we jumped into the back as the Hells Angels emerged through the pub's entrance and headed across the parking lot to their bikes.

"Mow them down!" ordered Pete.

"What, the bikers?" answered Andy increduously.

"No, you idiot, the bloody bikes!"

The bikers saw the vehicle charging towards them and jumped out of the way just in time to see Andy ploughing down their precious machines like a row of dominoes before screeching out onto the main road! As we headed south, two police cars, sirens blaring headed in the opposite direction towards the pub.

A year later we returned. We were curious to know whether the bikers had ever come back and what had become of the landlord and his family. As we approached the bar dressed in our civis, the publican looked at us and leaning over it he said, "I remember you boys, welcome back! You will be happy to see that we are still in business and no, the bikers never returned. Apparently two of them were wanted for GBH and the gang has all but broken up." '

The next morning he met *Carmela*. *Pepe* had put on some *Mariachi* music and as he was singing to *La Malaguena*, the door opened and *Carmela* burst in, and taking *Pepe*'s hands began to dance around the room before collapsing onto the bed in laughter.

'So this is our famous guest?' she asked in Spanish, turning to James. 'They didn't tell me how handsome you were!' and she screeched again.

Carmela was about 21 years old with dark black hair, full lips, high cheek bones and smooth chocolatey skin and her brown eyes were deep and lively. She was dressed in a traditional embroidered *huipil* and wore open sandals on her bare feet. James had never met anyone quite so beautiful in his life. She seemed utterly without pretention or affectation. She was smaller than him, about five feet three inches tall with a womanly hourglass figure.

'I love that song,' she said to *Pepe* getting off the bed, 'but every time I hear it I want to cry!'

'So what would you like today?' she asked as *Pepe* translated.

James thought it a strange question. He felt like saying, 'I want to get out, I want to go home and be free,' but didn't think it was appropriate.

'Some of those *huevos rancheros* would be nice,' he replied 'and maybe an orange juice.'

Carmela's face split into a huge smile revealing a row of pearly white teeth, 'Of course *Senor*, I will be back in just a moment,' and with a flourish she swept out of the door.

'Isn't she wonderful?' *Pepe* said. 'If I was a woman I would want to be like *Carmela*.'

The jumpmaster on board the Hercules C130 aircraft finished checking the task unit's equipment minutes before the drop. Sitting with their backs to the cold sides of the plane's fuselage were seven men who routinely risked their lives in the service of their country. Each of them had experienced a rite of passage: they had volunteered and passed the U.S. Navy SEALS' gruelling selection process, thus gaining entry into one of the toughest warrior elites in the world. They were not in it for the glory or the citations and few outside the Pentagon were aware of their deadly missions. Even their own families and loved ones did not know the full extent of the dangers they regularly faced, fighting to protect and preserve a way of life that most Americans took completely for granted.

On the night of July 14th, the task unit was being sent into the jungles of Southern Mexico to rescue Monica *Gonzalez*. As the huge mouth of the Hercules plane yawned open, the seven commandos shuffled to the rear of the aircraft and waited for the green light. Each man carried over 100 pounds of equipment and each was a highly trained specialist. In SEAL team nine, Burrito Platoon that night, there was an armourer, medic, sniper, radio operator and navigator in addition to two experienced officers. When the red light turned to green, the team jumped as one out of the Hercules into the dead of night, 3000 feet above the jungle and minutes later landed in a field of maize in a forest clearing within seconds of each other. No one spoke. Using only hand signals to communicate, they dumped their parachutes, and moved stealthily into the cover of thick trees and tangled undergrowth. Here they strapped on their body armour and operational gear and prepared their weapons. Between them they carried some impressive hardware: M48 machine guns; an M46 belt-fed 556mm machine gun, a 40mm grenade launcher, stun grenades and 9mm Sigg Sauer side-arms. The sniper carried an MK12, a suppressed version of the M4 assault rifle, which was equipped with an optical sight. Before setting off for the target zone, under orders from the platoon's chief, the radio operator called in their successful insertion; they were ready to go. In single file and in a modified skirmish line, they moved stealthily through the jungle following the task unit's navigator who had planned the route the previous evening in the Tactical Operations Centre back in San Diego, California. Using an enhanced Garmin GPS 720 and wearing night optical devices, the seven man team were able to navigate directly to their destination, a remote and disused coffee warehouse on the *Usumacinta* River, situated five miles to the south.

That very same day, leaving their daughter with Lucy, the Cooper-Browns flew from London to *Benito Juarez* Airport in Mexico City. The KLM flight stopped briefly in Amsterdam before crossing the Atlantic in just under 10 hours. They flew business class, and arrived in Mexico at approximately nine o'clock in the evening, local time. Back in Berkshire, they had reserved a room for two nights in a boutique hotel called the '*Santa Maria*' in *Polanco* and were in bed by 11 o'clock.

Over the previous week and during the flight, they had planned their visit meticulously. Their aim was to retrace James' last known movements. They knew from information provided by the Foreign Office, that James had withdrawn money using his credit card twice in Mexico City before journeying south. They also knew that he had stayed for three nights in the Hotel Montecarlo. This would be their first port of call.

The Cooper-Browns had deliberately not informed the Foreign Office of their plans to visit Mexico because they knew what the response would be.

'The *Madrigal* Cartel might see this as an opportunity to kidnap you too,' Piers could almost hear Edward Hutchinson advising them. After a continental breakfast of croissants, orange juice and coffee, they ordered a taxi through the hotel's concierge and were at the Montecarlo by half past ten armed with an A4 envelope containing some enlarged photographs of James.

The duty manager did not recognise their son – he had been on leave the three days that James had stayed but he confirmed from the register and the hotel's files that James had paid the equivalent of £60 in cash for the three nights and had stayed in room 34. He told the Cooper-Browns that he had heard about the kidnapping and was deeply sympathetic.

'You must not believe *Senores,* that all Mexicans are like these thieves and murderers; they bring shame on our country!' he said apologetically.

The Cooper-Browns asked to see the room. They knew that they would find nothing of interest there, but Virginia in particular wanted to try to visualise where exactly he had been and stayed. There were tears in her eyes as they closed the door to the room and took the lift to the ground floor. Virginia could almost see her son sitting on the bed, reading, browsing over maps and guidebooks, and taking in the city's sights from the bedroom window.

Having pictured him at rest in the old hotel, they flagged down a taxi and asked to be taken to *Coyoacan*, the second location where James had apparently withdrawn cash from a branch of *Banamex*. Knowing her son's artistic interests, Virginia knew that James would not have gone to *Coyoacan* without visiting *Frida Kahlo's* house, so after browsing around the square, where tourists mingled around an array of stalls selling jewellery, clothing and CD's, the couple headed there. The woman who ran the gift shop, which sold art books, cards and souvenirs, recognised James instantly. She had spotted him poring over a book on *Monte-Alban* and suggested he visit *Oaxaca*. He had replied that he was planning to travel south the following day.

0044 DAYS

CHAPTER 12

"The war against drug trafficking, hasn't worked and it's turned migrants into merchandise for organized crime," said Sanchez, a reporter for La Nacion. "Actually, what the governments of the United States and Mexico have done is to turn over the administration of migration to organized crime."

✝

Monica lay on a rough wooden pallet. Her hands were shackled with chains to the wall and her feet were bound together with course rope. She was filthy, bruised and bloodied. Clad only in her underwear, she had been gang raped. Barely conscious after an horrific ordeal, she was covered in cigarette burns and both her knees had been capped by a drill with a 1/16 inch bit.

At the other end of the warehouse, *Diego* and *Sergio* sat on two old coffee crates watching a Steven Seagal video on a decrepit television set. They were smoking marijuana and drinking Bacardi. If it had been up to them, they would have wasted the *gringa* and dumped her body in the river for the alligators to eat, but they were waiting for orders from *Cesar*.

'We could sell her for good cash to some other group; everybody likes to screw an American, even a damaged one,' he had said, chuckling.

Throughout her lengthy interrogation, *Gonzalez* had revealed nothing of use to the cartel other than to confirm her name and that she worked as a paediatrician out in *San Juan Bautista*. She had confessed to being a CIA agent but did not give any details of the numerous reports she had filed over the months providing Langley with information on the cross border narcotics trade or the photographs she had taken of various members of the cartel, including several of *Madrigal* on a rare visit. He had arrived one evening in a convoy of 10 vehicles and got out of a black Range Rover, dressed in a dark suit and open shirt. He chatted to some customs and excise officers briefly and there was a lot of back slapping and laughter and then after 15 minutes *Madrigal* had got back in the car before being escorted north towards *Tuxtla Gutierrez*.

Two hours before dawn, the seven-man SEAL unit approached the warehouse from the north. A high chain-link fence surrounded the compound and at the entrance were a sentry post and gate and a sign that read *'Café Lacondon – El Sabor del Sur'*. Both were guarded. Through his optical scope, the sniper scanned the target zone. In addition to the two guards on the road, he spotted two others. One stood outside a side door at the bottom of a metal fire escape smoking and another was posted at the main entrance. They were armed with AK47 assault rifles. They were dressed in jeans and boots and checked shirts and wore straw hats. They were dark skinned and looked poor. None of these men would have had any military training. They were probably malnourished, badly paid and unfit but nonetheless, potentially dangerous and unpredictable. To the south was a wooden jetty where three speed boats were moored on the riverside. There was some dim external lighting but no evidence of alarms or trip wires. Parked outside the warehouse were two Ford pickups, one of which had a mini gun mounted in the bed of the truck. The vehicles were old and rusty and the sniper doubted whether either of them could top 50 miles an hour. They waited a further 15 minutes to see if any other hired guns arrived on the scene. Apart from the cicadas chirping in the languid air, it was silent.

Waiting downriver was a U.S. Marine Corps Special Boat Team consisting of two, four-crew rapid response river crafts that had been airlifted in that same night from a Sikorsky Super Stallion helicopter stationed on board the U.S.S Stealth out in the Gulf of Mexico. Their mission was to extract SEAL team nine, Burrito Platoon and Monica *Gonzalez* just after dawn. Each boat carried a formidable arsenal which included a grenade launcher, a mounted 7.62mm

Gatling gun and a light anti-tank assault weapon. Just before five o'clock in the morning, the officer in charge of the Special Boat Team received a radio call the from the SEAL unit to stand by. They were about to go in to rescue *Gonzalez*. The estimated duration of the operation from entry to extraction was given as approximately 15 minutes. Slamming their throttles on full, the coxswains directed the boats up river, travelling at 40 knots per hour, their twin 440 Yanmar diesel engines roaring into action.

Back at the warehouse, the sniper had already neutralised the two men stationed outside the building's entrances. The guard smoking at the side door had slumped silently to the ground less than a second after the hollow tipped bullet passed through his skull. The man at the main entrance had been hit between the eyes and fell backwards onto a grassy bank. The sniper then turned his attention to the two sentries posted at the gate. The first went down noisily whereupon his companion reacted immediately by firing erratically in the SEAL unit's direction. Taking aim and breathing in calmly, the sniper squeezed the trigger and almost simultaneously, the last guard reeled back and crashed into the side of the hut. With the sniper covering them, six SEALS moved stealthily towards the fence and after cutting their way through, approached the building. The Special Boat Team was now less than 12 minutes away.

Inside, the warehouse was dark save for a thin slit of lighting coming from beneath a door at the end of a long hallway. Two SEALS went in first and cleared the four rooms along the narrow hall. Three rooms were padlocked and the other one was being used for storage. Signalling back to the remaining four SEALS who stood close to the main entrance, guarding the approach, they gestured for them to take the side entrance. The sniper meanwhile was scanning the target zone for tangos when he spotted a fifth guard with a Rottweiler on the end of a lead. They were patrolling the perimeter fence. The sniper knew it would be seconds rather than minutes before he discovered his dead *compadres*. He caught the guard in the cross-hairs of his scope and pulled the trigger. A mist of red exploded from the back of his head as he fell, releasing the dog. Dragging its lead behind it, the Rottweiler turned and picking up the sniper's scent, charged towards his cover in the dense undergrowth. The sniper dropped his rifle and quickly withdrew his Sigg Sauer hand gun and shot the hound moments before it was about to leap on him.

Back inside the warehouse, the four SEALS who were securing the side entrance discovered that it opened up directly into a cavernous hall piled high with old wooden crates. They heard muffled conversation from the far end and the distinct sound of a television. They then spotted *Gonzalez,* shackled and motionless on the opposite side of the warehouse. Just then, another door opened and five men ran in shouting something urgently in Spanish. They were heavily armed. The SEALS took this as their cue to attack. Pitching in three stun grenades they entered the hall and spreading out, opened fire with their machine guns, spraying the area in a maelstrom of bullets. Within less than two minutes three tangos lay dead, spread-eagled on the floor and four more had retreated to the cover of some crates to return fire. The two SEALS clearing the corridor were about to enter the hall when they were trapped in the narrow space by three tangos who smashed the glass in the entrance door and began firing in. One of the commandos went down, shot in the back of the neck. The other managed to dive through the open doorway of a room he had just cleared and returned fire through the fragile stud wall that separated him from the hallway and his assailants. Hundreds of bullets splintered the rotting boards peppering two of the tangos in the upper body and face. For a moment all firing in the back of the warehouse ceased; and then the lone SEAL, trapped in the side room, heard the unmistakable sound of a grenade rolling across the floor. There was a huge explosion as the walls caved in and the ceiling collapsed. Less than five minutes after entering the building, seven tangos were dead, including *Diego. Sergio* lay mortally wounded, his life bleeding out of him into a dark puddle on the concrete floor of the warehouse. The medic, who had been shot in the arm, ignored his own wound and immediately attended to *Gonzalez* who was unconscious and barely alive. The armourer shot the chain off its housing in the wall using his side arm and the two soldiers carried Monica outside where they were covered by the sniper. The remaining two SEALS completed a final sweep of the building before hauling the body of their fallen comrade out. They were unable to reach the navigator who lay dead under a mountain of debris in the side room where the grenade had exploded.

Outside, an orange sun was rising slowly over the river and the Special Boat Teams were waiting at the jetty to extract the SEALS. As the unit was loading Monica onto the first boat, two pick-up trucks skidded through the compound entrance sending up a cloud of dust, and eight men jumped out the back and began firing. The Special Boat Team, expecting hostilities, returned with rapid staccato fire from the heavy Gatling gun and anti-tank weapon. When the smoke cleared seconds later, and the air was filled with the smell of cordite, the warehouse compound was a scene of utter carnage and devastation.

0042 DAYS

CHAPTER 13

*The AK – 47, popularly known as El Cuerno del Chivo
(the goat's horn) is the preferred weapon for Mexican
drug cartels. In 2003, 30,000 were smuggled
in from former Soviet Republics.*

✞

The Cooper-Browns left the Federal District after two nights and headed by bus to *Oaxaca*. It took them an hour and a half to clear the city's sprawling suburbs and shanties. There were endless roads lined with garages, shops selling auto-parts and dingy looking diners. Scrawny children played football on dusty pitches between electricity pylons and emaciated dogs roamed the streets. There were only a handful of other passengers on the air-conditioned coach heading south. It was meticulously clean and smelt of lemon air-freshener and seemed to Virginia and Piers like an island of luxury amidst so much squalor. A Bruce Lee video was playing at the front of the bus but the Cooper-Browns paid little attention to it. Virginia read a novel by *Isabel Allende*, whilst Piers looked out of the window as the city's outskirts gave way gradually to green upland pastures spotted with magueys and poppies.

Every hour or so, the bus would stop in a grey town and itinerant salesmen would board.

'These pills costing only 100 *pesos* will get rid of dandruff, haemorrhoids and penal warts,' shouted a man dressed in a faded cream linen suit as he passed up and down the aisle.

'Chewing-gums, chocolates, sweets, sandwiches and sodas,' hawked a bare chested little boy dressed in shorts and a pair of open sandals.

After three hours the bus began climbing through a range of barren mountains interlaced with deep ravines. Piers loved this kind of scenery and it reminded him of the mountains of Oman where years before he had fought insurgents whilst serving in the Sultan's forces with an SAS unit seconded from the British Army. He wondered if James was somewhere out there. These were the kind of hills where bandits, reprobates and fugitives would take refuge.

To Virginia, the terrain seemed hostile and inhospitable and reminded her of James' cruel situation. There was nothing friendly or welcoming about the brown canyons and thorny cacti: she hated the country already for it seemed like a horrible metaphor of the violence that was tearing her family apart. She longed for the lush greenery of England and its tranquil countryside.

At dusk they pulled into *Oaxaca*'s bus terminal and took a taxi to the *Hotel Francia*, which had been recommended by the woman they had met at *Frida Kahlo's* house.

Their hotel was sandwiched between two chocolate factories from where the delicious smell of cinnamon and cocoa wafted. The neighbourhood was buzzing with activity around the city's huge indoor market and at night, prostitutes in stilettos and tight miniskirts gathered in doorways chatting and waiting, their cigarettes glowing like fire flies in the dark. As Piers and Virginia sat in a bar in the *Zocalo*, drinking their coffees and poring over guidebooks, a small army of buskers, clowns, basket makers, rug peddlars and souvenir hawkers pursued their trades under the porticoes. In the square, children roller skated and balloon and candyfloss vendors lingered around the restaurants. Virginia could understand why James would have loved *Oaxaca*. It was colourful and vibrant with shops selling jewellery, hammocks, embroidered garments and ceramics.

After breakfast the following morning, they returned to the *Zocalo* to plan their day. Whilst Virginia studied a map of the city, Piers decided to wander around the streets and alleys leading off the main square. He was impatient to find out as much as he could about his son's last known movements.

'I am just going to walk around for a bit with copies of James' picture to see if anyone recognises him,' he said to Virginia, downing his coffee and rising from the table. 'I won't be long.'

Virginia nodded and smiled before returning to the map.

James' credit card records showed that he had used a *Bancomer* ATM near the post office to withdraw cash, so Piers went there first.

He popped into one or two bars that were adjacent to the post office and asked waiters and the barmen if they recognized James but none of them had. And then he spotted a small internet café across the square where young back-packers and tourists were milling around the doorway reading the notices posted in the window. Inside, all the computers were being used as travellers from different parts of the globe emailed friends and family. Behind the counter was a young woman with dark braided hair, dressed in a tie-dyed shirt and long skirt. She was pretty and looked like a typical hippie and smiled as Piers approached.

'Can I help you sir?' she asked in a Californian accent.

Piers explained that his son had been kidnapped somewhere in *Oaxaca* and although the authorities were doing everything to locate him, he and his wife were trying to retrace where their son might have been. The woman looked shocked.

'I am terribly sorry to hear that!' she said. 'Yes, I do recognise him, that's James isn't it? He came in here several times for coffee and to use the computers and we chatted a lot. He told me he was heading to the beach and asked me to recommend somewhere off the beaten track. I suggested he go to *Puerto Sal*, a tiny little village on the Pacific with beautiful unspoilt beaches and an off-beat charm. It's down the road from *Puerto Escondido*.' Tears had begun to well up in her big brown eyes. 'I'm so sorry,' she said again.

The *molé* that *Carmela* cooked that night, accompanied by *tortillas* and rice, was one of the most delicious meals James had ever eaten. She had also prepared a dark rich drink called *jamaica* made from hibiscus petals which was refreshingly sweet and cold. *Carmela* insisted that it was most healthy.

'It's full of anti-oxidants and is good for all kinds of ailments including hepatitis,' she said.

After the meal, James, *Pepe* and *Carmela* sat in the tiny room chatting. *Pepe* and *Carmela* were eager to share their knowledge of Mexican food with him.

'Each *barrio* in *Oaxaca* boasts the best *molé*,' *Pepe* said, 'and every year there is a big *fiesta* to celebrate all the different types!'

Later that night, whilst *Pepe* slept soundly in the corner, James got up to relieve himself. Stepping over *Pepe*'s legs he opened the door quietly and wandered down the dark corridor to the bathroom. The house was silent and through the front door he glimpsed the very first rays of dawn. In his bare feet he padded further down the hallway and placing his hand on the door handle, he pushed it down. To his complete surprise, it opened. James looked out as the cool night breeze blew in. There was a patch of stony ground and then a concrete parking lot where two old trucks were parked. He could hear cicadas chirping in the undergrowth and looking up he saw a star filled sky and clear, full moon. To the east, the night was retreating. James could not remember feeling so liberated. He stood for a moment in the open doorway, letting the cool air run through his long matted hair. The thought did not occur to him immediately: he was too wrapped up in his enjoyment of being outside and the smell of fresh air.

'Shit! I need to get out of here!' he suddenly said to himself. He looked beyond the parking lot to a small wooden gate and track that meandered downhill through thick woods. There was no one about: no guards, no dogs, just him and *Pepe* and possibly *Carmela* sleeping in one of the other rooms. And then he realised he didn't have his flip-flops on or his shirt. He would need to go back for them. He felt exhilarated as adrenaline began coursing through his veins. 'I could be free, out in those hills within 10 minutes,' he thought. His mind was racing. 'There's bound to be tracks out there, a village where someone will take me in, give me a lift to a police station.'

He walked slowly and quietly back down the corridor passing the open door of the kitchen where the fridge whirred like an insect and he could still smell the nutty *molé*. He was about to put his hand on the door to his cell when it opened. *Pepe* stood there, silhouetted by the moon light, holding up James' flip-flops and his shirt.

'Go,' he said in a tired voice, 'if you want to! No one will stop you. *Carmela* is sleeping next door and although I have a gun, I could not shoot you James.'

James wanted to grab his things and run, but something held him back.

'You should go,' repeated *Pepe*, 'I would', and then he added. 'But if you do, *Carmela*, *Manolito* and I will all die. *Cesar* told me the other day that if you escaped no one could protect me from the gay bashers that have been itching to get at me. He told me he would deliver me to them himself; watch as they castrated and crucified me against a tree in the park as a warning to other *maricons*. Worse would happen to *Carmela* and they would feed *Manolito* to the sharks.'

'What about *Carlos?*' James asked, as if his fate suddenly mattered to him.

'*Carlos* is different; he's one of them,' answered *Pepe*.

James stood for a moment and then he pushed passed *Pepe* and fell back onto the bed.

0040 DAYS

CHAPTER 14

On July 10, 2003, the Mexican government announced plans to nearly double the size of its Federal Police force to reduce the role of the military in combatting drug trafficking. High ranking officers in the Federal army have been accused of complying, abetting and even supplying drug cartels with intelligence, weaponry and communications.

✟

The bus from *Oaxaca* to the coast rattled south through the *Sierra Madre* Occidental. They passed signs for *Mitla* and *Monte-Alban* and then climbed for an hour through wooded hills. Unlike the coach from Mexico, this one was old and oily and full of *indigenas* returning to their villages for the *fiestas*. The windows were dirty and cracked and there was no air conditioning. Instead of videos, the driver played *ranchero* music. Their companions sat silently clutching boxes and baskets of fruit. They were small and dark with noble, hard faces. Occasionally the bus stopped at remote villages to let passengers on and off: *San Juan Del Rio, San Gabriel Mixtepec*, and *Chilpancingo*.

Whilst Virginia sat absorbed in her novel, Piers made notes in a small leather-bound book about the people they had met and places they had been. And then he began drawing up a list. First he wrote down four names followed by a question mark. One was his own and then he wrote; Loftie McGregor, Marty Schultz and Matthew Waterman, his partner at Risk Factor, before compiling a detailed list of equipment:

4 balaclavas
4 pairs of black Asolo Italian made mountain boots
4 Motorola radios
4 Garmin GPS wrist devices
1 satellite phone
1 RPG
1 sniper rifle, scope & bipod
4 Glock handguns & suppressors
2 second hand SUV's
US Navy F1N canon Camera
Grappling hook

4 M16 semi-automatic rifles / shortened
4 SOG Special Forces knives
Ammunition
2 Persuader shotguns
1 pair of binoculars
4 night optical devices
4 70 litre Berghaus rucksacks
Abseil rope and climbing gear
Box of flash-bangs
Duct tape & nylon ties
Battlefield First Aid Kit
Box of grenades

James wanted to hate *Pepe* but he couldn't. When he had first been kidnapped he would not have given *Pepe*, *Manolito* or *Carmela* a second thought. They were part of the conspiracy and had he had the means he would have killed them. But since then, they had become his friends. Like so many of the nameless poor with whom he had shared cramped buses and dingy diners, they too were victims he realised. Unlike *Cesar*, the two gangsters that had picked him up and even *Carlos*, *Pepe*, *Carmela* and *Manolito* were not free. They lived under constant threats with little control over their lives. James knew now that he would not try to escape again. He did not want to imagine what would inevitably happen to them if he got away. As he lay on his bed thinking in the early hours of dawn his thoughts went back to his days at university. He thought of the numerous people he knew who glibly took drugs, smoked dope and insisted naively that it was harmless. Many of these students professed to having social consciences and caring deeply about people less fortunate than themselves. They had voted Labour, joined organisations like Amnesty International and had driven down to Edinburgh and London on student protests and demonstrations. James wanted to drag some of those people over to Mexico to show them the so called 'harmless effects' of their decadent flirtation with drugs. He wanted to show them the misery and suffering it caused. He knew that the likes of *Madrigal* were responsible for peddling this evil trade but it was people like his fellow students and their parents (many of whom boasted holding cocaine parties) that were *Madrigal's* market and kept the wicked trade going. He recalled an argument he had had with Charlotte shortly before they broke up.

'Stop judging me!' she had said as she sat on a bean bag in her room, dragging on a joint. 'It's none of your business whether I smoke this stuff or not and anyway what harm is it doing anyone?'

He recalled the look in her eyes as she stared at him as if nothing else in the world mattered except her moment of ecstasy. He knew now that he didn't want to know these people anymore and couldn't ignore their hypocrisy.

And then he remembered his father telling him about how an ancestor of theirs had played a leading role in The First Opium War against China in 1839 when The East India Company confiscated vast quantities of the narcotic from the Cantonese to redress trading rights and to satisfy burgeoning appetites for the opiate in England. This conflict had involved British troops and ships and had been sanctioned by the British government. The hypocrisy of politics sickened him. He loathed those who took drugs and sold them but he hated the sanctimonious platitudes and policies of his own government towards countries such as Columbia, Peru and Mexico and their endless criticisms that

Latin America was not doing enough to stop the trade and export of narcotics. Only a year before the son of a Conservative politician had died of a heroin overdose in his final days at Oxford University. There were no innocent parties in this filthy business; no goodies or baddies – the whole world was corrupt and sordid.

Piers and Virginia arrived in *Puerto Sal* at three o'clock in the afternoon on July 18th. They discovered a village with little more than a street, a supermarket, *cantina*, fish restaurant and two small hotels but the beach had powder white sand and there was a distinct lack of tourists.

'*Bienvenidos!*' said the large man with a goatee beard as they entered the *Hotel Tres Marias.*' He proceeded to shuffle about behind the counter for the register and a pen.

They paid for a simple but spotlessly clean double room overlooking the harbour and were sitting in the fish restaurant less than 15 minutes later with plates of freshly-caught, barbecued tuna before them. The dish was accompanied by a huge green salad and a plate of chips. Some men sat at the bar, swigging down bottles of cold *Corona* beer and eyed them with interest. The couple who owned the restaurant could not do enough to make the Cooper-Browns feel more welcome. They brought a basket of hot *tortillas* wrapped in a cloth, dishes containing chilli sauces of one kind and another and sat behind the bar eagerly awaiting further orders. The meal was delicious and both Virginia and Piers were hungry and thirsty after the long bus journey from *Oaxaca*. The Cooper-Browns could see why the village would have appealed to James. It was quiet – a genuine fishing community, without any pretention and the beach was pristine, with rocky cliffs tumbling down on either side. When they had finished their meal and ordered coffee, Piers pulled out the photos of James and when the owner of the restaurant returned, he asked the thin man dressed in black trousers and a white shirt whether he recognised him.

'I sorry,' he said blushing slightly. 'I no speak good English. Dis man,' he said pointing at the photographs, 'he your son?' he asked. Piers nodded

'Dis man stay one tine in di *Hotel Paraiso* up di road,' he pointed. 'What happens is terrible,' he said raising both hands up in front of him.

'Some bad peoples take your son away, we can do nothing! This is very bad for you and for the village,' he went on frowning. 'Peoples in *Puerto Sal* wants to know what is happening with your son,'

The Cooper-Browns thanked the man for his help and concern and asked for the bill.

'No bill!' replied the man. His wife was now at his side nodding. She was small and buxom, clad in a large apron. Both of them had dark faces weathered by the sun and sea.

'While you stay in dis village I pay for everything,' the owner insisted. 'You come here for di breakfast, di dinner, everything!'

After thanking the couple once again, Virginia and Piers left the restaurant and wandered out into the evening sun. They walked up and down the street looking briefly into the *cantina* and supermarket and then turned back to the *Hotel Paraiso*. They quickly discovered that the place was dingy and uninviting and wondered if the owner was aware or even cared about the irony of its name. They found a grumpy, unshaven man behind the cheap wood and glass reception desk watching football on the television. He did not look up until Piers rapped his knuckles on the surface of the desk. On seeing Piers however, he was clearly startled and unsettled – as if he had seen a ghost. Piers picked up on the look immediately. He had seen the same fear on the faces of a group of Omani insurgents that he and his unit had captured down an isolated wahdi.

'*Senores*,' he said rising from his seat and turning off the television with the remote control device. 'I no have rooms tonight. We are closed for the weekend.'

'We are not looking for a room,' answered Piers abruptly.

'We were told that our son James stayed here before he was kidnapped,' interjected Virginia.

'Yes, yes, the *gringo* stay here, but I no see what happen to him, I swear,' replied *Alberto* gesturing the

Cooper-Browns to the door. 'I sorry,' he went on, 'but the hotel is closed: I cannot help you.'

The Cooper-Browns left without protest but Piers knew that he had found his man. After a night in *Puerto Sal*, they returned to Mexico City and two days later were back in Mosscombe.

0038 DAYS

CHAPTER 15

Between 2000 and 2003, 42 journalists were murdered in Mexico for covering drug-related stories

✝

*C*arlos never returned to the house. Three days after James had considered escaping, *Carmela* brought him his breakfast without saying a word. She had been crying and her eyes were puffy and swollen with tears. An hour later, *Manolito* came in and silently sat down with his back to the wall, the AK47 nonchalantly balanced on his knees.

'What's wrong with *Carmela*?' James asked him.

Manolito pushed the brim of his straw hat up.

'*Carlos* died last night,' he replied without any emotion.

'What? How did he die?' James had never really liked *Carlos,* but he was only young and the news came as both a surprise and shock.

'The *pinche pendejo* was playing roulette with some friends down at the *cantina,* like the *bandidos* used to do in the olden days. He blew his head off with a Colt 45. They will bury him tomorrow. His body lies in *La Hermita de Santa Ana*. His friends say he had a death wish. He had been melancholic after he and some of *Cesar's* men were ordered to execute some *campesinos* a while back,' and he was silent again.

A blanket of depression descended on the house. Even *Pepe* was silent and subdued. He sat quietly in the corner, his headphones in his ears, refusing to eat or talk. *Carmela* continued cooking for everyone but she too rarely spoke and remained sullen for days. For James, this was the hardest time. He knew the deadline for the ransom was approaching and he longed for his family. After three days a tall slim man called *Ramon* joined the rota. He had been ordered to tighten up the regime inside the house and seemed determined to do so. Once again James had to be escorted to the bathroom and the magazines, cassettes and books were confiscated. *Ramon* carried an Uzi machine gun and a Smith and Wesson pistol in a holster and he rarely smiled. *Carmela* was confined to the kitchen and was prohibited from visiting James.

Loftie McGregor was stacking shelves in a B&Q store in Milngavie, Glasgow when he received the text from Piers Cooper-Brown. Loftie was five feet seven inches tall, wiry and built like a whippet. Born in the Gorbals district of the city in 1958, he had grown up fighting: first with his fists, then with knives and clubs and broken bottles. His arms and body were covered in tattoos and scars.

Loftie was regarded as a legend in the Gorbals. On June 14th 1976, he had been drinking in his local pub down in the docks when he went to assist a girl who was being slapped about by her boyfriend outside the toilets. The boyfriend was a known brawler by the name of Angus. He was six feet four inches tall with huge arms and legs like tree trunks. He was a dock worker by trade but spent most of his time drinking and fighting. The previous year he had killed a Belgian sailor in a bare-knuckle street fight with a single punch to the head.

Approaching the young woman but ignoring Angus, Loftie had said:

'Are you ok lassie? Seems like the hippo is given ye some trouble?'

The girl nodded, her eyes full of tears but she was clearly distressed.

'Who wants to know?' Angus had replied. 'You should be getting back to the circus,' he said laughing. 'The midget act starts in 10 minutes!'

Loftie returned to the bar, downed his pint, stubbed out his cigarette and picking up a wooden bar stool smashed it over the giant's head. The stool fell apart on impact but Angus barely flinched. Pushing the young girl aside and kicking the remains of the stool away, he clutched Loftie in his huge paws and raising him above his head, threw him across the bar into a shelf lined with glasses and bottles. The barman was quick to respond. He grabbed his double barrelled shotgun which he kept behind the counter and aimed it at the big man.

'Angus McLeod, if ye ever cast a shadow over this place again, I'll decorate the walls with ye blubber!'

Loftie spent six weeks in hospital. He had a fractured skull, broken jaw and numerous cuts. When he recovered six months later he joined the army. In July 1977, Angus' bloated body was found floating in the murky waters of the Clyde. A thin white gash across his neck, washed clean of blood, revealed that he had been garrotted by a length of cheese wire. No one was ever arrested or charged for the murder but it was widely suspected that Loftie McGregor had been involved.

The army saved Loftie from a life of crime and a premature death. He was half way up a ladder and two hours from the end of his shift when the phone in his pocket buzzed. Loftie read Piers' message smiling, descended the ladder and walked out the front entrance.

'McGregor, where the hell are you going?' shouted the manager after him as he strode across the car park towards his motorcycle.

'None ya fuckin' business!' shouted Loftie back, 'and you can stick ya job too!'

Loftie had been a corporal in the Scots Guards when he decided to take the selection course for entry into the Special Air Service. He had never heard of Hereford before and thought hitherto that the Brecon Beacons were a rock band. Out of the 35 volunteers, who willingly submitted themselves to the most gruelling physical tests known to man that freezing weekend in February 1981, Loftie McGregor was the only one to pass.

The house on *Juarez* Street was over 200 years old. Once the former residence of a wealthy Spanish landowner, *Madrigal* had bought and renovated it back in the early 1990's restoring it to its former glory. Behind a huge stone wall now covered in bougainvillea, a gravel drive snaked its way through trees, a mile and a half to the old two storey *hacienda* built around a courtyard and fountain. On the ground floor, all the rooms opened out onto spacious colonnades, and grassy terraces sloped down to a 20 metre pool hewn out of the rock. This was the *Madrigal* home where *Lorenza* lived and their two beautiful daughters had grown up. For a man, whose own family had been fractured and dysfunctional, the house was a symbol of unity and gentle domesticity, though ironically from the early 2000's onwards when the house was under constant surveillance by various federal agencies, *Madrigal* himself was rarely there. It was rumoured that a network of tunnels ran from the house under the *sierra* emerging out into the *Oaxaca* canyon-lands. Years later, *Madrigal's* biographer would write that all his passions, his psychopathy, lust for power and wealth stemmed from a deep desire for security and a desperate need to protect his family. Those who knew *Lorenza* and the girls well, described them as cultured, educated and sophisticated women untainted by the sordid world that *Madrigal* inhabited. *Madrigal* and *Lorenza* were never married, a deliberate decision, his biographer explained, that meant that *Lorenza* and his daughters would not be associated with *Madrigal's* business and criminal dealings. It was also said that he had signed over most of his wealth to his partner and the girls in the form of trusts to further cushion them from his criminal activities. Aged 11 and 13 respectively, *Paloma* and *Alondra* had been sent to The Sacred Heart boarding school in Sussex for a Catholic education and did not see either of their parents for months on end. They learnt to play hockey and lacrosse, were popular amongst the other girls, gained excellent academic grades and both went on to university. *Alondra*, the eldest, read international law at Princeton whilst her younger sister *Paloma* studied fashion in Milan. They mixed with the jet set crowd, spending winters skiing in the Alps and at Aspen in the Rockies and their summers touring Europe and further afield and for years they remained blissfully unaware of their father's crimes or his notoriety.

0036 DAYS

CHAPTER 16

*In May 2003, a submarine carrying a cargo of cocaine
from the Columbian port of Cartagena was intercepted
by U.S Navy Seals off Huatulco Bay.*

✠

The day after their return from Mexico, Virginia
and Piers were opening the stack of mail that had
been waiting for them on the hall floor. Among the letters of sympathy from friends and strangers alike was
one posted in London from *Javier Ernesto Madrigal*.
It had been neatly handwritten in ink on expensive,
heavy cream coloured letter-writing paper. There was
no address or date.

It began:

Dear Mr and Mrs Cooper-Brown:

*First I would like to apologise for the pain and suffer-
ing caused by the kidnapping of your son James. Believe me
when I say that I have nothing personal against you or your
family; I too have a wife and two beautiful daughters whom
I value more than anything else in the world. But here in
Mexico we are fighting a war of survival and abductions and
demands for ransom money are some of the many weapons we
must use in order to fight our cause.*

Although this will come as no consolation to you, my associates tell me that James is being looked after well; he is healthy and well-nourished and has access to books and music.

You will be aware that we are asking for a fee of $5 million in exchange for your son. The deadline set for this payment was a month from the day he was taken. However, contrary to what you might think of me, I too have feelings and am a compassionate man. I am therefore willing to extend this period for a further two weeks to enable you to raise these funds on the condition that they are paid in full. For you and your son's sake, please follow the instructions below to the letter. If you fail to do so, you will never see James again.

- *The money must be in untraceable bundles evenly distributed into 5 black Samsonite hard shell cases. These can be bought at either Liverpool or Sambourne stores in Mexico City*
- *Once the cases have been packed, they should be delivered to the parking lot in the <u>Desierto de los Leones</u>, a popular recreational spot and forest on Avenida de Toluca on the south-west of Mexico City*
- *You must leave the 5 cases in the large, green waste disposal units there at precisely 11:00 on August 30th. That will give you plenty of time to get there.*
- *The delivery must be made by Mr or Mrs Cooper-Brown or both together BUT no one else. You must*

drive a VW white Passat which you can hire from any rental agency in the city.

- *You will identify yourself by flashing your car lights 3 times before getting out of the car and leaving the cases in the designated drop*
- *When the ransom has been collected and counted, we will contact CNN in Mexico City with instructions of where to pick up James*

Please heed my warning and follow these instructions. Any attempt to involve the police or the military or sabotage the drop in any way will result in your son's execution.

Sincerely,

Javier Ernesto Madrigal

CEO Madrigal Cartel

That same evening, Virginia confessed to Piers that she had already begun the process of raising the necessary funds.

'I couldn't just stand by and wait for the Mexican authorities to do something. As it is we have heard nothing for weeks and I was terrified they would kill James unless we paid up,' she said sobbing as they sat on the sofa; her head nestled in on his right shoulder. Piers kissed her on the forehead and played with her hair.

'I knew you were up to something,' he said and they both laughed, 'but don't go selling my Range Rover. I have spent half my life dreaming of owning one!'

Virginia looked up at him. 'Actually it was third on the list after the two houses,' she replied. 'After all they are just things. If there is one lesson this whole dreadful experience has taught me, it is that material possessions are not worth craving for in life. People and relationships are so much more important,' and Piers nodded.

The second person to receive a message from Piers was Marty Schultz. He was corralling a herd of Mustang horses on a ranch in California when his Samsung cellular vibrated in his pocket. Handing his lasso to one of the stable bucks, he leant against the wooden gate and read the text.

Piers had met Marty in Kuwait City over a game of pool at the end of the first Gulf War. He and Matthew Waterman had been with SAS patrol, Tango 3.1 deep behind enemy lines, tracking and monitoring Saddam Hussein's mobile Scud missile launchers and were due to return home within a few days. They had gone to the Joint Forces Mess for a drink one evening when they had bumped into Marty Schultz.

'We will whip your limey asses,' goaded the tall lanky soldier dressed in faded fatigues. He had a mop of blonde hair and clear blue, laughing eyes. 'Teach you boys how to really play the pool' he said chuckling as he racked up the balls.

'Bring it on!' replied Matthew and he and Piers downed their pints and picked their cues. The tall Marine introduced himself as Marty Schultz.

'Oh, and this shrimp of a Mexican here is *Santiago!*' he said pointing down to his companion, a stocky, dark man with a crew cut who had just taken the first shot of the game.

Santiago potted a spot on his first shot and then two more. Matthew cued off for the British pair and potted three stripes in succession but on his fourth shot he sunk the black and had to concede the game. Piers and Matthew clawed back the next frame and went on to win the third but as the beers went down, the Brits lost their grip and Marty and *Santiago* ended up winning five frames to two. They had been roundly beaten by the Americans. After countless Budweisers, the pool game had been forgotten and the four soldiers were enjoying trading war stories and sharing their experiences.

'I won $200 in an arm wrestling contest the other day,' Marty boasted. '*Santi* and I were invited to join some Kuwaiti mechanics we had got to know out at the base and they took us to this seedy coffee bar in the old part of town. We had just entered the place and Abdul had ordered Arabian coffee and dates for us when this huge guy wandered over and challenged me to arm wrestle with him. "Not here," he said, "in the back room," and he gestured through a beaded curtain. He must have weighed close on 250 pounds and looked like Bluto. He was hairy and sweaty and had hardly any teeth. I told him I would finish my cup of coffee with my friends and join him shortly. So anyway, a few minutes later we go back into this dimly lit, smoke filled room where we see two huge Kuwaitis battling it out. Each was desperate to win, because they were competing over candle fire. Whoever lost was going to have his arm burnt badly. By now it was too late to back out. We sat down and gripped each other's hands and the umpire put the two candles in place. Bluto's hand felt like a huge piece of steak. His grip was like a vice and I knew I would lose. The room was crowded with spectators all gathering around to watch the American get his ass whipped. So we start and this guy is beating me big time. My arm is now at 45 degrees above the candle and I can feel the searing heat. So with my left hand, I reach under the table which was covered in a thick canvas cloth and grab the guy's balls and squeeze like hell. There was so much excitement and noise in the room that no one noticed me doing it! The next thing that happens is that the big Arab is screaming with pain and I have slammed his arm down on the candle, snuffing out the flame and the place has erupted into loud applause. Bluto meanwhile is now lying on the floor with his hands in his crotch and I am being handed my $200 prize money!'

At three o'clock in the morning, barely conscious from consuming so much alcohol, they stumbled out of the bar. Marty withdrew a penknife from his pocket, cut a line across his palm and insisted that the others did likewise. They then shook hands firmly and vowed to be life-long blood brothers. They had kept in touch ever since.

Schultz read the text message:

'Marty, your old limey friend needs a favour! Meet me at St Ermin's Hotel off Victoria Street in London on August 1st at 10 o'clock. All expenses paid including your return flight,' it ended enigmatically.

O ne afternoon, a week after *Carlos'* untimely death, *Pepe* opened the door to James' cell and with a smile said, 'I think something is about to happen my friend. There has been a lot of talk recently about you and everyone seems happy, especially *Cesar*. Maybe your ransom will be paid and soon you will go home!'

James was pleased that *Pepe* had regained his customary good humour but the news did not fill him with hope. He knew his father would never cave into a ransom demand even if his own son's life depended upon it and he doubted the British government would be paying it.

P iers and Matthew met Loftie McGregor and Marty Schultz in London as planned, precisely 29 days before the ransom was due to be delivered. Piers had told Virginia that he had business in London and caught the early morning train to Paddington. Neither he nor Matthew had seen Loftie for over 10 years but they recognised him instantly.

'Hey Buddy,' said Marty slapping Piers on the back, 'you're looking old. Be needing a Zimmer frame soon. Still got your teeth?' and the two of them laughed.

Marty and Matthew shook hands. 'It sure has been a while old pal!' said Marty affectionately, 'what has the old man got planned? Marathon pool challenge or is it snooker here?'

Matthew, with his mop of grey hair and bookish appearance, did not look like a former commando, but he had a steely resolve and his stamina and general toughness had been legendary. Years before, during a training exercise with fellow troopers out in Yemen, their patrol Landrover had broken down in the middle of desert. Unable to fix the gasket which had blown, Matthew and another soldier had volunteered to walk 70 miles to the nearest town for assistance. His friend collapsed and almost died of dehydration and Matthew had carried him over 15 miles of sand dunes and through the searing heat to the nearest oasis. Mathew Waterman still held the record for the fastest marathon yomp across the Brecon Beacons carrying a 100 pound Bergen.

'Something like that,' replied Matthew dryly, 'only it's in your part of the world – Mexico!'

Piers introduced Loftie. 'And this shrimp of a Scot here is McGregor, tough as a pit-bull and drinks like a whale. I spent two weeks with him in the desert behind Saddam's lines back in the good ol' days. But coming from Glasgow you won't understand a bloody word he says.'

'Howdi!' said Marty smiling. Loftie grunted back something incoherently.

Piers had reserved a small conference suite that came equipped with a white board, computer and over-head projector. They all sat down and moments later a waiter delivered a breakfast of boiled eggs, toast, coffee, fruit and bottles of mineral water.

Marty and Loftie had not changed much in the interim years. Marty still looked tanned but more weather beaten and his blonde hair was cut short. Loftie was still whippet thin and had picked up several new scars on his rugged, ruddy face and was missing a few teeth but to Matthew and Piers he looked exactly the same.

After exchanging pleasantries they got down to business. Both Loftie and Marty had heard about the kidnapping and expressed their heartfelt sympathy. And then there was a pause.

'This hasn't got anything to do with it, has it?' asked Marty with a wry smile.

Piers cut to the chase. 'You know where I stand with ransoms. I don't believe in paying them. If we give in to these bastards it will be someone else's son or daughter in two months time. Virginia is raising the necessary funds through some contacts of her sister's but we have a short window of opportunity. The money is not due until the 30th August. That gives us just over two weeks. The four of us with our skills, experience and expertise can handle these goons ourselves!'

'So it's 'us' now?' said Loftie sarcastically. 'Well if there's going to be any action boss, count me in. Beats stacking power tools in B&Q!'

'Are there any objections at this point before I go on?'

'I am in with you guys 100%,' replied Marty, 'but I can't be away from the ranch too long; Linda will crucify me. I'll need my expenses paying. Unfortunately Californian horse ranches don't bring in the money they used to in my old man's days. Quad bikes and 4x4's have made our four legged friends almost obsolete in my part of the world.'

Piers nodded. 'Of course. I understand. I'll be footing the bill for the entire operation.' He looked at Loftie.

'So when do we leave Boss?' asked the Scotsman

'The three of us will leave in two weeks and rendezvous with Marty in *Oaxaca*. All the information is in the files,' he said pointing to the ring binders he had handed the two men. 'I'm afraid Marty, I've got an additional job for you,' said Piers, pushing a buff coloured A4 envelope over towards the tall, slim former recon marine. 'As you can imagine, we will need one or two things not to mention a couple of vehicles and it's nigh on impossible to smuggle a bottle of shampoo onto a plane this end, let alone an RPG! Are you still in touch with *Santiago*? Do you think he could help us get a couple of old SUV's down there?'

'Sure,' replied Marty, casting his eye over the list he had taken out of the envelope. 'Consider it done,' and he held up a Western Union cheque for $10,000 that had been stapled to the sheet of paper. 'I could probably get most of this crap from my local K-Mart store. I will call *Santi* when I get back and see what he can do. He lives in *Cuernavaca* now; runs outdoor pursuit courses for corporate types, you know, team building and all that,' he said laughing.

The SEAL's assault on the warehouse on the *Usumacinta River* had not been entirely successful. Although much of the intelligence recuperated from the scene had been useful, Dr Monica *Gonzalez* died two weeks later from a blood infection caused by the torture she had endured. At the family's request, the funeral took place in Donna, Texas and she was buried with full military honours in the local cemetery. Many of her Langley colleagues attended including Mike Espinetti. Shortly before she was laid to rest, her parents were presented with the flag of the United States of America along with her badge, by George J. Tunnet, the Director of the CIA.

Among the items that were retrieved from the warehouse were a Toughbook computer, two mobile phones and some flash-drives which were bagged up securely and hours later were being processed and analysed by the geeks at Langley. They revealed a small treasure trove of intelligence. The same two assassins who had kidnapped James in *Puerto Sal* had murdered the pizza delivery boy and *Tarcisio Uribe* in *San Cristobal de las Casas* and had kidnapped Monica *Gonzalez*. They were *Diego Cossio* and *Sergio Sarabia*, assassins on *Madrigal's* payroll. Both had died in the SEAL's assault. The man charged with co-ordinating *Madrigal's* campaign of terror and kidnappings was one *Julio Cesar*, known as *El Jefe* who resembled a mild mannered bank clerk. There was also a plethora of information on *Madrigal's* narcotics operations but no information pertaining to the whereabouts of James Cooper-Brown, the young British tourist kidnapped in July. The CIA was particularly interested in a hit list they found that ran to over 100 names and included prominent Mexican politicians and members of the judiciary, authors, journalists, heads of police, U.S senators and even one or two Hollywood actors.

A month later, SEAL team nine, Burrito Platoon, was deployed to Manila in the Philippines to capture the leader of an Islamic Chechen terrorist cell who was planning on bombing the U.S embassy there. Unfortunately Medic Dave Williams who had helped rescue Monica *Gonzalez* from the warehouse was not with his comrades. Days after the raid, his right arm was amputated following the bullet wound he received which shattered his humerus, radius and ulna and damaged surrounding tissue. He refused to quit the navy and a year later re-trained as a computer analyst.

0032 DAYS

CHAPTER 17

Mexican cartels advance their operations in part, by corrupting or intimidating law enforcement officials. Often government officials, along with the police forces, work together with the cartels in an organized network of corruption.

✝

Two and a half weeks after their return from Mexico, Piers informed Virginia that he and Matthew were due to attend an annual trade show in Dubai on the 16th of August before going to Azerbaijan on business. These trips were not unusual given the nature of Piers' work and Risk Factor often took both men away from home for lengthy periods. On August 15th the three former SAS soldiers flew by British Airways business class from London Heathrow to Mexico City. They travelled lightly with only hand luggage though Piers had left Mosscombe that morning with a suitcase and suit-bag which he dropped off at the office on their way to the station. He gave his secretary instructions to inform any callers that he was away in the Middle East for two weeks. After an uneventful journey they arrived at *Benito Juarez* Airport at eight o'clock in the evening where they rented a sedan and arranged to drop it off the following day at Avis' offices on the outskirts of *Oaxaca*. Using a Garmin satellite Navigation device they negotiated their way through the city and within two and a half hours had reached the toll road heading south. Loftie drove with Matthew up-front whilst Piers had the back seat to himself. Half way, they stopped at a pristine service station where they filled up, bought cups of take-away coffee, bottles of *Tehuacan* water and a bag of Hershey chocolate bars. At three o'clock, they drove through *Oaxaca's* sleepy, deserted cobbled streets, and finding the *Hotel Francia,* (where Piers and Virginia had stayed less than three weeks before) checked in to their rooms.

The following day Loftie, Matthew and Piers met Marty Schultz at 12 o'clock in *Oaxaca's* huge elegant square. As they sat sipping their *Corona* beers dressed in short sleeved Hawaiian shirts, cheap stone coloured Chinos and dock-sider shoes, only one foreign tourist paid them any attention; a skeletal German clad in a white vest and blue Lycra shorts, who eyed them up through his shades over the top of his guide-book. And then he summed up the courage and mincing his way through the tables approached the group and introduced himself.

'Hi boys, I'm Axel, are any of you guys looking for some action?' he said smiling effeminately. There was a moment's silence before Marty turned to him and replied.

'Listen, my advice to you is go and cruise some Mexican sailors because the only action you are going to see around here is a fist in the gut!'

Back in Marty's room the four friends began planning their operation in earnest. On the floor were four large green canvas gunny sacks. Marty unzipped them and began laying out their contents on the bed, table and floor. Everything on Piers' list was there in addition to a small black laptop and the two SUV's which were parked outside. 'The first thing we need to do is go down to *Puerto Sal* and pay the owner of the Hotel *Paraiso* a visit. That will be your job Marty and Loftie. If he sees me again, he will run a mile or worse still, call in the cavalry,' Piers said. 'I suggest you drive the truck Loftie and wait outside whilst Marty, you play the innocent *gringo* looking for a room for the night. You will need to high-tail out of there as quickly as you can,' instructed Piers.

Piers spread an INEGI map on the bed and pointed to a wooded area just north of San *Gabriel Mixtepec* that he and Virginia had passed on their way down to *Puerto Sal*.

'Matthew and I will meet you here on the bridge at midnight. The hotel owner will give us the names and details of the people who took James and hopefully the location of where he is being held but I am afraid he won't be returning to his two teenage boys or his lovely hotel. I doubt whether his poor wife will miss him much, by the look of her. He's collateral damage. Does anyone have a problem with that?'

'Good,' continued Piers, 'We will dump his body here by the river. After the coyotes have seen to him and several days of rain, there won't be much left of him,' he said coldly. 'Depending on the quality of the intelligence he provides us with, we will then plan our next move.'

Alone in the barn back in Mosscombe, her husband away on business, her son still held hostage in Southern Mexico and Eleanor on holiday with friends, Virginia threw herself into organising the logistics of putting together the ransom money She knew from Piers' own experience of negotiating with kidnappers, that demands often changed; hostage takers were not predictable and a request for £3 million might escalate to an even higher figure as the deadline approached. She began to file through the hundreds of letters they had received from all over the country since the kidnapping. In addition to letters and cards, there were even cheques and cash sent by well wishers. Many of them moved Virginia to tears. The chancellor of St Andrews University had organised a whip around the student body and raised £1000.

'The enclosed is for James to spend on the holiday of a lifetime on his release,' the chancellor had written, optimistically.

Virginia found the comment ironic. James, she believed, had set off less than a month before on what was meant to be just that!

There was a letter from a Mrs Kenyon from Wales aged 83 who described the heartache she and her husband endured when their son, a university lecturer, was kidnapped in Beirut in 1988 by Hezbollah.

'Fortunately for me, my son Paul was released in 1992 but my husband never saw him again. He died of a stroke induced, the doctors claimed, by anxiety and stress just three months before Paul returned home,' and the letter ended with the words, 'my prayers and thoughts are with you and your family.'

Among the envelopes and cards that arrived in the morning's post was one written in a distinctly feminine hand. Virginia opened it with the silver letter knife she had inherited from her grandmother and unfolded the neat sheets of Basildon Bond. It was from Charlotte.

'I was devastated to hear that James had been kidnapped whilst travelling in Mexico,' it began. 'I meant to write to you as soon as I had heard the news but lacked the courage to do so because I felt both guilty and partly responsible for why he went to Mexico. James will no doubt have told you that I broke up with him days before the end of the summer term and

I realise now how hard it must have been for him. As you know we had been together for six years, since we were both in Lower Sixth at Wellington. Looking back I know I behaved atrociously. I let myself become besotted with a young man called Julian whom I met at a summer ball. I don't really know how it happened. I think I had begun to take James for granted, wanted some excitement and got carried away. I should never have broken up with James. As it happens Julian treated me appallingly (deservedly perhaps) and we broke up shortly after our holiday in Thailand. Toby confessed to me that he had persuaded James to travel to the States with him as a way of trying to get over me but he had no idea that James had continued south into Mexico after he returned to the UK following his father's untimely death. I cannot imagine how you are both feeling with James so far away, held hostage by members of a drug cartel, the worry and anxiety you must be enduring. I myself have not slept for days thinking about him. This letter is therefore an apology for having treated your son in such a terrible way. I regret doing so more than anything and still love him deeply. I hope in time that James will be able to forgive me and that perhaps we can be friends again. My thoughts and prayers are with you and your family.
Yours sincerely,
Charlotte Priestley.

Virginia read the letter and then read it again. There were tears streaming down her face when she folded the sheets and placed them in her file marked 'friends.' She had always liked Charlotte whom she had known for several years. Charlotte had stayed with them a couple of times and had spent a week with them at their house in Aldeburgh during the Easter holidays. She knew James had been very upset when the relationship ended but had never got the full story of what exactly had happened between them. Now she felt even more upset imagining James' loneliness as he dwelt on the past and Charlotte. Closing the file, she began planning her trip back to Mexico. James would need clothes and toiletries, there were flights and hotel rooms to pay for and she wanted to email all his close friends to inform them of his imminent release.

0030 DAYS

CHAPTER 18

In 2003, at least two prominent drugs cartels in Mexico established bases in 11 West African nations.

✝

*E*l Jefe, Julio Cesar, had known *Madrigal* since childhood. Both had grown up in *Oaxaca* and had been born into poverty and both had risen quickly to positions of power and influence in the streets gangs of their respective neighbourhoods. Although *Cesar* looked innocuous and dressed like a respectable business man, he was, like *El Alacran*, ruthless and known for his spectacular, violent outbursts. A week after James was kidnapped he shot a man in cold blood in a restaurant for bringing him the wrong drink. *Cesar* and some of his henchmen had gone to a roadhouse one evening for a meal. It was a cold, wet night in the middle of the rainy season and the men were tired after a routine inspection of a drugs depot in *Ariaga* on the *Chiapas* border. A huge consignment of cocaine had come in via Panama and Guatemala and *Cesar* had dropped by to check that it had not been tampered with by the Mexican DEA. A year before, a similar container had arrived which had been planted with a DEA transponder device traceable from the air by helicopters which had resulted in the confiscation of several tons of narcotics and the arrests of key players in the *Madrigal* Cartel.

It was past midnight and the owner of the diner was about to close up for the night when the three gangsters clad in suits and sleek black raincoats pushed open the doors and ordered *cafe Americanos* and plates of *Enchiladas*.

'*Amigos*, the place is closed now!' said the owner smiling, as he wiped down the tables and straightened the chairs.

'Well asshole, we have just re-opened it,' replied *Joaquin*, a diminutive, dark skinned man with a livid scar from a knife wound on his left cheek. He grabbed a chair and threw it across the room.

The three men sat down.

'Bring us the coffee and the food quickly or as of tonight you and this shitty excuse for a *cantina* will no longer exist,' threatened *Andres*. He was taller than *Joaquin*, about five foot ten inches in height, but square and built like a quarter back. He had piercing blue eyes, and fairer skin than both *Cesar* and *Joaquin* and boasted an Irish ancestry.

The owner of the restaurant scuttled back into the kitchen where he switched on the lights and muttered something incoherent to the two waitresses who had been standing behind the counter putting on their *ponchos* when *Cesar* and his men had entered.

'Next week that *pendejo Miguel De Toledo* who calls himself a politician and a future president of Mexico, will be history,' *Cesar* said nonchalantly. '*Madrigal* wants him out of the way. He is getting too cosy with the Americans and making all kinds of promises to them,' he went on.

'I tell you,' said *Andres*, 'if the *gringos* send their Delta Force people down here to try to flush us out, they will all be going back in body bags.'

'He is promising to build an army of Special Forces troops trained by the *Yankees* with the sole purpose of wiping out our businesses and those of our *compadres* in *Sinaloa* and *Veracruz*,' interjected *Joaquin* who had been cleaning his teeth with a toothpick. 'How stupid are these politicians?' He continued. 'Don't they know that it will be our Mexican brothers that they send down here; families who have settled north of the border, call themselves Americans to enjoy the good life but would never lift a finger against their cousins south of the border. The U.S. Marines and Rangers are full of *Mexicanos*, like my uncle *Eduardo* – he's a corporal in the Corps. Washington sends all the *Hispanicos* down here thinking they will infiltrate our organisations easily but they are too stupid to realise that most of them will end up helping us not sabotaging our businesses and selling us out,' and he laughed.

Presently a timid looking waitress arrived carrying plates of steaming *enchiladas* on a tray and three cups of coffee. She was about 15 years of age, dark like an *indigena* and dressed in a white apron. She placed the tray on the table and hastened back to the kitchen.

'What is this shit?' asked *Cesar* rhetorically, stirring his cup of coffee with its sweet smell of cinnamon. He picked it up, sniffed it and then threw it violently against the wall. He then proceeded to sweep the tray and its contents onto the floor. He was in a rage.

'What is wrong with this fucking country? You ask for a cup of coffee on a cold night and the stupid *Indio* brings you some shit made from coffee dregs and spices as if he is serving a beggar!' He turned towards the kitchen counter.

'Yes *cabron*, I am talking to you!' he shouted furiously at the restaurant owner who had stepped forward to see what was going on.

'Did we or did we not ask for *cafe Americanos*?' He didn't wait for the answer. 'Do you know who we are, you fucking peasant? And you bring us shitty *cafes de olla* like we are some *mendigos* that have crawled off the street!'

Almost in one swift move, *Cesar* pulled back his raincoat and whipped out a long barrelled Magnum 44 with an ebony handle from a shoulder holster, aimed it at the window and fired. The huge glass pane shattered in one piece and the cold night air and rain swept in. And then turning around he aimed the revolver at the restaurant owner and a second later shot the man in the head. No one said a word. The girls were too terrified to speak. *Cesar* walked slowly to the counter, stepping over the broken crockery and spilt *enchiladas* that lay in a mess on the floor. He leant over the bar and fired five more shots into the dead man's chest.

'Get the fuck out of here!' he screamed at the two girls. They fled out into the dark night leaving the door banging in the wind behind them.

'*Joaquin*, bring the car around to the front,' *Cesar* ordered angrily, 'and *Andres*, torch the place before leaving. Let's get out of here!'

Whilst *Cesar* and *Joaquin* waited in the car, *Andres* strolled into the kitchen, unplugged the butane gas cylinder from the range, turned it full on and setting fire to a paper table cloth, waltzed out of the restaurant. Moments later, as the car swung back onto the highway, there was a huge explosion and the roadhouse went up in a ball of fire.

Two weeks later, on the 25th of July, the PDR's presidential candidate *Miguel De Toledo* was gunned down outside the town hall in *Tijuana Baja California*, whilst giving a keynote speech. *De Toledo* was an educated middle class Mexican who had grown up in San Diego and graduated from Berkley University with a master's degree in politics and economics. The son of a

Mexican ambassador to Washington, he had been educated at Valley Forge Military Academy in Pennsylvania and had spent most of his life in the United States. He married Laura Wesley, a New York heiress and the couple had two sons and a daughter aged ten, eight and six respectively. *De Toledo* was bilingual in both Spanish and English in addition to speaking French and Italian fluently. Despite his affluent background and upbringing, *De Toledo* had entered Mexican politics and the PDR (Party of Democratic Revolution) in particular, with a burning desire to clean up corruption in Mexico's corridors of power and modernise its bureaucratic civil service. At the top of his personal manifesto was a pledge to deal with Mexico's drug cartels 'once and for all!' he had vowed. He was hugely popular amongst the country's educated elite and at the time of his death was topping the polls. Both the White House and Downing Street liked him and promised to support his 'war on the cartels' should he assume the mantle of president in six months time. These credentials alone made him the cartels' number one enemy and weeks before *De Toledo* embarked on the campaign trail they had put out a contract on his life.

Rodrigo Casablanca was a former Green Beret sniper and mercenary. Born in Miami in 1971 into a family of Cuban, anti-Castro dissidents, he had excelled as a cadet at Westpoint Officer Training

College, passing out top of his class and winning the prestigious Superintendent's Award for Excellence. After serving in the U.S. army's First Infantry Division he joined the Green Berets having passed its arduous selection course in 1998 at the age of 23.

Cesar met *Casablanca* in the Crowne Plaza Hotel, Miami on the 27th June 2003. The former U.S army sniper was offered $500,000 to carry out the hit on *Miguel De Toledo*. The precise details of the assassination (the date, time and location) were left to *Casablanca's* discretion but the contract was to be completed before the first of September. During his brief career as a mercenary and hired gun, *Casablanca* had accrued some high profile hits to his name, among them a former African warlord and a Russian oligarch. *Cesar* paid him $250,000 in cash as an advance, the remainder of the balance to be paid on completion of the assignment into an account in the Cayman Islands.

Miguel De Toledo was killed with a single bullet to the head as he stood on a podium outside the *Tijuana* town hall addressing a large crowd of supporters and party loyalists. It was a glorious sunny afternoon and the square and surrounding streets were festooned with yellow PRD flags and banners. There was no sound of a gunshot. One moment *De Toledo* was standing smiling, waving to the crowd, his wife by his side and a moment later he had fallen sideways off the stage into the applauding masses. The bullet that killed him had been fired from an Israeli made H-S Precision Pro Series rifle with a four inch silencer from 1000 yards. The killing caused mass panic amongst the crowd that had gathered, making it easy for *Casablanca* to escape from the roof of a four storey car park without being detected. He simply melted away, a lone assassin dressed casually in a blue Lacoste polo shirt, jeans and trainers, a black canvas bag in his right hand.

The assassination of a prominent Mexican presidential candidate made headline news across the globe. Within Mexico and the CIA it was widely believed that the hit had been funded and co-ordinated by the *Sinaloa* Cartel and its connections with the southern states of the U.S.

The head of the *Sinaloa* Cartel was a charismatic man called *Carlos Puentes*, now aged 65 and a former colonel in the Federal army. He was considered untouchable by the Mexican authorities who had tried on numerous occasions to arrest him on tax evasion and money laundering charges but evidence, testimonies and witnesses against him had an almost mystical habit of disappearing. Following *De Toledo's* assassination, Mexico's Judicial Police hatched an elaborate plan to kidnap *Puentes* one morning as he was leaving his *hacienda* on the outskirts of *Culiacan* but the operation was a disaster and *Puentes* once again evaded capture, this time by undergoing plastic surgery in a private clinic in *Puerto Vallarta* run by his cronies and escaping incognito to *Bogotá* in Columbia. Little did the CIA or the Mexican Secret Service know that the assassination had been planned by the lesser known *Ernesto Madrigal*.

0028 DAYS

CHAPTER 19

*The U.S Justice Department spent $7 billion
in its war against drugs in 2003 alone.*

✟

TV Cortes, owned by *Grupo Salinas,* was the second largest multi media company in Mexico and in 2003 its chief executive was *Tere Saldariaga,* a charismatic broadcaster and veteran journalist. She had made her name at the tender age of 24 covering the *Tlatelolco* massacre which had occurred in the *Plaza de Tres Culturas* in 1968, days before the opening of the Olympic Games. *Saldariaga,* now aged 58, had iron grey hair, clear green eyes and an uncanny resemblance to the American actress Ann Bancroft. She wore thick tortoise rimmed glasses and always dressed elegantly in tailored business suits. Unusually for a middle class Mexican, she had fallen in love with and married an impoverished but talented artist 15 years her senior and the couple lived in a gated compound in *La Herradura* a leafy suburb of the city. Their two grown-up sons, Alexis and Herman both resided in Canada where they owned and ran a successful graphic design company. Politically, *Saldariaga* described herself as being left of centre and *Cortes* had recently aired a series of highly acclaimed polemic programmes documenting the social and economic effects of the country's inter-cartel feuds and the damage this violence was causing to Mexico's image as a First World nation.

Saldariaga and her husband *Felicano Hernandez* hated living in the exclusive neighbourhood, behind high walls with razor wire fencing and security guards at the gate but these domestic arrangements were part of her contract with TV *Cortes* since *Saldariaga* had, on more than one occasion, been the recipient of hate letters and death threats.

On the evening of August 16th she was returning home from her offices in *San Angel* when she was kidnapped. Her black, chauffeur driven Mercedes Benz M-Class sedan had just turned onto *Avenida Tehuacan* when a grey Toyota Land Cruiser rammed the rear of the car forcing it onto the hard shoulder. Four men dressed in black, wearing balaclavas jumped out of the SUV, shot the chauffeur through the tinted glass window and hauled *Saldariaga* violently out of the vehicle and into the Toyota. It was six o'clock in the evening and the abduction took place amidst the heavy traffic and in full view of dozens of motorists.

Feliciano Hernandez aged 73, was by 2003 one of Mexico's most accomplished artists exhibiting his work in New York, Sydney and London and through his own modern art gallery in *San Angel*. He was widely regarded as one the country's most outspoken intellectuals and it was he, not TV *Cortes* that was the first to hear of his wife's abduction.

'If you wish to see your wife again,' said the flat voice over the phone, 'you will do exactly as I tell you,' it had warned ominously.

Hernandez was working in his studio at home when he received the call which came through on his mobile.

'*Mrs Saldariaga* is being held by the *Madrigal* Cartel in retaliation for the negative, warped lies that TV *Cortes*, through its television documentaries, has been spreading about our organisation. You and your sons, *Mr Hernandez,* are lucky that we didn't kill your wife for her betrayal and the only reason she has not been executed is because at this moment in time she is more useful to us alive than dead. In return for our continuing mercy, TV *Cortes* will pay \$10 million in addition to broadcasting a public apology retracting all adverse propaganda that has been broadcasted about the *Madrigal* Cartel. Failure to comply with these demands within two weeks will result in a catastrophic assault on the city which will culminate in massive loss of life and you will never see your wife again.'

The first thing James Cooper-Brown knew about *Tere Saldariaga* was that she was now his new cell mate. At three o'clock in the morning of August 18th the door opened and a woman he had never seen before dressed in a dishevelled business suit was rudely shoved into the room.

'Make up your own sleeping arrangements,' said *Ramon*, silhouetted in the open doorway. 'Sleep together for all I care,' he continued laughing, 'you could probably do with a good shag after all this time, that's if grandmothers do it for you,' he said addressing James and chuckling loudly before slamming the door shut.

For a moment the woman stood in the centre of the room, straightening out her crumpled skirt and playing with her hair.

'And you are?' she asked in perfect English.

'I'm James,' he replied sitting up in bed and rubbing his eyes sleepily, 'Cooper-Brown. Who are you?'

Saldariaga didn't answer him immediately. Instead she said, 'This is no good! Two of us in this tiny room and only one bed. When they come back in the morning I will demand a different arrangement. I am *Tere*,' she said extending her right hand. '*Tere Saldariaga.*' The two shook hands. And then she sat down on the end of the bed.

'Do you mind?' she asked 'I've been on the road for almost two days and I'm exhausted!'

Tere kicked off her shoes and sat with her back to the wall. There was silence for a moment and then James heard her heavy breathing and moments later she was asleep, her head slumped to the side over her left shoulder. James took the thin blanket from the end of the bed and gently draped it over her before getting back under the filthy covers.

*A*lberto, the owner of the *Hotel Paraiso*, had not been expecting guests on the night of August 17th. The rainy season had established itself and since the disappearance of the young *gringo* and the unexpected appearance of the boy's parents who were clearly still in shock, the town had largely shunned him. They suspected now that he had played a part in arranging the kidnapping and certainly profited from it. How else could *Alberto* suddenly afford to buy his lazy sons computers and the latest games and who was paying for the swimming pool that was being installed in scrubland beyond the dilapidated hotel? The citizens of *Puerto Sal* knew *Alberto* was not a successful hotelier. He was too lazy. So when an old grey 1998 registration Jeep Cherokee drew up outside the hotel and a tall *gringo* dressed in jeans and a T-shirt stepped out into the damp air and crossed the street entering the *Hotel Paraiso*, no one cared or bothered to ask why.

Approaching the tatty reception desk in the dimly lit lobby, Marty addressed the grubby looking man behind the desk in Spanish.

'I am looking for a single room for the night and wondered if you had any,' he said.

'Sure,' replied *Alberto* putting on a rare smile and rising from his plastic chair behind the television.

'We have plenty of rooms my American friend. But if you are looking for some pussy, you are out of luck. All the good ones left years ago. Now the only women we have here are old dried out hags, I should know,' he said nodding in the direction of the kitchen, 'I am married to one. No my friend,' he went on languidly, '*Puerto Sal* is a little shit hole at the end of nowhere with one nice beach and that's about it, but if you want a room you have come to the right place.'

'So where is your wife?' asked Marty, peeking through the kitchen door, 'the place seems kind of quiet.'

'She and my two useless sons have gone to the cinema in *Huatulco* to see some *gringo* film, so you see, it's just you and me. You are not a *maricon* are you?' he added laughing.

It was the second time that day that someone had asked him if he was a homosexual, so Marty thought he would make the most of it.

'As a matter of fact I am and you are kind of attractive. How about you and I go upstairs and have ourselves a little fun?' he said and then with one deft move he leant over the desk, grabbed Alberto by the hair and smashed his head into the table. Shards of broken glass and bits of wood splintered into his face before he collapsed to the ground. Stepping over the debris, Marty walked around the desk and bending down, yanked the hotelier to his feet and marched him out of the door to the jeep.

'Yeah, me and maybe a couple of local hill-billies are going to have a really good time with you tonight,' whispered Marty into *Alberto's* ear, before tying his hands behind his back and pushing him into the back seat of the car. Two skinny youths playing pool in the *cantina*, looked up momentarily as the jeep drove away before returning to their game.

'Hotel for sale!' said one of them and chuckled.

0026 DAYS

CHAPTER 20

In 2003, the U.S. authorities reported a spate of kill-ings, kidnappings and home invasions in southern states connected to Mexico's cartels and 19 U.S citizens were killed in their homes due to drug related crimes.

At midnight Marty and Loftie met Piers and Matthew at a remote forest lay-by five miles out of *San Gabriel Mixtepec*. There was no traffic on this desolate stretch of road but a cacophony of insect sounds emerged from the forest as the four men and their captive stepped out of their cars into the darkness. Unshackling his legs, Marty dragged *Alberto* out of the jeep and down a steep slope towards the swirling river and there tied him to a tree. When his blindfold was removed, *Alberto* saw the terrifying spectacle of four silhouettes in black, their heads and faces masked by balaclavas. They stood in a row in front of him, their legs set slightly apart, their hands behind their backs in silence. The tallest of the four stepped forward. He was standing about a foot and a half away from *Alberto* and was holding a large hunting knife with a serrated blade in his right hand. The blade glistened in the moonlight.

'Like I said,' whispered the man in Spanish, 'me and the boys here would like to spend a little time with you, but first we have some questions that need answering.'

Alberto recognised the voice. He was clearly terrified. His eyes were wide open and unblinking, his mouth agape, in a dumb scream and then the words came tumbling out.

'Why do you do this to me? I know nothing!' he said howling.

'You say you know nothing?' Marty replied, 'yet you do know that the young *gringo* that stayed in your hotel about a month ago was kidnapped in *Puerto Sal?*'

'Yes, I know that, but he was just a guest in my hotel, I do not know the men who took him, I swear!'

Marty took two steps forward. The two men were now inches apart.

'My friend back here has a stop watch. He will set it to five minutes and then you will hear an alarm. For every question you fail to answer correctly, I will cut off a toe or a finger, you can choose. The clock starts now!'

'Ok, ok!' replied *Alberto* panic rising up his throat. 'I swear, I was just the messenger. A man called *Cesar* came to me one day and told me he needed a *gringo*. He would pay me good monies if I informed him of any foreigners staying in my hotel, that is all!'

'You are wasting time,' replied Marty ominously. 'I haven't asked a question yet and you have less than four minutes remaining. Now tell us who took the *gringo* and where they are keeping him.'

'*Senor*, please – I cannot say no more or this man and his men will come back to my hotel and burn the place down. They will kill my wife and children.'

'Oh!' said Marty chuckling, 'and you think we have come out here into the woods for a picnic? Do you think we won't kill you and burn down your hotel? Be right about one thing my friend. We will hunt down anyone who was responsible for the kidnapping and kill them all and tonight we will start with you. If you provide us with the information we need, I will promise to protect your family. You have two and a half minutes left.'

'The man who came to *Puerto Sal* was called *Cesar* and he works for the *Madrigal* Cartel,' sobbed Alberto. 'I do not know for sure where they are keeping the *gringo* but some say he is at the *Monasterio de San Blas* high up in the *Sierra*. You can only get to it on foot or on horseback from the *pueblito* of *Santo Tomas de Los Platanos.*'

'Describe this place to me!'

'*Senor*, I do not know it well, my grandfather took me many years ago when I was a boy,'

'Well think hard, you have just over two minutes left.'

'It is high on a cliff, built like a fortress with thick walls and a big gate with views of the whole *sierra*, but that was many years ago, it might have changed for all I know!'

'How many men does this *Madrigal* have up there?'

'I do not know *Senor*, but he will have at least 20 armed guards, maybe dogs too.'

'How well armed will they be?'

'*Senor, Madrigal* has better weaponry than some of the federal regiments! They will have everything.. machine guns, grenades..everything!'

'Who else was involved in the kidnapping? This *Cesar* guy could not have taken James on his own?'

'There were two men with *Cesar; Sergio and Diego*, but both *Senor,* are dead now. There is a rumour they were killed by some U.S Navy Seals in a recent raid, this is all I know!'

'Why are they kidnapping *gringos* and why in *Puerto Sal* and not *Puerto Escondido* or *Huatulco*?

'I am not in command *Senor* but maybe because, *Puerto Sal* is quiet, there are no police or *judiciales* there and *gringos* have lots of money.'

'The man you took was not a *gringo*. He was English!'

'We know that now *Senor*, but at the time we assumed he was an American.'

'You stupid fuck, you had the man's passport, that was a big mistake my friend.'

Just then the alarm in Loftie's gloved hand went off.

'Thank you,' said Marty, 'you have been most helpful,' and he stepped back into the line of three men. There was silence for a moment before a second man stepped forward. He was shorter than the first but stocky. He removed his balaclava and in the dim moonlight, *Alberto* saw that it was the young *gringo's* father, the man who had visited his hotel three weeks before. He spoke in English and Marty translated.

'You had a choice between good and evil, between hard work and greed. You chose greed and evil and the result of that choice is that my son was kidnapped and for all I know may well be dead. Let me tell you that you made the wrong decision.'

Piers withdrew a black Austrian made Glock from his pocket and attached a silencer to the barrel. He raised the gun, took aim and fired a single shot into *Alberto's* forehead. Moments later the four men were back in the jeeps and heading for *Oaxaca*. They left *Alberto's* body tied to the tree for the *coyotes*.

When *Concepcion* and her two sons returned from the cinema they found the hotel's reception in disarray and *Alberto* gone. There was shattered glass on the floor, the register was upside down and *Alberto's* plastic chair was on its side. At four o'clock in the morning as the first glimpse of the orange dawn could be seen in the east, *Concepcion* was awoken by four strangers dressed in black standing in the hall-way. She was about to scream when she saw a pistol in the tallest man's hands.

'We have not come to hurt you or your sons,' he said gently placing the gun back in his shoulder holster. 'Is there somewhere that we can sit down and talk?'

Still looking terrified, *Concepcion* gestured towards the kitchen where there was a large table covered in a plastic cloth and chairs. She sat down first and fidgeted with the hem of her *serape*.

'Where's *Alberto*?' were the first words that she said, followed by, 'Not that I care.'

'*Alberto* will not be coming back,' replied the tall American as the four men pulled out chairs and sat down.

'I am afraid that your husband was a very bad man,' Marty continued.

'You do not have to tell me that,' replied *Concepcion*. 'He raped me when I was just 13 years old. It was such a dishonour for my parents they told me I would have to marry him. He never loved me. How could he? Shortly after we were married he beat me and there were more violations. Before the boys were born, I tried running away but he would always find me and then I really suffered. What did you do to him?'

'Let's just say he will never touch you again,' said Marty. '*Alberto* was instrumental in the kidnapping of my friend's son,' and Marty pointed at Piers. Piers nodded back. 'Didn't you ever wonder where all the money suddenly came from?'

'Of course I did, but it was not my place to ask.'

'I am sorry but you cannot stay here anymore. The men who paid *Alberto* for information will be back for you soon. You must get away tonight. My friends and I are here to take you to wherever you want to go,' Marty said softly. 'You've got 15 minutes to pack a bag and then we are off.'

'Thank you,' replied *Concepcion*. 'You can take us to the bus station in *Puerto Escondido*. We will go to *Tabasco* where I have family,' and she added, 'Is the young *gringo* still alive?' and she looked sadly at Piers. 'He was polite and well mannered and spoke gently to my sons.'

'We hope so, but until we see him, we won't know.'

An hour later the two cars drew into *Puerto Escondido's* bustling bus terminal. It was six o'clock in the morning on August 18th. *Concepcion* thanked Marty for the lift and moments later had disappeared into the teeming masses, a large colourful string bag in each hand, her two teenage sons by her side.

0024 DAYS

CHAPTER 21

There are three types of kidnappings in Mexico. The kidnapping of foreign tourists, the sequestration of children and the abduction of wealthy businessmen.

✟

When *Tere Saldariaga* awoke it was six o'clock in the morning on August 18th. Her neck ached, she was stiff and cold and she found herself sitting at the end of an old wooden bed. A young man with a mop of blonde hair wearing a dirty T-shirt lay asleep beneath the thin bedding – mouth open. The room had no windows and no other furniture. She was miles away from her home and her office, her loyal chauffeur called *Juventino*, who had worked for the company for over 20 years was dead and she was now a hostage; of whom? She did not know yet. She got up and banged on the door.

'Who are you? And what is it that you want? Please open the door; I need to use the rest room!' There was no response for a minute or two and then she heard a key turning in the lock. The wooden door opened and the early morning light flooded in from the hallway.

'I will take you to the bathroom,' replied *Ramon* sleepily. 'In there you will find a bag with toiletries and some clothes. You will have 15 minutes to wash and change. Knock on the door when you have finished.'

The bathroom was small and cramped with a dirty basin and cracked mirror, a toilet and walk in shower behind a green plastic curtain. She found a blue canvas bag on the floor containing a pair of plastic flip-flops, a toothbrush, soap, toothpaste, a comb, underwear, blouse, socks and a green tracksuit roughly her size and a black towel. The water was tepid and brown and the place smelt of blocked drains. *Tere* showered first and then brushed her teeth twice and combed her hair. She looked in the mirror and didn't recognise herself without her makeup on. Her face looked pale, drawn and tired. Her eyes were bloodshot and her hair was a mess but at least she was alive. She was determined to have her full 15 minutes of privacy. It was six twenty two. She waited a further three minutes and then knocked loudly on the door. This time a different guard opened it. He looked young, almost girlish and smiled at her before escorting her back to the room. It was *Pepe*. When the door was closed behind her, she found James sitting on the edge of the bed putting on his flip flops.

'Did you manage to sleep at all?' he asked

'What do you think?' she answered laughing. 'Actually I believe I did, from sheer exhaustion,' and she quickly changed the subject.

'Sharing a room as small as this is unacceptable. When I next see the guards I will complain. It is not right that a woman of my age or indeed a young man like yourself should be subjected to such conditions. What were they thinking? That we will take it in turns to use the bed?'

Just then the door opened and *Pepe* came in carrying a tray with two plates of scrambled eggs and cups of *cafe de olla*.

'My name is *Pepe, Senora,*' and he paused for a moment, '*Mucho gusto*. I am sorry we are meeting under such circumstances, but James here will tell you that I am a good person. I believe you will not be here long,' he continued. 'I heard *Cesar* saying you will both be moved today.'

They sat on the bed, in the small cramped room eating their breakfast and talking

'They kidnapped you a month ago didn't they?' *Tere* asked James.

'Yes, that's right, though I am beginning to lose track of time. How did you know?'

'Well I happen to work for one of Mexico's big TV networks and we covered the story. We have of course, always been very critical of the drug cartels here in Mexico, which is probably why I am here, though I don't know as yet who exactly is holding us.'

'I've heard the name *Madrigal* a few times,' said James, 'Does that mean anything to you?'

'*Ernesto Madrigal* has a monopoly over much of the narcotics that come through Mexico's southern border.

He is one of the most powerful men in the country. I assumed I had been taken by the *Sinaloa* group, which remains the most dangerous and influential cartel in Mexico. TV *Cortes*, of which I am the CEO, recently aired a series of programmes criticising the violence and mayhem which it's largely responsible for,' and they continued to talk.

Tere asked James about his family and background. She wanted to know how he had ended up in Mexico and in *Puerto Sal* of all places. James told her about his breakup with Charlotte and his subsequent travels through the States and of how he had always wanted to visit Mexico.

'We learnt about the Aztecs in primary school, funnily enough,' he said laughing. 'I remember doing a drawing of the pyramids and one of *Quetzalcoatl*. Little did I imagine aged nine, that I would one day visit this great country.'

'This experience must have marred your image of Mexico?' *Tere* asked him.

'On the contrary, I always knew Mexico had an edginess to it. I had read Graham Greene's account of his travel here during the revolution and more recently Mexico's inter drug cartel wars have been featured in the news back home. I just never thought I would get caught up in it. I love Mexico, particularly the old colonial towns.'

They chatted on for most of the morning. *Tere* told James about her work as a journalist, the stories she had covered over the years and her role as CEO and then at midday the door opened and *Ramon* told them to get ready to go.

'We are taking you to another refuge,' he said. 'This place is not big enough for both of you and is no longer safe. We will leave in five minutes.'

The hostages were blindfolded and led outside to two waiting pick-up trucks. *Tere* was put into one and James into the other. They were bound and hooded and pushed down onto the floor.

They drove for about 15 minutes before the cars stopped and *Tere* and James were pulled roughly out of the vehicles and their hoods removed.

'I hope you two can ride,' said *Ramon* laughing and pointing to some horses tethered to a fence. He stood with four other young men. They were dressed in jeans with checked shirts, bandanas around their necks and straw hats on their heads. They were dark skinned with thin wispy moustaches and unsmiling faces. They carried pistols in leather holsters on their hips and shotguns protruded from long gun cases attached to the saddles.

They all stood on a flat piece of rocky ground by the side of a road surrounded by deep pine woods. A river's white waters tumbled somewhere beneath them into a canyon.

'It's three hours on horseback from here and then a further two hours on foot,' said *Ramon* pointing up towards some jagged peaks of the *Sierra Madre*. 'The horses will all be tethered together so don't even think of escaping,' he said smiling menacingly.

Tere was adamant. 'We can't ride in flip-flops and my young English friend here is wearing shorts. The horses will rub terribly against his legs!'

'That's not my problem,' replied *Ramon*, 'Now saddle up!'

'Don't worry about me,' whispered James quietly into *Tere's* ear. 'As a kid I used to ride bareback in my swimming trunks. My grandparents had a hill farm with lots of horses in Devon.'

They mounted up and *Ramon* tied them together. A sullen looking *indigena* took the rear and holding the reins in one hand removed his shotgun which he held barrel pointing up in his other hand. He tethered James' horse to the pummel of his saddle. In between James and *Tere* rode a second buck followed by another young cowboy and *Ramon*. James was unfamiliar with western saddles with their hard pummels and long stirrups and single looped reins but found riding comfortable enough. *Tere* looked quite at home on her steed. The ponies were small in comparison to English hunters but they were as strong and as sure footed as mountain goats.

0022 DAYS

CHAPTER 22

*For every kidnapping registered, anti-crime groups say
that up to ten go unreported as family members are
scared that the gangsters will hurt the victim
if they go to the police.*

✝

Two days after his wife was kidnapped *Feliciano
Hernandez* penned a strong worded letter to the
president himself. He had met *Victor Medillo* once,
at a reception held by the trustees of TV *Cortes* and
thought him a bland man devoid of any personal cha-
risma, charm or vision.

*'Dear Mr. President,' the letter began. 'It is a dis-
grace that a country like Mexico with all its resources and
wealth, with its colourful traditions and history, to all extents
and purposes a First World nation, cannot find a way to deal
with its drug problems that threaten to drag us back into the
Middle Ages.. How many more young men and women, some
of them foreigners, many of them poor, will perish in terrible
ways before your government will take the necessary action
to eradicate this plague that is engulfing our nation and
destroying the moral fabric of our communities and society?*

You will be aware by now that Tere Saldariaga, the CEO of TV Cortes and my wife of over 30 years, was recently brutally kidnapped in broad daylight on her way home. Her driver, a loyal employee of the broadcasting station for over 20 years, a man with a wife and five children, was gunned down in cold blood. I hold you personally responsible for these and the continuing atrocities that ravage Mexico and demand that you take immediate action to secure Tere's release and deal once and for all with these criminal gangs.

I have forwarded this letter to the editors of all our major broadsheets, radio stations and TV networks.

At the very least I would expect a personal response to this missive.

Yours sincerely,
Feliciano Hernandez

Three days after receiving the letter, *Victor Medillo* invited *Feliciano Hernandez* to the *Los Pinos* palace in *Chapultepec Park*. A chauffeur driven limousine was despatched to *La Herradura* to pick up the artist who was dressed casually in a dark suit and open white shirt. Now into his 70's *Feliciano* had a mop of grey hair, large bushy eyebrows and round spectacles. As a young man he had been small and slight in stature but age had made him thick waisted and somewhat rotund. The two men met in the presidential office. They shook hands and then *Medillo* addressed *Tere's* husband by his first name gesturing him to sit down.

'*Feliciano*, it is not only you and your family who grieve at this latest atrocity. The whole country is in mourning not only for this kidnapping but for all the victims of these dreadful cartels. Our thoughts and prayers are with you and my government will do everything in its powers to secure *Tere's* early release.'

Hernandez was silent for a moment and then looking the president hard in the face he replied, 'Mr President, please cut the crap! These are just empty words, phrases we have heard countless times not only from your lips but from all politicians. What I want to hear right now is exactly and in detail what measures are being taken by you to hunt these people down and bring them to justice. I will not leave this building until you have given me a satisfactory answer!'

On the 20th August 2003 Mexico's Special Forces, known as The Elite Corps launched co-ordinated assaults on the drug cartels. The Corps, a regiment of the Federal Army, had been formed in 1994 during the presidency of *Carlos Salinas de Gotari* and had been trained by members of the U.S army's Delta Force. Initially it had been established as part of the NAFTA agreement to stem the passage of immigrants and most notably, criminal gangs crossing the border illegally into the Southern United States. The force amounted to approximately 500 specialist troops trained in counter insurgency and counter terrorism but as yet had not been deployed on any active operations.

The offensive against the cartels, known as Operation Lightning had three major objectives: to kill or capture the cartels' leaders, to confiscate their narcotics and to freeze their assets. Washington was also demanding the extradition of the kingpins to face trial in U.S courts for drug trafficking offences, something the Mexican government had hitherto resisted.

When *El Alacran* got wind of this new offensive, he went into deep hiding. His lieutenants were ordered to move any hostages to remote inhospitable locations away from urban areas and to unleash another campaign of terror. A car bomb exploding in the colonial town of *Guanajuato* outside a branch of *Banamex* bank, destroyed the building killing 10 pedestrians and injuring more than 30. Among the dead were women and children. A *Pemex* petrol tanker was sabotaged and set on fire on the outskirts of *Guadalajara* and the resulting explosion incinerated 15 motorists as they sat in their cars, injured dozens of people and caused mayhem in the city centre for 48 hours. A prominent judge was assassinated in a drive-by shooting as he was leaving his apartment and three police officers who had refused to take back-handers from the *Madrigal* Cartel in return for inside information on DEA anti narcotics operations, were gunned down as they left their Police

Department building in *Taxco*. The message from the drug cartels was clear. 'We will not surrender and any attempt to flush us out will be met with more violence and terrorist attacks.'

But the Elite Corps also had its successes. They prevented *Madrigal* from having any contact with his family by maintaining constant surveillance on his various residences and tracked his family's every move. *Madrigal* was forced to live the life of a fugitive, never spending more than a night at a time in the same place. He was surrounded 24 hours a day by loyal henchmen and bodyguards who ferried him across the country from one hiding place to the next. It was even rumoured that he was living in the sewers beneath the city of *Puebla*. The Corps rounded up many of *Madrigal's* middle men and killed at least 30 of his hired guns in a savage fire fight at one of his cocaine processing plants located in *Neza Chalco-Itza,* a sprawling slum on the outskirts of Mexico City with a population of four million inhabitants.

The tragic irony of *Feliciano's* plea to the president to confront the cartels was that in doing so, he unwittingly sealed his wife's fate.

Two weeks before the ransom was due to be paid, Piers was still not back from his trip to Azerbaijan and Virginia began to worry. Her son was a hostage in Mexico, and now her husband had disappeared.

Although he was often away from home for extended periods, Piers always kept in close contact, calling home regularly and rarely returning home late from his business trips. Picking up the phone after breakfast, she called Molly, his secretary at Risk Factor.

'Mrs Cooper-Brown, I was just about to call you,' she said apologetically. 'Matthew called about an hour ago. A strategic meeting to be held somewhere in the Caucasus has been delayed. Matthew says Piers tried calling you last night but couldn't get through for some reason. He will arrange to meet you in Mexico City on the 28th of August at the same hotel you both stayed in. He will email his itinerary through to you tomorrow morning. Once again, I do apologise!'

Virginia thanked Molly and put down the phone. Something wasn't right. She had a sinking feeling in the pit of her stomach that things would go horribly wrong. Piers would be delayed, they would miss the deadline and she would never see James again. She tried dispelling these negative feelings. She thought ahead. In a month's time the nightmare would be over and James would be home. They would have to move to a smaller house and there would be no more holidays in Suffolk, but none of this mattered to her anymore. They would be a family again. She picked up the phone and called Robert, her brother in law.

'Please don't worry,' he said reassuringly, 'Everything is in hand. An old friend of mine from

Insead is now a director of the merchant bank Dakota Holdings in Mexico City and will handle things for you when you get out there,' and he went on to give Virginia *Tato Labastida's* contact details.

'I will wire the funds to Dakota the day before you arrive,' Robert explained. 'There, the cash will be counted into fifty thousand, $100 notes which in turn will be made up into 250 cellophane wrapped bricks each worth $20,000. Do the maths and you will see it will all be there. *Tato* will pick up the five black Samsonite cases which will each contain 50 bricks. The cases will then be securely padlocked and stowed away in the bank's vaults until the day of the drop,' and he continued. 'You will then stay with *Tato* in the bank and Piers will make the delivery, it will be safer that way. I will be at the end of the phone if you need me for anything, and I mean anything Virginia. *Tato* can set up a conference call so it will seem as if we are all there with you. You will have to be strong and we have to believe that these murderers have some sense of honour – that they will make the exchange!'

Virginia was almost in tears but she listened to Robert's wise words and thanked him profusely.

'Robert, we will never be able to thank you enough for what you have done for us. I know I misjudged you in the past – maybe even thought you were not right for Lucy, but I take it all back. You have done a wonderful thing!'

'The truth is Virginia that I have always been in awe of Piers. Silly really, but you know, his military background, his SAS experience etc. I think when I was younger I thought myself a lesser man so tried to compensate by coming across as cold and intellectually superior. Oh the follies of youth,' said Robert, and they both laughed.

0020 DAYS

CHAPTER 23

The Mexican state with the highest number of kidnappings is Chihuahua, home to the murder capital of the world: Ciudad Juarez.

✝

From the road, the two hostages and their captors dropped steeply down towards the river and crossed the foaming waters over a makeshift bridge of tree trunks bound together with chicken wire. No one spoke. As they rode up the steep bank to join a muleteer's track that rose from *Santo Tomas*, they could hear a curlew's shrill call high above them and a woodpecker hammering against a tree. When they were free of the woods they began riding through mesquite and wild rosemary, the horses picking their way carefully through the prickly magueys and boulders. Soon the river was far below them; a silver slither of mercury running into the canyon.

'We will rest for five minutes when we get to those trees over there,' shouted *Ramon* pointing up to a rocky outcrop where two lone pines stood swaying in the breeze.

'Then there will be no stopping for at least two hours. If you need to take a piss after that, you will have to wet yourself,' he said and *Tere* translated for James.

An hour later, they were riding up a steep switchback when *Tere's* horse suddenly stopped, dropped its dappled head and began pawing the ground with its hoof. Its eyes were wide open, ears pricked back. *Tere* tried pulling her reins up, but her horse responded by backing up and kicking the pony behind her. They were on a knife edge with steep scree descending to the path on one side and rough ground giving way to a cliff on the other.

'Woman, control your fucking horse!' shouted *Ramon* as pandemonium broke out. The horse that had been kicked bucked violently throwing its hapless rider, who tumbled down into some chaparral. By now all the horses were backing up on the trail, kicking each other in a frantic effort to find space on the precipitous path. *Ramon* spotted what had spooked them and shouted, 'It's just a bloody rattlesnake, get those horses under control or we will all be dragged over the *barranco!'*

James saw it too; a large Mojave greenback coiled on a flat rock below the trail, and heard the unmistakable sound of its rattle.

The fallen rider was now up and grabbing his horse by its bit, was trying to calm it down. *Tere's* horse was bucking and rearing violently but she clung on, gripping its flanks with her thighs and grabbing the pummel. James was caught in the middle; his horse had nowhere to go and was desperately trying to get off the trail and up the steep scree, pulling *Ramon*'s steed with it.

'We need to untie the *caballos jefe*,' shouted one of the bucks, 'or someone will get dragged off the cliff,' he shouted to *Ramon*.

'Well what are you waiting for, *idiota*!' screamed *Ramon*, 'Cut the lassos!'

The fallen rider withdrew a short stubby hunting knife from a sheath on his belt and slashed the thin rope tying his horse to *Tere's* and at once it bolted up the scree slope finally coming to a halt 400 yards above the trail where it stood neck craning, neighing into the wind.

There were now two strings of horses on the narrow path. *Tere* was at the front tied in a line to two of the cowboys. The fallen rider was scrambling up the scree to retrieve his horse leaving *Ramon*, James and a fourth buck tethered together at the other end of the trail. *Ramon* withdrew his shotgun from its cover and pointing it at *Tere* ordered her to bring her horse up:

'Get up here now,' he bellowed, 'or I will blow your head off!'

But *Tere* seized an opportunity. Seeing that one of her guards was still having difficulty controlling his horse and was between her and *Ramon*'s line of fire, she lunged across and pulled the pistol from his holster and without a moment's hesitation shot the rider in the head. His skull exploded in a mist of blood and brain matter, his body sliding sideways off the horse and over the cliff, the terrified mare bucking and rearing uncontrollably. In an instant she turned and shot the second guard who was fumbling with his reins in one hand and desperately trying to free his revolver in the other. The bullet caught him in the chest and he too reeled back falling over the sides of the precipice. *Tere* did not wait. She spurred her horse and cantered off down the path, pulling the two guards' ponies with her, leaving *Ramon*, James and the two remaining guards screaming after her.

'Go, go!' shouted James at the top of his voice whilst *Ramon* cursed and swore into the wind warning *Tere* that they would find and kill her.

'There is nowhere to run!' he roared, 'If we don't find you, the others will.'

He was furious. Riding up to James he took his revolver out and pistol whipped him across the face, knocking him off his horse onto the stony ground.

'I swear on my mother's grave, I will kill both of you like dogs,' he screamed.

'And you,' he said pointing at the two bucks, who sat silently on their horses, '*Cesar* will deal with you!'

James was aware that he had lost consciousness when he felt cold water being poured over his face. His hands were sticky with blood and when he raised them to his head he felt a deep gash just below his hair line. His nose had been broken; he had a black eye and on falling off his horse had hit his head hard on the jagged edge of a rock.

One of the cowboys was bending over him, dabbing his wound with a damp bandana.

'*Jefe*,' he said addressing *Ramon*. 'The boy will need stitches, the cut is very deep and bleeding badly.'

'Do you see any hospitals out here *cabron*!' answered *Ramon* angrily. 'The best we can do is cover it up, stop it bleeding until we get to *San Blas*. *Cesar* can call in a doctor. Now get him up and back onto his horse.'

The two bucks lifted James gently back into his saddle. He felt dizzy and was almost certainly suffering from concussion but was just able to hold onto the pummel of his saddle before being violently sick over the side of his horse.

'We need to get going!' shouted *Ramon*. 'We only have four hours of daylight left and we have not even started the climb yet.'

The two cowboys mounted their horses and once again James was tethered to *Ramon*.

Tere was three miles down the trail when some of *Cesar's* men spotted her from a watch tower.

As she rounded a rocky promontory before the trail entered thick woods, four men on horseback blocked her way. They were dressed like the other cowboys with the addition of sunglasses and they carried AK 47 rifles.

'This is where your little adventure ends, *Senora*,' said one of them addressing her. 'Now get off your horse and throw us that pistol you've got there!' *Tere* did as she was told. Another man dismounted and lashed her hands together with a lasso before getting back on his horse.

'From here on up you walk. Don't stumble or fall or we will drag you all the way to *San Blas* and by the time we reach *el monasterio* you will look like a packet of minced meat. You should have done what you were told and stayed with *Ramon*,' and turning their horses, they continued up the trail, dragging *Tere* on foot behind them.

0018 DAYS

CHAPTER 24

Known as 'the beast,' the massive cargo train from Honduras is mounted by hundreds of illegal migrants every day who perilously cling to the sides and roof on the ride north. They then risk capture by Mexican drug cartels who traffic them as slaves.

✟

James could recollect very little of the journey up to *San Blas*. He was concussed and only half conscious as he hung on to the pummel of his saddle. Forty minutes from their destination, the men abandoned all but one of their horses in a fenced corral and continued on foot. James, too weak to walk, was led by one of the cowboys. He was occasionally aware of sounds around him, heard voices in Spanish, felt his horse stumble once or twice and an intense throbbing pain in his head and at last he felt strong arms lifting him to the ground where he was laid on a makeshift stretcher before he blacked out.

For *Tere Saldariaga*, the two hour trek up to the monastery was torture. She constantly fell on the rough stony ground and had the horses been going any faster would not have been able to get up without the use of her hands. Her face and knees were covered in bruises and scratches; her throat was parched and sore and she was desperate to relieve herself but refused to be humiliated in front of her thuggish captors. She was exhausted, almost delirious – aware only that she was placing one foot in front of the other. She was only able to rest once, when the men stopped to take swigs from their water bottles and to leave their horses in the corral, but the reprieve from pain and weariness lasted minutes before she was rudely pulled along the trail by one of the men, the lasso's tight grip cutting sharply into her raw wrists. Just when she was about to give up and let herself fall to the ground and to the mercy of her captors, they rounded a bluff in the barren hillside and above them rose the monastery like some medieval fortress 200 yards above them. Dark rain clouds were billowing in from the south and lightning split the early evening sky in two.

The construction of *San Blas* took almost 300 years to complete. Begun in 1570 by Dominican monks and finally finished in 1857, this magnificent building had withstood civil war, earthquakes, fire and revolution. Originally built of wood as a mission station among the *Zapotec* Indians, it had been used as a barracks by *Hidalgo's* insurgents during Mexico's War of Independence and later by *Francisco Madero's* troops in the revolution of 1910. With walls more than eight feet thick, the monastery was built around a central cloister and consisted of a chapel, 10 or so spartan cells for the monks, a refectory, kitchen, and a small herb garden. The bell tower rose 50 feet above the main structure commanding a panoramic view for hundreds of miles. To the south, the Pacific Ocean could be seen; to the north the rugged hills, cliffs and canyons of the *Sierra Madre*.

On the night of the 19th of August, the Monastery of *San Blas*, silhouetted against the dark sky, a crimson sunset to the west and thunder echoing about the hills, looked menacing and inhospitable; the perfect hideout for fugitives and the ideal prison for hostages. By the time James was brought in unconscious and badly injured, *Tere* had been within its dark walls for an hour. Her cell had a wooden pallet and dirty blanket for a bed and a bucket for a latrine. James was held captive in an identical cell next door but she did not know this. *Pepe, Carmen and Manolito* arrived at one o'clock in the morning, cold and drenched by torrential rains.

James awoke to the sound of a Huey helicopter landing somewhere outside and minutes later the door opened and *Cesar* and a man he did not recognise walked into the room.

'This is Doctor *Chiro Trejo*,' said *Cesar* introducing the shabbily dressed man in a raincoat. He had greasy black hair and steel rimmed spectacles. 'He treated you for amoebic dysentery a few weeks ago when we all thought you were dying,' he said smiling wryly.

'So what is it now young man?' asked *Trejo* bending down to inspect his patient. James was aware of the stench of whiskey seeping from the doctor's pores. *Trejo* lifted the bloody bandana that had been wrapped around the wound.

'This is a serious injury,' he said turning to *Cesar*. 'Not only does he have a broken nose but the trauma that caused this gash could have fatal consequences. He needs an MRI scan. Didn't you say he lost consciousness and was dizzy and sick?'

Cesar did not answer him directly. '*Trejo,* just patch him up as best you can,' the boy's future welfare is not my responsibility.' And he left the room banging the door behind him.

Trejo sighed and opening his leather bag removed a packet of antiseptic wipes and began cleaning the gash. James closed his eyes and clenched his teeth. The alcohol from the wipes seeping into the wound stung and he could feel the doctor lift a flap of skin to inspect how deep the cut was.

'Son,' he said soberly, 'This goes right down to your skull. I will clean it and then stitch it up but first I will inject an anaesthetic into your forehead which should numb the pain.'

Forty minutes later, the doctor was gone. James felt his face gently with his fingers. His nose was puffy and he could feel where the bridge was broken. His right eye was half closed and he picked dried blood off his forehead and cheeks. He touched the jagged gash, beneath the bandage and imagined he looked like Frankenstein's monster. And then the door opened again and *Carmen* came in bearing a tray with eggs, *tortillas* and re-fried beans. She put it down on a crude wooden table in the corner and crossing the room she flung her arms around James.

'I have missed you so much,' she said, hugging him tightly. 'It's good to see you again!' she said and kissed him on the cheek.

'They told me you had had a terrible accident that you fell off your horse?' she said touching his bandage gently.

'I fell off the horse because *Ramon* clubbed me with his pistol breaking my nose,' James replied adamantly, still holding on to *Carmen*. The smell of her skin and hair and the feel of her body next to his filled him with warmth and longing.

'And *Pepe*? Is he here too?'

'Yes and *Manolito*, we came up last night. *Cesar* said we had to; that the house in *Los Alamos* is no longer safe, and she kissed him on the cheek again before handing him his breakfast.

'Do you know what happened to *Tere*?' James asked her.

'*Dona Tere* is next door, I saw her just now when I brought her breakfast. She looks exhausted and has the most awful cuts and bruises on her wrists!'

'I am so relieved that she is okay,' replied James. 'Did you hear that she tried to escape on the trail coming up here and that she shot two of the guards?' James asked her.

'No!' *Carmen* said, horror registering in her voice. 'I knew nothing of this, but then I am just the cook, no one tells me anything. What happened?' James went on to describe the terrible journey.

At noon *Cesar, Joaquin and Andres* convened in the refectory.

'It's what I feared,' said *Cesar* addressing the two killers. 'The Elite Corps is hunting us down, *Madrigal* is on the run and they have all his houses and depots under surveillance. Our terror tactics did not have the desired effects we had hoped for. People across the country are demonstrating against the violence, the world's media is against us and the Europeans and our friends to the north have had enough.'

'This could be an opportunity for you,' said *Joaquin* smiling 'An opportunity for us all!' he went on. '*Madrigal* has proved himself to be a liability; he has got too big for his boots. Man, the guy has become such a megalomaniac he actually believes he is *Emiliano Zapata* reincarnated. And now this that he has brought on himself; and we too have to run and cower!' *Cesar* was now listening.

'Make a deal with *el General* and *Jimenez* in *Veracruz* and call a truce and when you have done that, sell out *El Alacran* to the CIA on the condition that they stop their covert operations down here sabotaging our assets. Once things calm down you can help the Yankees bring down the other cartels. Within five years you could have complete control of the cocaine market. That way, everyone looks good. The Americans can take credit for clearing up the mess south of the border. *Medillo* can smile because there is peace between the cartels and you slip into *Madrigal's* shoes.'

'In the meantime,' asked *Andres*, 'what do we do with the hostages?'

'We wait,' replied *Cesar*. 'The Englishman's parents will pay up or their son will die and that bitch *Saldariaga* – well we'll make an example of her. She whacked two of my men and her meddling husband is partly responsible for this latest crackdown so we will waste her in a day or two.'

A fter a breakfast of *huevos rancheros*, bacon, fruit juice and coffee, the four former commandos met up in Piers bedroom in the *Hotel Francia* to plan the next phase of the operation.

'Now we know where they are holding James, we can kill two birds with one stone. We will rescue my son and neutralise this *Cesar* bloke and anyone who helped him at the same time.'

Loftie interjected. 'Boss, I know you're impatient to get James out as soon as possible, but we cannot just go in all guns blazing. This monastery sounds very remote and inhospitable, the perfect fortress probably and if *Alberto* was telling the truth it will be defended by a small army of heavily armed tangos. I suggest Matthew and I recce the place first; we will take photos and scout the best route up there and possible approaches for an assault.'

'Loftie is right,' agreed Matthew. 'We need to plan this thing properly. We will only get one opportunity and if things go wrong you will never see James again!'

They spread out their INEGI map of the *Sierra Madre* and located the village of *Santo Tomas de los Platanos*. The closely knit contour lines informed them this was mountainous country and the monastery itself was perched on a high cliff. It reminded Piers of Agia Trias Meteora near Kalabaka in Greece, over a thousand foot of sheer granite accessible only on foot or on horseback up a treacherous path. Members of the Greek resistance had planned attacks on the Nazi's during the Second World War from its precipitous height.

'We will have to consider our extraction route too,' added Marty. 'We have no idea what condition James will be in. He might be ill or injured in which case we will have to carry him. With a load of tangos on our tail things could go pear shaped pretty quickly!'

'Ok, I am with you,' said Piers. 'You're right, it's a while since I did anything like this and I'm allowing my impatience to get James out to safety to cloud my judgement. Marty and I will stay here and prepare all the gear. Now let's go out and enjoy a few beers!'

They folded the map away and strode out towards the city's huge square again where they found a bar in the sun and ordered bottles of cold *Corona*. The waiter had just brought them their drinks when Axel, the skeletal German tourist, spotted them and approached their table.

'Changed your minds boys?' he said smiling at them provocatively. 'The city has a great scene you know – I could show you all a good time,' he said winking at Marty.

'Now listen good! If I ever see you again, I will ram your head so far up your butt you'll think you've been fucked by a freight train.'

'Ooh! Someone's tetchy' replied Axel. 'Must be your time of the month?' he chuckled effeminately before walking away. **0016 DAYS**

CHAPTER 25

*Despite the fact that Mexican drug cartels and their
Columbian suppliers generate and launder up to
$39 billion each year, the U.S. and Mexican
governments have been criticized for their
unwillingness to freeze or confiscate the
cartels' assets.*

✝

In the early hours of August 22, Virginia woke up in
a cold sweat. The light from the full moon was filter-
ing through the gap in the curtains as they fluttered
in the warm night breeze. She knew what had woken
her. She had just had the most horrible, vivid nightmare. James was standing on a forest track surrounded
by dark woods. He was clad in a familiar T-shirt that
he had bought sixth months earlier at a rock festival
and had on a tatty pair of shorts and flip-flops. He was
filthy and covered in blood. In his hand, by his side he
held a black pistol and he was grimacing. And then
four cowboys on black horses rode by laughing. It was
so shocking, she felt she had to share it with someone
and after breakfast she called Lucy.

'You know I am not superstitious, but it felt so real I cannot help thinking it's a bad omen,' she said down the phone.

'Virginia, you have been through harrowing, anxious times recently and your thoughts and feelings are bound to be troubled. The dream was just a manifestation of your state of mind, your worries about James. Think nothing of it and try to forget about it,' she advised her younger sister.

Next, Virginia called John Mullholland, the family GP in Lambourn, who had been a friend for over 15 years.

'Ginny,' he said affectionately. 'James may well be traumatised by his experience. He was kidnapped and he has been held captive by people he doesn't know and in conditions we cannot begin to imagine. He might have been ill, injured or tortured. He will probably be malnourished and these are only the possible physical implications of his experience. The mental and psychological scars may run very deep and even if they don't manifest themselves immediately, his reactions maybe delayed. Hard though it is to accept, do not expect James to be the same young man who went away travelling two months ago.'

'I know you are right John and I have considered all this.'

'What I suggest is a consultation with a psychologist at Reading General Infirmary as soon as you get back.

I know a good man there, Charles Clarke; and James will need a thorough medical. Can Robert's contact in Mexico City arrange one before your return?'

'Yes, I am sure he could. You know John,' she said changing the subject, 'every waking moment I have longed to see James, to hug him, to have him home again and yet another part of me is dreading seeing him. I am afraid of finding a son who has been permanently damaged by all this!'

'I can empathise,' replied John, 'but you must be prepared for this. How has Eleanor reacted?'

'Not well, I have to say. She was finishing her A'levels when James went away and since the holidays began and the news of James' disappearance she has lost her appetite and has no energy to do anything. I worry that she will not cope well while I am away. She will be staying with Lucy but she is very concerned that something might happen to all of us.'

'My advice would be that you all seek counselling when this is over; even that hard man of a husband of yours. It has been deeply traumatic for the whole family.'

After speaking to Mullholland, Virginia drove into Swindon where she bought some clothes for James at Next and booked a return flight to Benito Juarez Airport and two single flights for James and Piers back from Mexico. She purchased some *pesos* at Barclays Bank and some toiletries from Boots. Her trip back to Mexico now seemed tantalisingly close.

For the first time since she had been kidnapped, *Tere* felt afraid and very lonely. Until now she had barely had the time to process all that had happened to her: the violent manner in which she had been seques- tered, the cold blooded murder of her driver *Juventino*, the long journey down to *Oaxaca* and the horrendous trek to *San Blas* during which she had killed two young men. All that seemed like one long nightmare that had become a certain reality. She felt clammy and could not stop her hands from shaking. She wondered where James was and thought of *Feliciano* and her two sons hundreds of miles away. She didn't want to betray her principles of never caving in to terrorists but she des- perately wanted to be free so that she could return home to her loved ones and to her perception of normality.

When *Pepe* brought in her lunch of pasta soup and *tortillas* she requested a favour.

'*Pepe*, I know from what James has told me that you are not like these other villains,' she began. 'Can you do something for me?'

Pepe put down the tray of food and turning to her replied, 'What is it *Senora*?'

'Can you get me some paper and a pen and smuggle a message out to my family?' she implored.

'I do not know *Senora*,' he answered. 'If I get caught helping you or James, *Ramon* will kill me.'

'I understand *Pepe*,' continued *Tere*, 'but you know in life we have many choices to make. If you believe kidnapping people and taking them away from their families, selling drugs and corrupting our youth can ever be justified and your conscience is clear helping men like *Cesar* and *Ramon*, then of course you cannot do this for me. But if deep down, you know that you are helping wicked men to commit terrible crimes, I ask you to think again,' she said smiling gently.

Pepe turned away and fumbled with the dishes. 'I am not like you *Senora*. I lack the courage to stand up to these people. All my life I have been afraid. I fear what will happen to me if I act against them.'

'It is all right *Pepe*, I understand,' said *Tere*, rising and patting *Pepe* on the back. 'What these people are capable of is terrifying – but you know what we are most afraid of is **Fear** itself. Instead perhaps you could tell me how James is?'

'*Senora*, he is well enough, though *Ramon* said he fell off his horse and broke his nose and he has a deep wound to his head. *Cesar* called out the doctor this morning.'

'Did you hear about the incident on the trail; how the two young cowboys died?' she asked him.

'I know only *Senora,* that you killed the two guards and that *Cesar* says you must be punished.'

'I was trying to escape *Pepe*, escape from men who took me away from my home and family and killed a loyal friend. I am not proud of what I did. Like you, I too am afraid, not of death itself but of dying. Do you know what they are planning to do to me?'

'*Senora, Cesar* does not confide in me but I have heard rumours that they want 'an eye for an eye' as the Bible say.'

'I feared as much, *Pepe* that is why I need to get a message out to my family. I do not want to die without them knowing how much I love them. I want them to know what has happened to me. Do you understand that?'

There was silence for a moment. When *Pepe* turned to face *Tere*, there were tears in his eyes. He put his arms around her and hugged her tightly.

'You know *Senora*, all my life I wanted to be like the beautiful women of *Tehuantepec*. I admired them so much. But now I see that there is another kind of beauty; a beauty of spirit. You have that *Senora*, like the woman who cared for me when I overdosed. You are so courageous and brave that I feel ashamed,' he said beginning to weep uncontrollably. When finally he had composed himself, he placed his hands on *Tere's* shoulders and looked into her eyes.

'I will do what you asked me to do – I promise to bring you paper and a pen and to get your message to your family,' and he left the room.

*J*uarez Street* is an antique avenue of cobbles that weaves its way between old colonial *Haciendas*, their walls covered in bougainvillea and honeysuckle. It is the road out of *Temascaltepec Del Valle*, a prosperous suburb of *Huatulco Bay*. In 2003 its most notorious resident was *Lorenza Martinez, El Alacran's* partner. Madrigal's biographer, the Spanish writer, *Fernando Garcia*, described it as a metaphor for Mexico: 'A place of opulence and luxury masking a terrible and truth.' On the night of August 22, at three o'clock in the morning, *Lorenza* and her two daughters were rudely awakened by the sound of helicopters landing on their lawn and looking out of the windows saw a platoon of commandos disembarking from two MH-53 rapid response birds. They were heavily armed and bore night vision optical devices. Three body guards standing outside the *Hacienda's* main entrance were gunned down despite raising their hands in a sign of surrender. Dozens of other hired goons fled on hearing the deafening roar of the gunships. Using a door breacher, the team were inside the *Madrigal* residence within minutes and had rounded up all the domestic staff along with *Martinez, Paloma and Alondra* whom they arrested on suspicion of aiding and abetting a dangerous felon. They did not expect to find *Madrigal* on the premises but checked every inch of the property, gardens and outhouses where they uncovered the entrance to the much rumoured tunnel that led five miles underground out into the *Oaxacan* canyons. Two hours after the raid, detectives and an entire forensic department were despatched to strip out all the furnishings, wooden panelling, carpets and fabrics. Antiques, and paintings, jewellery, vintage cars and horses; anything of value was immediately confiscated and impounded. Sniffer dogs trained to detect the odour of narcotics and human remains combed every inch of the five acre spread. The pool was drained, the tennis court and lawns dug up and the wooden stables dismantled. A week later the house on *Juarez* Street looked like a bomb site. The bodies of a young woman and two men were found under the tennis court and a fourth was discovered buried in lime in a cavity wall in the pool house. The woman was identified as *Micaela Manrique*, a hooker from *Puerto Escondido* who was reported missing by her mother in 1999. The cadavers of the three men were revealed to be those of *Alexis Rodriguez*, a known assassin on the *Madrigal* payroll, *Pedro Valdez* one of *Madrigal's* accountants and *Valdez'* 25 year old son, *Ricardo*.

Two days later, Mexico's Attorney General, Dr. *Jorge Pedregal* received a typed-written letter from *Ernesto Madrigal* offering terms of surrender.

'With my wife and daughter now in custody, my house in Juarez Street in ruins and under Federal jurisdiction, I am willing to admit defeat. My family has always meant everything to me. I am proud of what I have been able to do for them and proud of their personal achievements. I will plead guilty to the crime of drug trafficking but deny any involvement in the murder and disappearance of Micaela Manrique, Alexis Rodriguez, and Pedro and Ricardo Valdez. In the past I have been *accused of many crimes but more than anything I am a dedicated family man, patriot, philanthropist and entrepreneur. Despite numerous accusations put about by the media, I am not a murderer. I am therefore open to negotiating terms for my surrender.'*

He arrogantly went on to outline his demands:

'I am prepared to give myself in to federal agents on the condition that:

- *I face trial in the Republic of Mexico and under no circumstances am I extradited to the United States of America*
- *My partner Lorenza Martinez and two daughters Paloma and Alondra are released immediately from custody*
- *If found guilty I serve out my term in Saltillo secure penitentiary*
- *I should have certain privileges: access to television and a personal computer with internet and email*
- *I should be free to wear my own clothes and not the uniforms worn by common criminals'*

In a meeting with *Alejandro Mondragon,* the Mexican Secretariat of the Interior, *Pedregal* could not contain his outrage.

'How dare this street mongrel dictate terms of surrender to us!' he said slamming his fist on the desk. 'Who does he think he is?'

'Possibly the most powerful man in the Republic!' replied *Mondragon* ironically. 'He has played his ace my friend, because he knows that he can. This is the only opportunity we will get to bring *Madrigal* to justice (or call it what you want) and I am determined to take it. You will accept his offer!'

Mondragon had served as Mexico's ambassador to the United Kingdom from 1993 to 1998 and had a genuine fondness for the British. It had been almost six weeks since the young English tourist, James Cooper-Brown had been kidnapped and although he had personally vowed to do all he could to secure the young man's freedom, he had become frustrated at the lack of progress in ascertaining the precise details of his kidnapping and the young man's whereabouts. He also knew that his hands were tied. The man charged with leading the investigation into this and other high profile kidnappings, was *General Estefano Obregon* who commanded the army's nine infantry brigades. But six weeks before the kidnapping, *Mondragon* had received some intelligence suggesting that the general was corrupt and was secretly in league with the *Madrigal, Sinaloa* and other cartels in providing them with weaponry, information and communications in exchange for a cut of their profits. *Mondragon's* secret source had also informed him that *Obregon* and other high ranking officers, were using these illicit funds to plan a coup d'état. Under direct orders from the president, the Mexican Federal Intelligence Agency had launched a top secret enquiry into these allegations and had informed *Mondragon* that, under no circumstances was he to question or meddle in the General's affairs until the investigations were complete. *Mondragon* had a nagging suspicion that no efforts at all had been made into locating James and bringing his captors to justice. Now, with the Elite Corps closing in on *Madrigal,* he glimpsed an opportunity. He hoped that in arresting *El Alacran,* all hostages would shortly be released.

0014 DAYS

CHAPTER 26

Mexico is the kidnapping capital of the world

✟

It was two days after his arrival at *San Blas* and James and *Pepe* were talking after breakfast.

'They executed *Ramon* last night,' *Pepe* said almost nonchalantly, though he sounded upset. James did not answer at first and continued drying his wet hair with a dirty towel. He was deliberating on how he should respond. He had always hated violence and the mere thought of an execution sickened him but he had harboured an intense disliking for *Ramon* for several days, especially after he had been viciously pistol whipped. At night, as he lay in bed thinking, he had grappled with thoughts and images of revenge. He pictured himself beating *Ramon* to a pulp and imagined the man's surprised look as he pointed a gun to his head. Images of the two cowboys, who had been shot right in front of him on the trail up to *San Blas,* played out endlessly in his mind despite his efforts to dispel them with happy memories of home. They were like images in slow motion: the pistol kicking back in *Tere's* hands, the flash and smoke and smell of gunpowder from the barrel and the explosion of blood and bone matter and the two limp bodies sliding over the sides of the canyon into the abyss. He admired *Tere* for her courage and wondered if he would have done the same thing, but nonetheless the brutality of the killings appalled him and filled his dreams with terror. His response to *Pepe* when it came surprised even himself.

'I am glad,' he finally said sitting down on his bed to eat his plate of scrambled eggs. 'The threats he made to *Tere,* the way he assaulted me were unacceptable. Men like *Ramon* live by the sword and therefore must be prepared to die by the sword too,' he said coldly and he suddenly felt ashamed. It occurred to him in an instant that he had already changed. A month of captivity, tales of extreme violence, threats, *Ramon's* cruel beating and the sight of two young men being blown apart had confused his moral compass and clouded his sense of right and wrong. He had become anaesthetised to other people's pain and suffering – even his own.

'*Ramon* had a young wife and a two year old son. Now *Luz* is a widow and *Alfredo* has no father. I can't help feeling for them in their loss,' said *Pepe.*

'*Pepe,*' said James, 'I want to tell you something I have never told anyone else, not even my old girlfriend. My father was a soldier, but not just any old soldier. He served for five years with the British Special Forces. My father was a trained killer. He killed men much like these goons have; only he was sanctioned to do so by the British government. I have never been like him. I never wanted to join the army but what I do know is that whatever happens to me, he will not rest until the men who took me are brought to justice and by that I don't mean to a court of law. Men like my father, like *Ramon* and *Cesar* live by a code. They are bound to each other by concepts such as loyalty and trust. They learn to put their lives in the hands of others and they hold other men's lives in theirs. When bad things happen to their friends and comrades and family, when they are betrayed they take it very personally. Although my father professes to being a Christian, he has no notion of forgiveness. He will want to hunt *Cesar* and the others down and kill them and anyone who stands in his way. *Pepe*, although I have spent my life trying not to be like my father, I think I have inherited some of his ruthlessness. I feel no sympathy for *Ramon*. I hope he rots in hell!'

Pepe was clearly disturbed by what had happened to *Ramon* and was holding back tears.

'But James,' he said. 'They killed him like a dog! One minute he and all the others were sitting down eating their dinner in the refectory, chatting and laughing. The next minute he was dead. *Cesar* came in, nodded to *Roberto* and *Felipe* and seconds later they were dragging him outside. *Cesar* made us all watch. *Ramon* was screaming and begging for mercy. He had wet himself and the men were laughing. They threw him to the ground and without a word *Cesar* shot him, first in the leg and watched the poor man for a moment and then again in the head. And then he ordered *Felipe* and *Roberto* to throw his body over the cliffs before turning to us and saying "let that be a warning to you all!"' *Pepe* was quiet for a moment.

'James, without forgiveness we are all damned. An eye for an eye and the whole world ends up blind!'

At lunchtime, *Pepe* brought *Tere* two sheets of crumpled A4 paper and a biro pen.

'*Senora*,' he said greeting her, 'I brought you what you asked me for. I am sorry the paper is not good. I folded it up and hid it in my shoe! Please be careful. If the others find it we will all be in trouble.' And then he paused. 'How will I get the message to your family?'

Tere hugged him affectionately. '*Pepe*, you have done a very brave thing!' she said looking into his eyes. 'I will give you the address to send it to. Can you buy a stamp and get to a post office?'

'There is no post office in *Santo Tomas*. The nearest one is in *Huatulco*, that's two hours away by bus. *Cesar* will wonder where I am, why I am not here on duty and he will interrogate me when I return. I am very afraid *Senora*!'

'Is there anyone you trust that you could give it to?' *Pepe* thought for the moment.

'The only person is *Carmela*, but I love her too much to ask her to do a thing like this.'

'I understand *Pepe*,' *Tere* replied gently. 'You have done more than enough bringing me the writing materials. I will ask *Carmela* myself.'

When *Tere* next saw *Carmela* it was on the evening of August 22.

'I know what you are going to ask me to do *Senora*,' said *Carmela* as she closed the door behind her. '*Pepe* has already told me,' she said turning to face *Tere*. '*Pepe* and I are not like the others. We did not choose this way of life like *Cesar* and some of his men. We did not volunteer to cook and guard you and apart from getting our meals free, we are not paid a single *centavo*. Did you know *Senora*, that *Madrigal's* men kidnapped me and my mother six years ago when I was only 15? One afternoon when my father and older brothers were working in the fields, a pick-up truck arrived in our village and men with guns jumped out and rounded up all the women.

"Your lives as you have known them, no longer exist," said one of them. "You are now the property of the *Madrigal* Cartel." They took us to this huge warehouse where there must have been at least another 200 women some as young as 12, others as old as 60. We were confused and in shock and our fate; to live or die was in the hands of men we had never seen before and knew nothing about. I clung to my mother and we cried all night. That first evening many of the women were raped. Some disappeared altogether. My mother and I were fortunate for 48 hours but then in the night some men came for us. It is a terrible admission, but I was actually relieved when they only violated me. I thought they had come to kill me. After three days we were divided into groups. Some women like me were sent as prostitutes to work for pimps in *Acapulco*. I never saw my mother again. I heard rumours that she and others were sent to work in cocaine processing plants. After working in a brothel for a year, I was taken to a strip bar where they injected me with all kinds of drugs and I was forced to perform obscene acts. Thankfully, I was so drugged up, I cannot recall much of that time. And then two years ago a man I had never seen before told me that I was too old for the bars, that the punters wanted younger, prettier women. He told me I was being sent to work as a cleaner and cook for one of *Madrigal's* lieutenants. That's how I met *Cesar*. He raped me the first night I was in his house even though his wife was asleep next door. Although I hate the man and know one day that he will go to hell, he actually saved my life. Many of the girls were murdered and buried in mass graves. That's how I ended up here. When the first hostages were taken, *Cesar* said he needed a cook and a housekeeper. So *Senora*, I know about loss and pain, suffering and sacrifice. I have lost everything and have nothing left to lose. My mother once told me that there is only one certainty in life; and that is that we will die. What we don't know is how and when. What I do know is that when I die I will go to a better place where my mother waits for me. I will take your letter to the post office, *Senora,'* said Carmela and the two women hugged like mother and daughter.

0012 DAYS

CHAPTER 27

Federal authorities discovered 49 dismembered bod-
ies along a highway in northern Mexico, the latest in a
series of mass murders that security analysts
blame on escalating tensions between
warring drug cartels.

At midday on August 23rd, *Javier Ernesto Madrigal* turned himself in to the federal authorities after several hours of lengthy negotiations between his law-yer, *Mateo Casas* and the Attorney General's office. It was agreed that if found guilty he would not be extra-dited to the U.S but instead he would serve out his sentence in the Maximum Security Prison in *Saltillo*, in the North Eastern state of *Coahuila*. He was to be allowed certain privileges; namely to have access to a personal computer, the internet and email and he was to be exempt from having to wear the obligatory orange boiler suits worn by other inmates. In addition to these demands, all charges against *Lorenza* and his daughters were dropped. His material assets such as his various residences and all their contents, his fleet of Lear jets, cars etc were confiscated and impounded. At

Jorge Pedregal's insistence, *Madrigal* would be tried by a panel of three judges, without a jury and in camera. There would be no public access.

Madrigal was formally charged at Mexico City's Central Police Department in *Venustiano Carranza* Street with the crimes of four accounts of murder; drug trafficking, money laundering, rape, extortion and attempting to pervert the course of justice. If found guilty, the sentence would be 125 years. Pending trial, *Madrigal* was held in a purpose built, subterranean cell made of steel and reinforced concrete, constructed within a Diebold bank vault. It was located next to the barracks of the Elite Corps beneath the Ministry of Justice. The date of the trial was scheduled for April 15, 2004.

Late at night on August 23rd *Tere* sat on her bed and penned a letter to *Feliciano* and her two sons. Hot tears streamed down her face onto the thin cheap paper as she wrote.

'All my working life,' she began, *'I have tried to use writing and journalism to fight evil and injustice,'* and she went on to outline what she had tried to achieve in her long and distinguished career. *'Now, looking back,'* she commented, *'I wonder if in fact I have failed, that my work was in vain - for I believe that this Country that I love, is more corrupt than when I first set out as a young journalist. Then, we had a sense of community and our nation was not*

ravaged by this dreadful plague of drugs, gang warfare and violent crime.' And she concluded her missive. '*But now I realise that my work was actually irrelevant. My greatest success in life was my family: being married to a wonderful man and having two wonderful sons. If something terrible happens to me, if I never see you again, please remind yourself every day that I loved you all so very much.*'

As she finished the letter, *Carmela* came into the room. 'Is it ready *Senora*? Tomorrow morning I will walk down to *Santo Tomas* and from there catch the bus to *Huatulco*. I will do everything I can to get your letter to your loved ones.'

Tere folded the paper and put it in the envelope *Pepe* had given her and then wrote her address on the back of it.

'I feel so much better now,' she said, rising from the bed and handing the letter to *Carmela*. 'You are doing a wonderful thing for me,' she said putting her arms around the young woman and hugging her tightly.

*C*esar came for *Tere* at three o'clock in the morning. She was already wide awake, unable to sleep, tormented by fear and a desperate longing to be with her family and loved ones. She knew at once what was about to happen and almost instinctively she composed herself and the guise of the unruffled veteran journalist took over. She rose, combed her hair and slipped on her flip-flops.

'*Senora,*' *Cesar* said addressing her. 'You know you could have been going home to your family and to your work. Instead you chose stupidity. In killing two of my men you signed your death warrant and that meddling husband of yours put the nails in your coffin by interfering and appealing to the president.' *Tere* didn't respond at first. A few moments of silence passed.

'Do what you need to do!' she said. 'But you will never win this war: soon people will tire of the evil that men like you peddle for a living. They will tire of the violence and corruption and you too will die a violent death. And then you will need to explain your life and your actions to God. What will your defence be?'

Cesar nodded to the two guards waiting outside the door. They were young; probably still teenagers, with sullen grim faces.

'Take her to the woods and do it quickly and don't forget to take shovels with you.'

As they passed James' cell, *Tere* shouted out almost jubilantly. 'If you get out, James, tell the world how they killed me like a dog. God bless and good luck my young friend!'

It was dark and cold outside but the sky was filled with stars and a wisp of cloud passed across a crescent moon. *Tere* forced thoughts of her husband and two sons into her mind. Her hands were shaking and her teeth were chattering. She had an almost overwhelming urge to vomit, a symptom she knew, of her abject fear. And then to boost her spirits, she began singing the Mexican national anthem, quietly at first and then louder as her confidence returned. Her two guards walked silently, one behind her and one in front. From the monastery they descended into thick woods, their torches illuminating the tangled branches and undergrowth. After 10 minutes they came to a small clearing. One of the guards threw *Tere* a hood and told her to put it on.

'I don't want the hood!' she replied indignantly. 'I want to look up into the faces of the cowards who would kill a woman like this! May God forgive you.'

They did not reply. She was told to kneel down, which she did and a moment later it was over with a single bullet to the back of the head that echoed through the dense forest.

James was awoken by the muffled sound of a pistol shot and knew immediately what it was. He jumped out of bed and banged furiously on the door.

'Murderous bastards!' he screamed. 'You fucking cowards, killing a woman like that!' he bellowed at the top of his voice, but his protestations fell on deaf ears. The rest of the monastery was silent and after 10 minutes he gave up and fell back onto his bed. Now more than ever he wished that his father was out there somewhere to exact revenge on these mobsters.

The following morning CNN's offices in Mexico received the message that *Tere Saldariaga*, former

CEO of TV *Cortes* had been executed. The story was all over the Mexican and global media within minutes. *Feliciano Hernandez* was in a meeting with executives at *Cortes* discussing the possibility of raising the ransom money for his wife's release, when the news came through. The whole building fell silent for a few seconds before pandemonium broke out as journalists scrambled for notepads and the channel began preparing their own investigation into the tragic death of their CEO. *Feliciano* sat in silence for a moment, the colour draining from his face and then he picked up the phone and called his sons in Canada.

Piers and the boys were in their hotel room planning their assault on the monastery when the news flash came up.

'That's got to be our cue to do this thing,' he said. 'They might decide to execute James next.'

That same night, Loftie and Matthew set out to reconnoitre the monastery. They left their old black Jeep Cherokee in a side street in the sleepy village of *Santo Tomas de los Platanos*. Before leaving the city, they had pulled into the car park at Carrefour on the outskirts of the city where they parked next to a Ford Explorer and quietly changed the number plates.

Both men knew that a Jeep parked in a remote mountain village with a *Cuernavaca* registration would be sure to attract unwanted attention. They also assumed that the small town would be riddled with spies and informers and that everyone from the local police chief to the barber would be on *Madrigal's* payroll. Before leaving the truck they swept it clean of any evidence that might incriminate them as hostile. Everything was bagged and binned including the car's manual and a Hershey bar wrapper that had fallen down the side of the seat. At one o'clock in the morning, *Santo Tomas* was silent save for a dog barking somewhere in the distance. Apart from a single street lamp that glowed in a corner of the square, the village was dark. Wearing black tracksuits and balaclavas and their NOD head gear they set out into the hills, up a cobbled road that climbed up past the church to a wooden gate.

Alberto had informed them that the Monastery was a 15 mile climb up from the village along a narrow track. They started up the muddy trail which had been drenched by the recent rains and they travelled lightly. In their black packs they carried a *US* Navy F1N Canon Camera with a wide angle and zoom lens, two SOG Special Forces knives three cartons of 9mm parabellums, two Glock handguns with suppressors, platypus water carries for hydration, climbing and abseiling equipment and a handful of glucose-high chocolate bars. On their wrists they wore Garmin GPS devices and tucked into their pockets were small Motorolla radios.

After two miles of steep walking, they dropped down off the path to avoid being spotted. Here the undergrowth was thick and tangled between patches of chaparral and mesquite trees and it was strewn with rocks and boulders. Cicadas chirped in the night air. They made good progress climbing briskly in silence, Loftie leading the way and after two hours and 10 miles of walking they could see the path above them again where a wooden bridge crossed a ravine. They spotted two guards leaning on the railing and heard their distant voices. Matthew removed his Canon camera and began shooting stills. Zooming in on the two men, he could see that they carried AK 47 assault rifles and one of them had a large German shepherd on a lead. Avoiding the bridge they dropped down into the gulley emerging above a waterfall.

'We will have to abseil down to the bottom in order to get to the other side' whispered Loftie. They removed the harnesses and a figure of eight and secured the rope around the base of an evergreen oak. Matthew descended first, jumping away from the cliff side into the void above the swirling waters of the cascade and within seconds had reached the bottom, whereupon Loftie pulled up the rope with the descendeur attached and followed swiftly. They pulled the abseil rope down, coiled it up and packed the gear back into their rucksacks before crossing the swirling, bitterly cold river where the water pooled up to their waists. Once on the other side, they resumed the steep climb beyond the bridge where they contoured the hillside for a further five miles. At last, the monastery was in sight, austere and dark in the pre-dawn light, 300 yards above them. Here Matthew took more photographs and spotted five more guards around the entrance to the old building and the stable block.

'We need to get as close as we can to work out the layout of this place,' Matthew said quietly. 'It's going to be murder getting James out of here and down to the village.' Loftie nodded in agreement. The two men were wet and cold after the river crossing and the dim light of sunrise could be seen on the horizon to the east. They had about 20 minutes left to reconnoitre the place.

0010 DAYS

CHAPTER 28

*35% of Mexicans live in poverty without access to
basic resources such as adequate housing,
education and nutrition.*

✝

On the morning of August 25th, the Elite Corps arrived at the infantry barracks in *Lomas Hipodromo* where they arrested General *Obregon* on suspicion of conspiring with drug cartels to overthrow the government in a coup d'état. He was sitting at his desk in his wood panelled office smoking a cigar when two commandos burst in. He offered no resistance and moments later the disgraced soldier was bundled into the back of an olive green Hummer and taken to the Corps' headquarters beneath the Ministry of Justice, where he was interrogated over three days. The General resisted at first; even after being water boarded. His interrogators then moved on to amputating his thumbs with a pair of secateurs. Finally, after being threatened with castration, *Obregon* broke. Amongst the details that he provided, was information pertaining to the whereabouts of the hostages. On the afternoon of August 26th, two CIA agents, dressed smartly in dark grey suits, arrived and informed *Obregon* that he was being extradited to the U.S to face charges for the crimes of human trafficking and drug smuggling. Still badly injured and wearing blood stained, army fatigues; he was hooded and transferred by helicopter to *Benito Juarez* Airport where a Hercules plane waited on the runway, its giant propellers revolving slowly in the torrential rain.

On the same evening that *Obregon* was being flown into U.S airspace somewhere over Texas, a unit of the Elite Corps raided the remote ranch of *Los Alamos* looking to free James Cooper-Brown and other hostages previously kidnapped by the *Madrigal* Cartel. They quickly discovered that the place was deserted. Doors and windows had been left open to the elements, the rooms were bare and leaves and other debris had blown into the hallway and corridors. In the stinking kitchen, where the sink was filled with dirty dishes and mice had already established a home, a commando found a tin of *Choco-milk* in an otherwise empty cupboard. On opening it he discovered a grubby piece of folded paper on which were written the words:

'Tere Saldariaga and the Englishman, James, are being taken to San Blas'

Within hours, *Mondragon* was on the phone to Sir Humphrey Phillipson, the British Ambassador to Mexico with the news that they had located the hideout where James Cooper-Brown and possibly other hostages were being held. He was also able to report that federal forces were rapidly closing in on members of the *Madrigal* Cartel and that *Javier Ernesto Madrigal*, its head and one of Mexico's most notorious criminals was also in custody. This information however, was to remain confidential until the official press release. The government needed to time the dissemination of the news carefully to avoid any potential backlashes by renegade members of the group or indeed other allied cartels. He counselled Phillipson against advising the Cooper-Browns of this news until James had been rescued.

Robert Swinton had met *Tato Labastida* at Insead Business School in Fontainebleau back in 1986. *Labastida* was an extremely bright student who had recently graduated from Yale with a degree in Economics. Although Robert did not know the young Mexican well, they had occasionally played five-aside football together, had bumped into one another a handful of times in local bars and had loosely kept in touch. Following his MBA, *Labastida* had returned to Mexico working for various banks before joining Dakota Holdings in the early 1990's where his rise to the top had been meteoric. Unbeknown to Robert however, *Labastida's* family had links to organised crime syndicates in Mexico and in particular to the *Veracruz* Cartel based in the east of the country. They used subsidiaries of Dakota and bogus companies to launder money.

Among the bits of information *Obregon* had spilled under duress were the names of various wealthy businessmen including that of *Tato Labastida*. Although the Mexican banker knew all the details of James Cooper-Brown's kidnapping, he was unaware that his old college friend was a relative of the young man and therefore it was a pure coincidence that Robert had contacted him to assist in putting together the ransom money. Responding to Robert's email for assistance, *Labastida* could not quite believe his good fortune and moments later was on the phone to *Federico Jimenez* his friend in the east.

'*Compadre!*' he said, 'you will be aware of the high profile kidnapping of the young British tourist in *Oaxaca* a few weeks back?' he had begun. 'Well it so happens that the man who is representing his family's interests was an acquaintance of mine at business school and has requested my help in putting the ransom money together. This could be a god-given opportunity to make some quick, easy cash,' continued *Labastida* and he went on to describe the details of the ransom drop as he understood them.

'I will arrange for someone to intercept the package before *Madrigal's* people get their filthy hands on it,' *Jimenez* replied chuckling. 'Email me through what you have got. With *Alacran* now in federal custody and *Julio Cesar* his right hand man working for us, it won't be long before we can monopolise the southern trade.'

Listening in on this conversation were the Elite Corps' technical geeks and the information was immediately forwarded to the Corps' tactical command. Another domino in Mexico's seemingly infinite chain of narcotics criminals was about to fall.

J ames felt drained and utterly exhausted and there were times when he wondered if he had the will to continue living or whether in fact recent traumas would eventually drive him mad. He had been shocked by the spate of violence: the death of the two cowboys on the trail and the murders of *Ramon* and now *Tere*, worked over and over in his mind.

A week after *Trejo* had seen to his wound, the alcoholic doctor returned to see his patient. He unwrapped the bandage around James' head and examined the gash and stitches.

'It's healing nicely young man,' he said reassuringly. James could smell whiskey on his breath again and his sweaty, musty clothes.

'If you can sit still I will take the stitches out. Unfortunately you will be left with a nasty scar, but your hair should hide it and in time it should fade.'

The procedure lasted less than 20 minutes. As *Trejo* was packing his bag and getting up to go he patted James on the back and whispered to him.

'It will soon be over son. Keep your head low; avoid confrontation for a few more days and I reckon you will be out of here. The news is that Elite Corps is rapidly closing in on all *Madrigal's* associates. With the big cheese gone they will be at each other's throats,' he said gesturing towards the door. James knew he was referring to *Cesar* and his henchmen.

'Thank you Doctor, I appreciate what you have done for me.'

When *Chiro Trejo* had gone, James ran his fingers over the scar on his forehead and felt his scruffy beard and long matted hair and wondered if his parents would recognise him. He knew that he had lost weight during his time in captivity. His shorts were baggy around his waist and legs and he had lost muscle tone in his arms. When he had looked at himself in the dirty bathroom mirror, he saw a gaunt hollowed face looking back at himself. His tan had gone and his face looked pale and pasty. He thought it ironic that he had gone away on holiday with the intention of getting some colour and swimming in the sea as much as possible. He had wanted to return to England in peak physical condition. Instead, he had picked up amoebic dysentery, been brutally beaten and scarred and looked half skeletal. Added to this, he felt alone and isolated with only fleeting visits from *Pepe* and *Carmela* who themselves often seemed quiet, preoccupied and reluctant to talk.

When *Pepe* brought him his lunch two days after *Tere's* execution however, he seemed eager to chat.

'James,' he said sitting on the bed next to him. 'I have been meaning to tell you something since we arrived here at *San Blas*. I truly believe that even if the ransom for your release is not paid, you will soon be leaving this place!' and he smiled.

'What do you mean? How do you know?' responded James.

'On the day they brought you and *Dona Tere* here, *Carmela* and I were ordered to clear up the house at *Los Alamos* where you were being held hostage. We were told that everything had to go: furniture, bedding, rubbish everything. So we spent the whole day clearing it out. We made a fire in the yard and burnt all the contents of the house. As we worked, *Carmela* and I talked about you and *Dona Tere* and then it came to both of us. We knew how we could help you to be rescued. *Carmela* said we should leave the kitchen in a mess, the dishes unwashed etc. We both knew that eventually the police or army would find the ranch and that they would search the house. They would notice first that most of the house was bare, no furniture, nothing. But coming to the kitchen they would see the dirty plates and smell the stench of rotting food and this might prompt them to look for other things. We found an old tin of *Choco-milk* and decided to leave a hidden message inside informing anyone who might find it that you had been brought here to *San Blas*. By now I am sure they have found *Los Alamos*.' And then he was silent for a moment. 'I also heard on the news the other day James, that *Madrigal* had handed himself in. I believe the net is his cartel. This could be a very good thing but we could now be entering dangerous times.'

James was suddenly aware for the first time that *Pepe* used 'we' instead of just 'you'. It was as if he was distancing himself further from other members of the group and associating himself and *Carmela* firmly with James.

'I say dangerous because, like wild dogs cornered in a corral, *Cesar* and his men could react unpredictably and violently to recent events. On the news they have been reporting that Mexican Special Forces have made some important arrests and discoveries over the last few days. If they find our note, they will rescue you soon,' and he laughed quietly and gestured to James to join him in a high-five.

0009 DAYS

CHAPTER 29

Mexican drug cartels in fight over drug route:
49 decapitated bodies found

✝

Two days before leaving for Mexico, Virginia received a phone call from Marty's wife Linda. Over the years, since their husbands had met back in 1991 at the end of Operation Desert Storm, the Cooper-Browns and the Schultz' had seen each other a handful of times both in the U.S and once or twice in London when Marty and Linda were over in the U.K visiting various horse fairs. Linda was typically Californian with long blonde hair and healthy outdoor looks and an effusive, bubbly personality. Virginia had taken to her immediately.

After exchanging pleasantries, Linda had gone on to express her sympathy and concern for the Cooper-Brown's situations and then she paused momentarily and said, 'Is Piers there by any chance?'

Virginia was slightly taken aback by the question but replied, 'No,' before explaining that he was away on another business trip but was scheduled to meet her in Mexico City in two days time.

'Why do you ask?'

'Because Virginia, I think something is up — I am pretty sure that as we speak Piers, Matthew and Marty are already in Mexico!'

'What do you mean? I am not sure I understand! Piers told me he was off to Dubai to a conference and then on to Azerbaijan. I heard only the other day from him that he would meet me in Mexico on the 28th!'

'Virginia, I believe he and Marty have been in Mexico for at least 10 days!'

'How do you know? And why Matthew and Marty?'

'I was recycling some paper the other day when I came across part of a travel itinerary and some other documents mentioning a return flight to Mexico, Piers, Matthew and someone I have not heard of — Loftie McGregor?'

'Loftie? Yes,' replied Virginia, concern and anxiety beginning to register in her voice. 'He was with Piers out in Kuwait. But what are they doing there?'

'I don't quite understand myself,' Linda replied. 'I have my suspicions though. Marty told me he was off to Montana and Wyoming for two weeks visiting various stud ranches up there. But I think now this all has something to do with James.'

'I am really confused Linda. How could it? I confessed to Piers the other day that I was raising the necessary ransom money. He wasn't happy about it but he understood.'

'You will not like this anymore than I do Virginia, but I think they are going to try and locate and rescue James. I had a curious phone call from a former Marine friend of Marty's on Tuesday - a really nice guy called *Santiago,* who has contacts down there. He said, "Did Marty get the message about the cars and where to pick them up outside *Cuernavaca?*" and then I think he realised he had said something he shouldn't have because he ended the call saying, "Forget it Linda, I will speak to him myself," and hastily called off.'

Virginia was close to tears. 'Linda I cannot believe what you are telling me. They are all too old for this. First James goes missing and now my husband is deliberately putting himself in harm's way.'

Linda tried consoling her. 'Virginia, I am afraid this kind of thing is in their blood. Why do you think Marty risks his life every day breaking in wild Mustangs? Because he loves the adrenaline rush of it. Why did Piers choose to run a security business where he is likely to meet some very undesirable types? Because it's the only thing he knows! We chose to be with these stupid men because deep down we know what they are like and that is what we find attractive. James being kidnapped has just made what they like doing very personal. The fact is they live by a code we will never understand. Men like Marty and Piers will lay down their lives for their friends and loved ones.'

'I am so sorry that Piers has dragged Marty and you into all this.'

'Please don't apologise. Marty is a big boy. He would not let himself be dragged into anything unless he really wanted to,' and she laughed before adding, 'Virginia, if it's all right with you, I would like to join you in Mexico. That way, whatever happens, we can support each other.'

'Linda, that would be lovely,' she replied and she went on to give her the details of her travel plans and where she would be staying. When she put the phone down she felt exhausted and overcome with worry. A few minutes later she called Robert and told him everything.

'This must remain confidential,' she told him. 'It's only a theory of ours and I don't want to compromise him anymore than he already is. If for some terrible reason, I don't see him on the 28th, we must still go ahead with the ransom drop,' she explained.

Among the witnesses subpoenaed in the prosecution's case against *Javier Ernesto Madrigal,* was *Enrique Ramos*, the administrator of the *Los Ninos* field hospital in *Chiapas*. When questioned by lawyers from the Attorney General's office, he acknowledged that he had known for some time that he was being paid indirectly by the cartel but fear of what might happen to his family had prevented him from coming forward with information. He described the afternoon back in March when he had been threatened by two of *Madrigal's* henchmen and how it had affected his life and work. He described the sudden disappearance of both *Monica Gonzalez* and *Tarcisio Uribe* and how he had been informed by the hospital's trustees that they had been sacked for embezzling funds and incompetency, charges, he of course, did not believe but was powerless to do anything about. He was also aware that *Antonio Torres* had been planted in the hospital to keep an eye on him and had wondered what had become of the young man. In return for his testimony he, his sister and his mother were immediately taken into protective custody and put on a witness protection programme in *Monterrey* pending the trial of the notorious criminal. Life as *Enrique Ramos* had known it, came to an abrupt end.

D espite handing himself in to the federal authorities, *El Alacran* had no intention of spending the rest of his life behind bars. A few days after he had been incarcerated, he claimed to be suffering from terrible headaches, nausea and sudden drowsiness. His peripheral vision, he said had become impaired, he was confused and was aware of a ghastly, persistent grinding noise in his head. A doctor examined him in his cell but could find no outward symptoms of any serious condition. When *Madrigal* was found on the floor of his cell the following day however, screaming and writhing in pain, both hands clutching the side of his head, the authorities had no option but to take him to the military hospital in *Tecamachalco* for an MRI scan.

On August 26th, *Madrigal* was transferred to an armoured prison van which had been commissioned as an ambulance. Four outriders on motorcycles from the Elite Corps, along with several armed guards on board, accompanied it. As they were driving up *Avenida Guerrero*, a highway patrol officer on the cartel's payroll stopped the vehicle at a road block claiming there had been an accident and diverted it down a narrow one-way street flanked by high blocks of flats and offices. As they were progressing slowly down the road avoiding parked cars and skips on the pavement, four snipers on the rooftops took out the outriders, and another cartel foot soldier shot a rocket propelled grenade at the armoured van, which blew off its heavily bolted door and sides. Armed, bandana clad men piled out of adjacent buildings and gunned down the stunned guards who were now piling out of the wreckage, hauling *Madrigal* with them. Moments later, a black numberless Range Rover reversed at high speed down the alley and picked up the cartel's boss. The transponder on the van registered that it had stopped and as the Elite Corps technical geeks followed what had happened on the CCTV playing out in front of them, a rapid response Apache helicopter was scrambled to give chase. For over an hour it tracked the car as it headed south west out of the city on the *Toluca* road. On board were a Corps sniper and two other commandos. Just after the Range Rover emerged from wooded hills on the outskirts of the city before the suburb of *Cruz Blanca*, the sniper was ordered to stop the vehicle at any cost and to capture *Madrigal* dead or alive. The Apache helicopter descended to 70 feet and followed the fleeing vehicle as it headed for the densely populated shanty town. Leaning out of the helicopter's sliding door on a harness, the sniper fired three shots. The first one missed the vehicle ricocheting off the tarmac. The second hit the car's right, front tyre which exploded on impact shedding rubber and debris all over the highway. For less than a minute the Range Rover limped on, slumping to its side, the bare steel wheel sending up a firework display of sparks as it grated along the surface of the road. The sniper then aimed at the rear right wheel and squeezed the trigger. A nano second later, the tyre exploded flipping the car into the air and onto a grassy verge where it rolled over twice before coming to a halt upside down. The Apache turned and circled and was about to land when the wreck exploded in a ball of orange flames and black smoke. *Javier Ernesto Madrigal*, two body guards and their driver were pronounced dead at precisely 11:42 am.

0008 DAYS

CHAPTER 30

"In this block of apartments alone, all the teenagers were either killed or disappeared," said Pedro Reyna Diaz, 46, whose two stepsons were among those swept up in the drug cartel warfare waged in this neglected neighborhood. "An entire generation was lost." The Dallas Morning News.

✝

After speaking to Robert, Virginia called Edward Hutchinson at the Foreign Office notifying him of her intention to go to Mexico and deliver the ransom money.

'I am sorry it has come to this, Mrs Cooper-Brown,' was his reply. 'Despite our best efforts we have been unable to negotiate with the cartel though Mr *Mondragon*, the Interior Minister, has hinted that that they now have some useful leads. I will of course convey your message to the cartel via our various channels out in Mexico and will make appropriate arrangements for you and your husband to be picked up at the airport and escorted around the city.'

At six o'clock on the morning of 26th August, Piers and the boys convened in Loftie's room. Matthew loaded the photographs onto the laptop and the others gathered around. Whilst Piers and Marty took notes, Loftie and Matthew described the ascent up to the monastery from the village and pointed out the various locations where they had spotted guards on the approach.

'*Alberto's* description of the place was pretty accurate,' said Matthew pointing to a picture of the building's outside walls.

'There is a large wooden door here,' he said. 'And the wall is about 15 feet high all around. Loftie scaled it and was able to get a good look at the general layout of the place.'

'Yes,' continued Loftie, 'the wall drops down to some flat roofs and then into the cloisters. There is a central courtyard with a fountain which all the rooms seem to open out into. There appear to be no outward facing windows so we will only be able to get in via the main entrance or over the walls and roof. Here, in the top right hand corner,' he said pointing to the photograph 'is the chapel and steeple which is being used as a watch tower. We spotted at least two sentries up there. The problem is, we have no idea where James is being held. There are probably 10 rooms in addition to the chapel and the refectory. In total Matthew and I saw eight well armed men but *Alberto* said the place was heavily fortified so we can expect at least 20; and there are only four of us.'

'I suggest you spot for us Loftie from a sniper's hide somewhere to the south here,' said Piers. 'It will be your job to see us three inside and then you will have to join us. I will sweep each room with Matthew whilst you two cover us from outside. I see the biggest issue being our extraction. It will be one thing to get James out of his cell but it will be another thing altogether getting him out of the building and off the mountain with a load of tangos on our tail.'

'Boss, that was Matt's and my concern. It's pretty hellish getting up there with a waterfall to ascend on the return journey,' responded Loftie. 'James might be injured or even unconscious. And then there's the village to negotiate. I think we can assume that there will be cartel people all over it,' he continued.

'There is nothing we can do about the extraction now,' interjected Matthew. 'All we can do is plan for the worst – that James is wounded, in which case we will have to haul him up the waterfall and carry him down to the village. Remember guys, the number of tangos is really irrelevant. They maybe well armed but I doubt whether any of them will have had military training. So long as we can get into the main building, I reckon with the hardware we've got, we can deal with any number of goons. We will also have the element of surprise.'

'Good,' responded Piers. 'We will do this thing tomorrow. Loftie will be our sniper. Matthew, can you guide us up there and back? I will take care of locating James with Marty covering from outside.'

'Have you considered that James might have made some friends in there – possibly allies?' Matthew asked.

'That's something we cannot afford to factor in to the assault,' replied Marty. 'We have to assume that everyone in there apart, from James is an enemy combatant and anyone who gets in our way will have to go down!' His friends nodded in agreement.

During August every year, the statue of *La Virgen de la Sierra* was carried from the hermitage of *Santa Ana,* high up in the hills back to the village of *Santo Tomas de los Platanos,* where it would remain for six months. For the local priest, *Padre Ruffo* and the inhabitants of the small hamlet, it was their most important feast day. Families would return from as far away as Mexico City to enjoy an evening of religious ceremonies, processions, fireworks and local specialities of punch and spicy *tamales.* By the evening of the 27th August the whole town was decked in colourful bunting and strings of fairy lights adorned buildings. Trestle tables covered in embroidered white clothes lined the high street ready for the feast and *piñatas* for the children were strung up in the trees. Widows dressed in black swept the church and outside a huge stage was erected for the arrival of a *ranchero* band from *Oaxaca.* The ageing population of *Santo Tomas* was about 700 but on the night of the *fiesta* it would swell to over 2000 as families returned to the village and the mountains would echo with the sound of fireworks and *Mariachi* music.

James lay on his bed, his face turned to the wall, his mind wrapped up with memories of recent events. His thoughts wandered back to his trip with Toby which now seemed to him like another lifetime. He wondered what his friend was doing. Less than three months before he had been taking his finals at university and was still going out with Charlotte. He recalled how one afternoon they had sat out on the beach revising, St Andrews' Old Course behind them and then they had wandered hand in hand back to the town where they had sat and had coffee in 'Cafe Rouge.' He thought about his future and what he wanted to do with his life and then it occurred to him that he might never return home; that soon *Cesar* would come for him in the silent hours and he would be taken outside somewhere lonely and desolate and shot like a dog. That is what they had done to *Tere*. He tried to blank his fears out and instead pictured himself at home in the large kitchen with his mother and father and Eleanor. He had successfully applied to do a doctorate in History of Art at Cambridge, a course that would start in October, but the study of art now seemed so meaningless and trite after everything he had experienced and witnessed. He knew his captivity had changed him: that if he returned home, he would not be the same person. He wished to live his life differently, more ethically if that was possible and then his silent thoughts were interrupted by the door opening on rusty hinges and *Pepe* and *Carmela* bounced in joyfully.

'James!' *Pepe* said. 'There will be a *fiesta* in the village tomorrow night. *La Virgen* is being returned to the church. *Cesar* has told *Carmela* to prepare a party for everyone. There will be *molé*, *chicharon* and *pozole* soup and music and dancing. *Cesar* has told the guards that they can bring their wives and girlfriends up. We will have a good time and soon, my friend you will be going home!'

Carmela nodded enthusiastically and hugged James. 'I will teach you to dance a *Sevillana*,' she shrieked, grabbing James by the hands and twirling herself around him.

'*Cesar* has told me we can have music again in the room so I have brought you a cassette of *Chavela Vargas* singing *Piensa en mi* and *Para toda la vida*.' He plugged in an ancient looking Hitachi cassette recorder and pressed play and seconds later the *Costa Rican* born singer burst into song.

'Do you know Don James,' Carmela said addressing him affectionately, 'that Mexico has more *fiestas* than anywhere else? Have you heard of *El Dia de los Muertos* – the Day of the Dead?' she asked him.

James said he had but did not know much about it. 'A few years ago one of the big museums in London put on an exhibition about The Day of the Dead, but I never went to see it,' he confessed.

'Well let me describe it to you because it's probably Mexico's most colourful *fiesta,*' she went on. 'The first and second of November are of particular significance in Mexico, combining the ancient pagan cult of *Mictlantecutli,* the *Aztec* Lord of the Underworld, with the observance of All Souls Day. The week leading up to *El Dia de los Muertos* is one of expectation as families prepare to welcome back the souls and spirits of their dearly departed. We build altars to our loved ones who have passed away, adorning them with photographs and particular items of memorabilia along with food and drink.

Cake shops and bakeries sell icing sugar skulls, with eyes of shiny paper for children to eat. Skeleton images are everywhere and the streets are decked out in *papel picado* – colourful tissue paper cut into skulls and skeleton shapes. Shops and roadside stalls sell skeletons playing football, smoking and drinking; skeleton matadors, skeletons driving cars and playing pool. The mood on The Day of the Dead, far from being morbid or gloomy, is one of *fiesta,* as families gather at twilight in the cemeteries to lay marigolds and light candles on their relatives' graves. We bring food and drink and sit on blankets and rush mats late into the night talking and laughing. Death is not a stranger to us. We grow up and see it all the time. I saw my little brother die of dysentery when I was ten years old. We buried my grandparents in the graveyard back in my village. Death to us is as familiar as birth.'

Before coming to Mexico, James had never seen a person dying, much less a corpse. Death for him had been something fictitious; the body counts in celluloid film. When real people died, they were rushed away in ambulances with tinted windows or wrapped in body bags. People he knew never joked about it and although the idea of a party celebrating death went counter to his Christian beliefs, he understood the sentiment behind it. For the pre-Hispanic, pre-Christian people of Mexico, death must have seemed terrifying and inexplicable. The only way to diminish its terror would be to joke about it, to caricature it, to rationalise it – even to welcome and celebrate it!

They continued to talk for most of the morning.

'James, my family did not always live in Oaxaca?' *Carmela* informed him. 'My grandfather was a *Tarahumara* and came from a small village called *Creel* in the Copper Canyon in the state of *Chihuahua*. He brought his family here in the early 1970's to look for work. They say that the Copper Canyon is bigger and deeper than the Grand Canyon in the United States. All over Mexico my people are known for their stamina and their ability to run great distances. In my language, *Tarahumara* means 'running people'. We are the only tribe in Mexico never to have been subdued. The *Aztecs* left us alone and when the white men came, the *Tarahumara* abandoned their homes on the plains and took refuge in the canyons where they have remained ever since. Now, their only enemy is progress itself. Loggers have moved in and cut down the forests and mining companies have dredged the rivers for diamonds and quarried the hillsides for metals.

I remember my grandfather telling me how at the age of ten he had to undergo an initiation. They called it the rite of passage to manhood. Along with the other boys from the village, he had to run 50 miles through the dry riverbeds in bare feet to the end of the valley and back again, with only eight hours of rest in between. Using sling shots and bows and arrows they were told to hunt a deer before skinning and cooking it. In the tradition of the *Tarahumara,* nothing was to be left. The meat was salted to preserve it, the hide dried and used to make mocasins and the bones and antlers, tools and weapons.

Our ways and traditions are no longer valued by men who do not respect nature and its natural cycles. My great grandfather once fought off a grizzly bear with only a knife and spear. It crept up on him whilst he was fishing in the creek. He told my father that he wept for three days after he had killed it. He lamented that he had slayed one of nature's great warriors. The cave painting of my people tell the story of creation before man brought wickedness into the world. The *Tarahumara* believe that once, man and beast lived side by side. They say there was no need for hunters and warriors because man ate the fruit of the land, that is why we respect the bear and jaguar, the deer and the wolf. They were our friends and roamed the earth with us,' and she paused. 'Tell me about the tribes in your country James,' she asked him enquiringly.

James had to stifle his laughter prompting *Carmela* to ask him what was so funny.

'We don't have tribes in England,' was his answer. 'You would have to go back a long way in our history to find them,' he said. 'But that is our loss. I find Mexico so exciting because it has so many layers of tradition and colour.'

'I cannot believe you do not have tribes,' *Carmela* said incredously. 'Here in *Oaxaca* alone there are more than 10 indigenous groups each with their own language and ways and everyone knows their ethnic roots. There really is no such a thing as a Mexican you know,' she said laughing.

*F*eliciano Hernandez received his wife's letter three days after her execution. His two sons were over from Canada and they had gone to TV *Cortes* to sort out her affairs, when *Tere's* teary eyed secretary handed him the filthy envelope. On recognizing his wife's handwriting, the 73 year old wept. 'What has become of this nation of ours where women are butchered like this!' he exclaimed hugging his sons. 'I will make it my life's work or whatever is left of it, hunting down her killers and bringing them to justice!' he vowed.

Under orders from *Federico Jimenez*, head of the *Veracruz* Cartel, plans were now underway to intercept the ransom money due to be delivered to *El Desierto de los Leones* on August 30th. The Cooper-Brown's every move would be watched as they arrived in Mexico City on August 28th. On the day of the drop, *Tato Labastida* would oversee the counting and packaging of the $5 million and ensure that it was safely stowed in the back of the white Volkswagen Passat. A transponder device would then be placed underneath the car making it easy to follow through the chaos of the city. As the Cooper-Browns left the head offices of Dakota Holdings in downtown *Polanco* and entered the outer fringes of the forest that marked the beginning of *El Desierto,* approximately two hours later, their car would be hijacked and the ransom money taken. Both Mr and Mrs Cooper-Brown were to be shot dead and their car torched. Their son James would then be executed. *Labastida's* cut of the ransom would be $2 million.

0007 DAYS

CHAPTER 31

Crime is among the most urgent concerns facing Mexico, as drug trafficking rings play a major role in the flow of cocaine, heroin, and marijuana transiting between Latin America and the United States.

✝

James woke up to a mood of celebration in the old former monastery. From down the corridor where he surmised was the kitchen, he could hear *Carmela* singing and when *Pepe* brought him his breakfast there was a large slice of pineapple sprinkled with cinnamon on a plate, a glass of orange juice and *huevos rancheros*. *Pepe* was positively buoyant with a distinct spring in his step.

'Tonight is *La Fiesta de la Virgen*,' he said cheerfully laying the tray down on a crude wooden table. 'The men of the village will carry the statue of our lady down from the *sierra* at dusk to the church where the women will receive it with incense and candles and then after mass there will be much celebrating. *Los Pistoleros* are coming from *Oaxaca*, they are the most famous *ranchero* band in the region and the streets will be lined with stalls and *piñatas* for the children. There will be dancing in the cloisters. *Cesar* said even you will be allowed out to celebrate.'

James ate his breakfast sitting on the end of the bed, savouring the sweet taste of the pineapple and spices and the hot eggs and their chilli tomato sauce.

'I heard on the news last night that the Elite Corps have arrested more of *Madrigal's* men. It won't be long my friend before they locate us here,' he said turning to James and smiling.

'*Pepe*,' James replied, a note of anxiety in his voice. 'Believe me, I desperately want to go home and see my family again, but I am worried that if a rescue attempt is made you and *Carmela* will be caught up in the ensuing violence. Have you considered that? You two have done nothing wrong and you do not deserve to bring that kind of judgement on yourselves. If you really believe that an assault on the monastery is imminent, is there no way that you and *Carmela* can get away before it happens? Can you not just disappear? Is there nowhere you can go?'

'James, of course I cannot speak for *Carmela*, but as for me, my place is here with you. I have made my peace with God and I know my role is to serve and protect you as best I can, and anyway I have nowhere to go. I am happy to do that and even if I am killed, it will be God's will. I have spent all my life running away in fear, escaping from myself. Now I know who I am and I want to die a dignified death not cowering in

fear again. *Carmela* told me something the day before
Tere died and I have thought about it every day. She
said that there is only one certainty in life and that is
that one day we will die. What we don't know is where
and how and when. James, I want to die a noble death
serving God.' *Pepe* was silent for a moment and then he
turned to James and said, 'Do you know what they did
to *Manolito*?'

'No,' James replied. 'I noticed that he had not been
around, what happened to him?'

There were tears in *Pepe's* eyes. 'I do not know for
certain but some of the men are saying *Cesar* ordered
him to be killed. They say that two of his associates,
Andres and *Joaquin* carried it out. They even volunteered. *Manolito* wanted to join his grandparents in
Texas. He apparently told a friend that he was leaving *Oaxaca* and that he would try to cross the border.
Cesar found out and was furious. They say *Andres* and
Joaquin invited *Manolito* out for a night on the town
down in *Puerto Angel*. Then, when he was drunk, they
told him they were taking him fishing. They comman-
deered a *lancha* and went out to sea, threw a bucket of
pigs' blood into the water and waited. And then, they
fed *Manolito* to the sharks. *Constantino*, the old boy
who took them out, said *Andres* and *Joaquin* sat there
laughing as the sharks circled in for him. He said
he cannot sleep now; that his dreams are filled with

Manolito's screams and the men's demonic laughter. I believe God has given these people over to Satan.'

On the night of the 28th of August, Virginia Cooper-Brown flew into *Benito Juarez* airport, Mexico City and an hour and a half later was sitting in the comfortable lounge of the *Hotel Santa Maria* in down-town *Polanco* sipping a gin and tonic with her old friend Linda Schultz. There was still no sign of Piers or Marty.

The day before, she had dropped Eleanor off with Lucy and Robert in London and spent the night with them in their comfortable home in Cheniston Gardens, Kensington. When Eleanor had gone to bed, the three of them had sat around the table with glasses of wine and talked late into the night.

'You must not worry about anything,' Robert had reassured her. '*Labastida* is a good man and will make sure everything is ready for the drop in two days time. If the Foreign Office has offered you a driver, you must take them up on it. Mexico, we all know is a danger-ous place so don't go hopping into taxis or taking any unnecessary risks. James will need you two to be there for him and so will Eleanor on your return.'

'My worry is that something might have happened to Piers. Stupid man. Love him dearly though I do, I fear he might try something drastic. He was never going to agree to pay the ransom, even if he led me to believe that he was okay with it.'

'For the time being, Virginia you do not have the luxury of thinking about Piers. I am sure he can look after himself. Your only focus must be James and ensuring the ransom is left in the right place at the right time. If Piers is not there, you will have to muster the strength to do this thing by yourself.'

The three of them gathered around the table and studied the map of Mexico City which Robert had bought the day before from Standfords travel bookshop in Longacre.

'Here is where you will be staying I believe?' and he pointed to an area marked *Polanco*. 'And Dakota Holdings is about here just down the road from you. The Foreign Office driver will take you there. *Labastida* said he will organise the hiring of the white Volkswagen Passat and will make sure there is a GPS device in it with the drop zone already keyed into it. You will then drive from *Polanco* to *Avenida de Toluca* here and then it's pretty much a straight route out of the city to the place they call *El Desierto de los Leones,* here,' he said pointing to the shaded area just beyond the city's outskirts that marked the beginning of the forested recreational area. 'It's important that you have your phone on at all times. Think positively. In less than four days time James will be home,' he said smiling.

Now, sitting with Linda in the lounge of the Hotel *Santa Maria*, Virginia could feel panic rising in the pit of her stomach.

'There is still tomorrow,' Linda said doubtfully. 'Our men might not have done a thing like this for a while but they are still as hard as nails. I reckon you and I should take full advantage of your driver and hit the city for some retail therapy tomorrow. I have always wanted to go to Mexico City's *Bazar Sabado* in *San Angel* and to have lunch or a coffee at Sambournes,' and she went on. 'The capital has some magnificent markets too. By the time we get back in the evening Marty, Piers and the boys will be sipping beers in the bar,' she said swilling back her drink and laughing.

Whilst Linda and Virginia were sitting comfortably in their hotel lounge, *Tato Labastida* was in his penthouse office putting the finishing touches to the hijacking plan. Just the previous morning he had spoken to his old friend and fellow student Robert Swinton in London who had confirmed that Mrs Cooper-Brown was leaving for Mexico the following day and would be at his offices early on the morning of the 30th August as planned. *Jimenez* had also been on the phone to inform him that James' mother had landed safely and was followed to her hotel from where her every move would be tracked. Two of *Jimenez's* most reliable assassins were being hired for the job and within less than 72 hours $5 million of easy money would be theirs. It did not trouble *Labastida* in the slightest that he was not only betraying his friend; he was signing the death warrants of three innocent people: a young man of 22 years of age and his parents. He had been brought up in a corrupt family with filthy, violent connections and although he had never killed anyone he had certainly sanctioned murder and torture and slept easily knowing his decisions had caused other people untold misery.

0006 DAYS

CHAPTER 32

There are 10.1 million indigenous people in Mexico of different ethnic groups, which constitute 9.8% of the population.

✠

It was just after 11 o'clock at night when the four men dressed in black loaded the two vehicles with their heavy rucksacks and left the city of *Oaxaca* heading south. Being a weekday, the streets were silent and deserted with only a few stray dogs picking at taco scraps in the gutters. It had recently rained and the cobbled roads glistened under the street lighting. As on their previous excursion to *Santo Tomas*, Loftie pulled in at Carrefour's quiet parking lot on the outskirts of the city where they exchanged the registration plate of the second vehicle with a solitary Nissan saloon. Matthew drove with Piers whilst Marty and Loftie followed behind. There was little conversation. Each man was wrapped up in private thought. Marty was thinking of Linda and of how he would explain his jaunt to Mexico. Piers thought of Virginia and felt a pang of guilt that somehow he had betrayed her trust by leaving her to sort out her travel plans and Eleanor.

He hoped and prayed that within less than 24 hours, he would be with her again in Mexico City along with James. Matthew focused on the dark desolate road ahead as it swept by the pre-Hispanic ruins of *Monte-Alban* and headed towards the barren silhouette of the *Sierra* and Loftie wondered what he would do on his return to Glasgow. There would be no job for him at B&Q, that was for sure.

After an hour of driving high into the mountains they came to a heavily wooded area with deep ravines sloping down to the coast. Occasionally a car passed driving in the opposite direction towards the city, its headlights illuminating the dark woods but apart from that the road was theirs. Just after midnight, and an hour and a half from *Santo Tomas*, they pulled in at a roadhouse for some refreshment. For miles they had passed no sign of habitation. The *cantina* stood out under pink neon behind a dusty parking strip and advertised food and drink. There was one other car outside: a 1981 Ford Galaxy saloon with *Policia* written across its side and lights on the roof. As the four men approached the swinging doors of the *cantina,* they heard laughter and conversation and as they entered were met by the pungent smell of marijuana and *tequila*. A group of five state troopers sat around a table shrouded in cigarette smoke. They were playing cards and swigging down shots. Piers, Loftie, Marty and Matthew quietly found a table in the corner by the window and sat down. They looked very conspicuous; four foreigners dressed in black sitting in a lonely roadhouse in the middle of the night, but the drunken policemen paid them little attention at first. Presently, a young waitress aged about 15 dressed in jeans and a sweat shirt arrived with menus. The men ordered a plate of beef *tacos* with *guacamole* and bottles of water. As she was returning to the kitchen, one of the policemen approached their table. He was an overweight man with a pock marked face and thin moustache. His belly bulged over his waistline and his navy blue trousers looked uncomfortably tight around his crotch. Hanging from a utility belt was a pair of handcuffs, a holstered Colt 45 and a long truncheon. He spat out the remnants of a sunflower seed. He was smiling; almost grimacing.

'We don't see many *gringos* in this neck of the woods,' he said by way of an introduction. 'Especially not four men all dressed in black at a cantina in the middle of nowhere. What are you guys doing and where are you going?'

Marty, the only Spanish speaker in the group, was quick to respond. 'We are all members of a scuba club back in California. We just finished a long dive off *Huatulco* Bay and are heading back to *Oaxaca*,' he replied smiling charmingly. 'You sure have some beautiful waters around here!' he added.

'The best in the world my friend, the best in the world,' replied the cop. 'But you boys need to be careful.

There are *bandidos* in these hills, men that do not care a damn who you are and where you come from. Enjoy your meal anyway,' he said returning to his colleagues.

The food was delicious accompanied by various sauces and after half an hour the men were ready to hit the road again. They had just requested the bill when the overweight policeman, stood up and slapping his revolver on the table, addressed his colleagues.

'Now let's play a little roulette like the *Zapatistas* used to do in the old days,' he said. '*Quique* you are the youngest, you go first!' he said addressing a young man with buck teeth and hound dog looking eyes. There was silence around the table and beads of sweat began to appear on the youthful policeman's brow. *Quique* picked up the gun, stuck the barrel against his forehead and pulled the trigger. The four *gringos* in the corner looked on appalled. There was a loud click as the hammer of the pistol shot forward and the chamber revolved and then the young trooper dropped the gun on the table and ran outside into the night where he was violently sick. His companions sniggered as he returned moments later, ashen faced with shock. And then the fat sergeant picked up the gun.

'To show you boys and our *gringo* friends here that I am not a pussy, I will go next,' he said arrogantly picking up the Colt and ramming it into his mouth. Just then the crackly, static sound of an incoming call was heard over his radio. He replaced the gun, picked up the radio from the table and took the message.

'They want us over in *Chilpancingo* now,' he said to his colleagues. They finished their drinks, picked up their weapons and were gone, their car screeching away into the chilly night.

In the monastery of *San Blas* the *fiesta* was in full swing and the cloisters and central courtyard were cluttered with couples dancing to the *ranchero* music blasting out of some large Bose speakers mounted on the old walls. *Carmela* was busy serving out bowls of soup behind a huge trestle table and preparing shredded pork tacos. Other tables were laden with slices of fresh fruit, tortillas, salad and steaming bowls of punch. *Cesar* languished in a big wicker chair puffing on a Havana cigar, his mistress draped across his lap. She was a dark, sultry woman with shiny black locks, full red lips and high cheek bones.

'That's *Lourdes*,' *Pepe* said to James as they sat on a bench on the opposite side of the courtyard. 'She used to be a whore up in *Acapulco* before *Cesar* claimed her. You know he has a wife and two kids back in Mexico City, but he never sees them!'

Cesar was talking to two men in dark suits who sat on either side of him.

'Who are the men with him?' asked James. 'I have never seen them before.'

'The one on *Cesar's* right is *Andres*; the other one is *Joaquin*, both former assassins on *Madrigal's* payroll but now that *El Alacran* is no more, the three of them are probably muscling in to take over the cartel.'

Carmela had a free moment and wandered over to join *Pepe* and James. Occasionally the clear night sky erupted into red, green and white sparks as fireworks were set off in the village far beneath them. *Carmela* brought James and *Pepe* a plate of *tacos* and some slices of melon sprinkled with chilli powder and she watched James with interest as he wolfed the food down hungrily.

'So James, after all this time, what do you think of my cooking?' she asked laughing.

'I think it's absolutely delicious,' he replied, his mouth full of beef and *salsa*. 'To be honest I don't think I have ever eaten such tasty food in all my life and that's saying something. My mother is a very good cook!'

'Do you like the melon?' she asked
'Well,
I would never have thought fruit and chilli would go together but it really brings out the flavour. When I return to England, I will have to introduce it to my friends and family. Maybe I will set up a Mexican restaurant and you can be the cook!' and the three of them laughed.

When *Pepe* got up to go to the bathroom, *Carmela* took his place and snuggled up to James and took his hand in hers. He did not resist. And then she looked up at the star filled sky and sighed.

'I think I am in love with a man I barely know!' she said in Spanish wistfully and she turned to look at James with her large brown eyes. But James understood her.

'Who is the lucky man?' he replied.

Carmela leant over and kissed him on the cheek. 'It is you,' she said, before getting up and returning to her *taco* stall.

Sitting on his own, James was still reeling from *Carmela's* confession. All his senses were being assaulted simultaneously. He could smell the delicious roasting meat and the sweet punch and his head was filled with the sounds of music, clapping and laughter. He watched *Carmela* sashaying gracefully through the dancing couples dressed in her white skirt and embroidered blouse, her bare brown feet clad in a pair of open sandals and he longed to hold her tightly in his arms and kiss her delicate mouth. For a moment he forgot that he was a hostage held by brutal killers and wished that this snapshot of time would last forever. And then his thoughts were interrupted by *Cesar's* loud arrogant laugh. James looked at him as he slapped *Lourdes* on her backside and told her to go away. He hated *Cesar*. He wondered if indeed the Elite Corps, that *Pepe* had spoken of, would eventually rescue him or whether, like *Tere* he would die like an animal here in *San Blas*. He thought of his life back in England which seemed so unreal now. He had lost track of time but knew that the deadline for the ransom must be approaching and then he felt *Pepe* slap him on his back and he looked away from *Cesar* and smiled at his friend.

'What time do you think the party will end?' he asked.

'You have not seen the half of it,' *Pepe* replied grinning. 'It will go on until dawn; until everyone is either too tired or too drunk to stand,' he said.

'Do you think the place is still being guarded?' James asked looking up at the Chapel tower.

'Of that you can be certain. *Cesar* will have paid 10 of his best men overtime to miss the *fiesta* and make sure the place is secure,' he replied sombrely. 'Do not be seduced by the air of frivolity my friend,' he said turning to James. 'Now is not the time to plan an escape.'

0005 DAYS

CHAPTER 33

Mexico has some of the most mountainous terrain in the world. In the early 1500s, when Spanish conquistador Hernan Cortez was asked to describe Mexico, he is said to have crumpled up a piece of paper and set it on the table.

✢

Jimenez's spy, stationed outside the Hotel *Santa Maria* in a small white Renault reported that Mrs Cooper-Brown had checked into the hotel and had met a fellow *gringo* for drinks in the lounge. The two women had spent an hour or so chatting before going up to their respective bedrooms. He had no idea who the second woman was and although he had tried bribing the hotel's concierge for information, none had been forthcoming. The spy also reported that Mrs Cooper-Brown had been picked up at the airport by a chauffeur driven car with diplomatic number plates.

On the basis of the intelligence gathered by the Elite Corps from the abandoned ranch at *Los Alamos*, they planned to launch an assault on the monastery at *San Blas* to rescue the young British tourist, James

Cooper-Brown on the night of the 29th August. Major *Pedro Alvarado*, the officer in charge of operations, had pushed for an earlier attack but had been persuaded to postpone the rescue mission on account of the local *fiestas*. Orders from the offices of *Alejandro Mondragon* explicitly counselled against an assault at a time of religious observance.

'The potential for huge collateral damage is too high to risk,' is how the missive from the Ministry had been worded.

The mission would involve a small force of 20 paratroopers especially trained in mountain warfare who would be dropped onto the *sierra* under the cover of darkness for a pre-dawn raid. They were told to neutralise all enemy combatants, including *Julio Cesar*, a notorious former lieutenant of the late *Javier Ernesto Madrigal*. No prisoners were to be taken.

Virginia did not sleep a wink. Still suffering from jet lag and tormented by anxiety, she tossed and turned until the early hours of the 29th of August wondering what could possibly have happened to Piers. She thought about Eleanor and how afraid and lonely she must be. She had no desire to join Linda on a shopping spree around the city the following morning but at the same time had to agree that it might take her mind off more important issues for several hours and Linda was probably right. By the time they returned to the hotel in the evening, Piers and the boys would have turned up. She thought about her husband's deception and wanted to feel angry and let down but then was reminded that it had been no worse than her own secretive plans to raise the ransom without his knowledge. In the end, she reassured herself that both of them had had James' best interests at heart; their respective approaches to the situation had just been different. Eventually, at half past three in the morning she fell asleep unaware that outside her window on the street below, her movements were being tracked and her fate was being decided. As she slept the nightmare returned. Only this time, James was not grimacing. His face was twisted into an ugly scream, his eyes were red and he was pointing the gun at an unseen assailant. A spot of blood on his white shirt gradually grew into a deep purple stain and his stubbly face and matted blonde hair were filthy.

From as far away as five miles they could see the fireworks exploding above the village.

'Shit!' exclaimed Marty as Loftie drove out of a hair pin bend and Santo *Tomas* came into view below them.

'There's a *fiesta* in the village tonight. *Madrigal's* men will be crawling all over the place.'

'A crowded village might work out in our favour,' Loftie commented. 'We will be less conspicuous.'

As they descended into the valley they could hear loud explosions and the distant sound of a band. Behind the hamlet loomed the *sierra*.

'The monastery is somewhere up there,' said Matthew to Piers pointing up.

As they approached the village, it became clear that they would have to park some distance from the square. Lines of ancient pick-ups and cars crammed the pavements and the main street was strewn with straw and horse manure. They parked the two cars behind a large fruit truck and geared up. They put on their mountain boots, checked the channel on their radios and night optical devices, both of which they would need once they got off the path and deep into the woods. Their weapons, ammunition and climbing equipment were packed away in their rucksacks which weighed in at 80 pounds per man.

'We will draw less attention to ourselves if we split up,' suggested Piers. 'I'll go with Loftie, Marty you go with Matt. We will rendezvous at the trailhead gate just beyond the church in 20 minutes.' As they were locking their vehicles, a group of *Charo* cowboys dressed in large *sombreros*, tight studded trousers, boots and spurs, rode by followed by a band of pilgrims dressed in white carrying a huge float mounted with effigies of various saints. They were accompanied by a brass band. The sound was deafening but no one paid the four *gringos* any attention. The streets were now thronging with people. Many wore ghoulish masks and straw hats and elaborate, colourful ceremonial costumes. Stalls lining the streets brimmed over with fruit and regional dishes, local arts and crafts, confectionary and numerous *piñatas* swayed in the night breeze. The air was filled with the smell of cordite and roasting meat and the sound of music, laughter and shouting. Children ran about with sticks of candy floss and corn on the cob and withered old *indigenas* in brightly coloured tunics sat on rush mats selling embroidered purses, and jewellery. Before splitting up the *gringos* stopped at a stall and bought straw hats, bandanas and *serapes* which they donned over their shoulders, obscuring their packs. They looked like hunchbacks, blending in perfectly with the rich pageantry of the occasion as they made their way slowly through the crowds towards the square. On nearing the church, the crush of people thickened and the band struck up. Many of the men carried pistols and were now firing them into the air. Loftie gestured to Piers to head towards the alley next to the church. Marty and Matthew were nowhere to be seen. They pushed their way through the masses and made their way up the narrow passage that led to the trailhead. Half way up, a group of children ran down carrying balloons on strings and pushed the two men to the sides, shrieking with laughter as they passed. The men reached the gate and ditched their disguises and a few minutes later were joined by Matthew and Marty brandishing sticks of pink candyfloss.

'We couldn't resist!' said Marty smiling.

*P*epe, *Carmela* and James sat laughing on the bench together. It was now one o'clock in the morning but the party showed no signs of slowing down. The music got louder and the number of people milling around in the cloisters, singing and dancing, had swelled to more than 80.

'James,' said *Pepe* leaning over and hugging him tightly, 'I believe it was fate that brought you to Mexico and to us! How else would we have met? A rich educated *gringo* like you and two *campesinos* like us: one of them a scarred *maricon* who dreamed all his life of being a woman and the other a truly beautiful *indigena*,' he said gesturing to *Carmela*.

'I think you are right,' said James smiling, 'though I would have preferred to have met you on a bus or in a market not under these circumstances,' he said laughing.

'But you would not have spoken to us,' *Carmela* replied. 'What would we have in common?'

'Believe it or not, when I was travelling by myself I used to strike up conversations with all kinds of people, not just other travellers,' James replied.

'Yes, but I would have been too shy to talk to you,' *Carmela* answered him smiling affectionately. 'This way we were thrown together, we had no choice but to meet each other. My mother once told me that God works in mysterious ways and I believe her now. He brings people together often briefly and with no apparent reason or motive in the most unlikely of circumstances. When would I have met a woman like *Tere Saldariaga*, God rest her soul, or a handsome *gringo* like you? I have been blessed in so many ways.'

James was quiet for a moment. 'Before coming to Mexico I led a very narrow existence and knew only people like myself, from similar backgrounds. Yet now I find I have more in common with you two than any of my friends back home,' and summoning up the courage he leant over and kissed *Carmela* on the lips. She responded, and putting her arm gently around his neck, she pulled him closer.

0004 DAYS

CHAPTER 34

Mexico has more public fiestas than any other Latin American country

✠

After two miles of steep climbing, Matthew led them off the track and they began the long descent to the waterfall. From their previous reconnoitre they knew it would be too dangerous to stick to the path leading up to the monastery and that there were sentries posted all along it at different stages. Four inches of rain had fallen on the *Sierra* in as many days and the steep sides of the canyon were strewn with huge boulders and fallen trees, dislodged by landslides. Despite all being in their early fifties, the four men were fit and scrambled briskly down the slope, negotiating obstacles with ease and a further hour of walking brought them to the top of the waterfall.

'As you can see,' shouted Loftie over the din of the cascading waters, 'we will have to ascend the waterfall with James on our return. We can assume that the track down will be littered with tangos.'

They dropped their rucksacks and took out the climbing gear: harnesses, the abseil rope, ascendeurs, some prussik loops and a figure of eight.

'Once we are all down, we will leave the rope in place and attach the ascendeurs. If James is ill or injured, it will be a nightmare getting up!' said Matthew soberly.

'Let's cross that bridge when we come to it,' Piers responded soberly.

They attached the rope to a thick pine tree before Loftie lowered himself over the edge of the cliff and into the void above the foaming waters of the waterfall. Seconds later he was down and calling for the rope and figure of eight to be hauled up. It took less than five minutes for the four men to descend the waterfall and gather up their gear. By now they were drenched in the icy cold spray coming off the torrent. Piers was the first into the bracing water which rose up circling around his waist, the fast current threatening to drag him down river and over the edge of a second fall. He found some sure footing on the river bed among the rocks and waded across to the opposite bank followed by Marty, Matthew and Loftie. They were cold and wet but numbed by the adrenaline now coursing through their veins. Again they dumped their sacks and took out their weapons, ammunition, and their NODS which they checked thoroughly. They were carrying some impressive hardware. Each man had a shortened version of the M16 assault rifle, a Glock pistol and a SOG knife in addition to flash-bangs and grenades. Loftie was also armed with an Accurac AW50 sniper rifle, (with a range of 2,000 yards) scope and bipod which were strapped in a green canvas bag to the top of his rucksack. These he would assemble on the approach to the monastery.

By the time they reached the top of the canyon, the dark forbidding walls of *San Blas* were in view silhouetted by the grey dawn and they could hear loud *ranchero* music, laughter and shouting.

'Damn it!' Piers whispered. 'Seems like they are celebrating the *fiesta* here too!'

'That's good,' responded Matthew. 'That means the last thing they will be expecting is a raid. Hopefully some of the men might be drunk and in no mood to fight.'

'The risk of collateral damage could be huge,' interjected Marty.

'That can't be helped,' said Piers coldly. 'Our first objective is to get James out at any cost.'

They found an overhanging boulder which gave them some cover and began preparing for the assault.

'We will stick to the same plan,' said Marty. 'Loftie, you find a good sniper hide and radio in your location. I will then join him,' he went on addressing Matthew and Piers, 'and cause a diversion to get you guys in over the wall and onto the roof giving you time to search and sweep the place for James. Once you are out with

James, Loftie and I will cover you until you are into the woods. We will rendezvous at the waterfall.'

'Make sure you are all switched on to channel 4,' Matthew reminded them. Loftie unbuckled the green canvas bag from the top of his rucksack and began assembling the rifle. He took out the stock and attached the barrel, butt, scope and bipod and adjusted the lens. He then inserted the 30 round clip. He slung his M16 over his head and around his shoulder, put on his rucksack and set off up the steep scree to the monastery. The other three waited in silence, checking their equipment, their breath forming tortured shapes in the chilly air. No one spoke. Far below them they could hear the rush of water over the fall and above them the din from the party. Within ten minutes Loftie had found the ideal hide among a pile of logs to the south side of the monastery from where he could observe the entrance to the building, the tower and walls. He then re-arranged the logs to give him cover and to set up his rifle in place. After nestling himself into position he spent several minutes scanning the target area for tangos. Just outside the monastery's main gate stood a group of five people: three women and two men. The men wore jeans and white shirts and straw hats and held AK47 assault weapons nonchalantly in their hands as they smoked and chatted with their girlfriends. Loftie then scanned the tower where he spotted two armed guards and a Gatling gun resting on the parapet. Next he quickly surveyed the rest of the building, noting three sentries on the roof and two others patrolling the outside wall. He concluded that there must be as many guards inside the building and sentries on the other side of the monastery which was hidden from view. That made a total of 20 armed combatants. The four former commandos would have their work cut out for them even if some of the tangos were drunk and in no mood for a fight. He got Matthew on the radio and briefed him with the intelligence, providing him with his precise GPS coordinates. Five minutes later, Marty had joined him.

'Sounds like a bunch of people inside that place,' Marty commented, nodding in the direction of the monastery. 'We need to get as many of them out of there so that Piers and Matthew can sweep it without too much enemy fire power coming their way. I say we lob a couple of flash bangs towards the entrance there, cause a bit of a stir, see what the response is and then follow it with grenades and heavy gunfire to take down as many tangos as we can. Whilst I am engaged in that, you neutralise the sentries. I will then join the boys inside.'

They radioed Matthew to say they were ready and in place.

Inside *San Blas, Cesar, Andres* and *Joaquin* who were all now well soaked, were scheming again.

'The Elite Corps did the work for us!' said *Joaquin* laughing. 'The sewer rat had it coming to him – someone should have stepped on *Madrigal* years ago and broken his puny little neck!' he continued.

'You say that now *Joaquin*, but much as I despised the man, he was ruthless and cunning and more intelligent than the three of us put together. How do you think he survived for so long and became so powerful? Anyway, he is not a problem now,' *Andres* said puffing on his cigar.

'With *Jimenez* with us, we can combine operations and set our sights on *Sinaloa*. They're a mess up there. *Puentes* is gone and they are all fighting for leadership. I say leave them to it. They can kill each other and then we will move in,' *Cesar* added, smiling menacingly. '*Jimenez* tells me he and his banker friend are planning on stealing our ransom money. It's peanuts anyway and a small price to pay for having the old man on our side. Give it 18 months and we will arrange a little accident for him. Get *Casablanca* to do the job and throw in an extra $500,000 to tie up any loose ends like this banker fuck!'

'So what are you going to do about the *gringo* boy?' *Andres* asked *Cesar*.

'I will waste him myself tomorrow. It will give me great pleasure. I'll tell him his parents are being whacked too. That will add some spice to his misery!' he said laughing and downing a shot of *tequila*.

0003 DAYS

CHAPTER 35

The Tijuana, Beltran, Gulf, Juarez, Sinaloa and Zetas Cartel: these are just some of the many criminal organisations fighting to monopolise the lucrative narcotics market in Mexico.

✞

Piers and Matthew scouted around the back of the monastery where the ground gave way to the steep sides of a precipice and decided this was the best place to scale the walls. Matthew took out the folding grappling hook, screwed the two serrated blades together and then clipped 30 feet of climbing rope into it with a karabiner. They removed their SOG knives from their backpacks and attached them to their utility belts along with their side arms and ammunition. Matthew slung his assault rifle over his head and shoulder and threw the hook up over the 15 foot stone wall, before trying the rope. It held. They radioed Marty to inform him that they were in place and to begin the diversion. They would take the sound of gunfire and the flash bangs as their cue to begin their rescue mission.

'On the count of three, I'll throw the first flash bang and you begin taking out the sentries. The boys are ready to go,' Marty whispered to Loftie as they lay behind the log pile.

'Roger that,' replied Loftie as he sighted in his first target in the church tower catching the man's head in the cross hairs of his scope. He breathed in and out steadily, his finger touching the trigger almost imperceptibly. Three was the only number he heard Marty call out followed seconds later by the sound of a huge explosion, shouting and screaming and gunfire being returned in the general direction of the log pile. He squeezed the trigger, saw the guard falling back and moments later had taken out the second guard and was targeting one of the sentries on the roof. By now Marty was on his feet and firing furiously into the group standing outside the Monastery's entrance. There were dozens of people piling out of the main gate and straight into his line of fire. The noise of grenades exploding, rapid gunfire, screams and shouting was deafening but Loftie remained focused, almost oblivious of the mayhem around him. He sighted in his third target and squeezed the trigger. The bullet ripped off the side of the man's head and he fell off the wall and over the cliff disappearing into thin air. The two remaining guards were alerted and kneeling on the narrow ledge at the top of the wall, they returned fire. Hundreds of bullets thudded into the ground next to the two *gringos* and into the log hide sending up splinters of wood into the air. Loftie kept calm even though bullets were whistling past his ears. As one of the guards stood up to fire down on the pair, Loftie caught him in the neck, sending him reeling back where he fell onto the roof, his life bleeding out him.

'One more to go!' the Scotsman said to himself. The guard was firing maniacally towards Marty from a kneeling position. Loftie aimed just above his head and when the guard paused to reload a clip into his AK47, he took the shot. It caught the man in his upper arm with such force that it sent him 15 feet off the wall where the hard ground finished the job.

With Piers covering him from the bottom, Matthew took the cue and began scaling the side of the monastery and two minutes later found himself standing on a terracotta tiled roof just below the lip of the wall. Bending down, he silently signalled to Piers to come up.

Meanwhile Marty and Loftie were engaged in a savage fire fight. Leaving the sniper rifle resting on the bipod, Loftie had jumped over the wood pile with his M16 and was firing at the string of tangos, taking up positions in the stables and outhouses.

On reaching the top of the wall, Matthew and Piers had a clear view of the cloister below them and the layout of the interior of the building where there was a central courtyard and fountain and various rooms opening out onto it. The party had well and truly ended and the empty courtyard was strewn with broken crockery, upturned tables and chairs and cauldrons of spilt soup and punch. In the shadows and cowering behind pillars and columns and in half open doorways they could see the shadows of heavily armed men waiting and no doubt guarding their valuable hostage. Somewhere down there, in one of those rooms was James.

With Loftie covering him and blazing his way towards the main gate, Marty took down anyone in his path. He didn't have time to think or even see if they were men women or even children for that matter. If it moved; he shot it and not just once, until it stopped moving. Reaching the open gate, he withdrew the pin of a grenade and threw it into the cloister before charging inside the walls. Piers and Matthew had already begun clearing and sweeping the rooms. The first one they had entered was the kitchen. It was empty. As they were emerging from it back into the cloister, a huge man wielding a rifle by its barrel lunged forward through the semi darkness at Matthew. He was clearly drunk with little co-ordination but the butt of the weapon caught Matthew hard on the side of the head knocking him out and sending him reeling onto the stone flags of the cloister. Raising his weapon again to deliver the killer blow to the top of Matthew's head, Piers moved out of the kitchen just in time and shot the man at point blank range in the face. Blood splattered all over the walls covering Piers' clothing in a huge dark stain. He quickly bent down and grabbing his friend by the scruff of the neck, hauled him back into the kitchen and closed the door behind him. He was on his own now.

Julio Cesar and his mistress were just getting into bed when they heard gunfire. Clad only in his underpants, *Cesar* pushed *Lourdes* under the bed and grabbing his pump action shotgun opened the door and ran down the cloister towards James' cell. When James later recalled the horrifying events of that bleak night, they seemed to unfold in slow motion. He had just been escorted back to his room by *Pepe* and the door had been locked, when they heard the first explosion. Seconds later, the door was blown apart and James saw *Cesar's* spectral figure standing under the lintel, his gun raised. And then *Pepe* stood up and threw himself forward towards the barrel of the Persuader and a second later a deafening shot rang out and *Pepe* landed on the other side of the room with a sickening thud. The gunshot had ripped through his chest, peppering his heart and lungs.

'No! No!' James heard himself scream, though his voice sounded curiously detached from his body. The next thing he knew, he had grabbed the gun and was forcing it up towards the ceiling whilst *Cesar* frantically tried to slide two more cartridges into the breach.

As the barrel went up, James rammed the heel of his hand into the Mexican's face slamming it hard against the wall and then bending low he charged into his midriff whereupon *Cesar* doubled over, the gun still in his hand and the two men fell sideways down onto the floor. *Cesar* was the first to his feet and managed to load another cartridge, when James kicked him hard in the knee sending *El Jefe back* onto the bed. There was a third blast as *Cesar* squeezed the trigger and part of the ceiling caved in bringing loose canes, adobe and plaster down into the room which was now filled with smoke and dust. Stunned and dazed, James was slow to move and as he was pulling himself up, leaning on the end of the crude wooden bed, *Cesar* grabbed the gun, slid a fourth cartridge into the breach and aimed it at James's head. He was a split second away from squeezing the trigger, when Piers appeared in the shattered doorway and fired a full clip into the cell. *Cesar* was lifted into the air by the force of the blast from the M16, the hail of bullets puncturing him like a sieve and he fell in a tangled heap by the side of the bed.

'Son!' Piers screamed into the smoke and dust and grabbing James by the arm pulled him out of the wreckage and into the cloister.

With Marty behind a large ornamental barrel just inside the entrance to the monastery, Loftie was left to provide cover fire as more tangos appeared from the outhouses and the pathway leading down to *San Blas*. He retreated to the log pile and bending down on his left knee shot into the stream of guards piling out of the barn and into his line of fire. Inside, the courtyard was deserted and then Marty spotted Piers and James stumbling towards him out of one of the rooms.

'Where's Matt?' Marty shouted over.

'He is unconscious in the kitchen. Cover me until I am out of here and then you and Loftie extract him as quickly as possible – we'll rendezvous at the waterfall!' Piers replied.

'Dad!' James shouted into his father's ear above the cacophony of gunfire, 'I can't leave without the girl; *Carmela*, she's completely innocent – they will kill her!' he shrieked.

'James, we don't have time – listen to me, we've got about three minutes. If we are not off this hill *pronto* we are all going to die. Do you hear me?' but James was already pushing his father away and running back towards the cloister.

'James!' Piers shouted back and turned to follow him.

James ran past the kitchen, past his own room where *Pepe* lay dead under a fallen beam, until he reached the third room along.

'*Carmela*!' he bellowed as he forced open the flimsy door which had been locked from the outside. At first he didn't see her in the gloom. As his eyes focused he noticed a figure under the bed clothes. The pillow was covered in a large red stain, a stream of black hair flowed out over the side of the bed. '*Carmela!*' he shrieked again, but there was no answer, no movement. He pulled back the sheets and lying on her back, her big brown eyes wide open, her soft lips slightly parted, showing her pearly white teeth, was *Carmela*, a jagged gash across her neck where her throat had been cut.

0002 DAYS

CHAPTER 36

*Probably the largest change in the entire history of
the Tzotzil people of Chiapas and the Tarahumara
of Chihuahua is happening today, as they are
being forced to abandon their traditional lands
to make way for logging companies.*

✝

For almost eight hours they drove in silence. They
were exhausted, filthy and covered in blood. At
Midday they stopped at a service station outside
Tepoztlan, 25 miles from Mexico City and finding the
toilets, they stripped off, washed down, changed and
binned their old clothes. Marty bought some soft drinks,
sandwiches, bottles of water and several chocolate
bars and then they hit the road again, their GARMIN
SATNAV directing them to the Hotel *Santa Maria* in
downtown *Polanco.* It was the 29th of August 2003. Their
faces were blank and pale with shock, their thoughts, a
nightmare of blood and noise and pain, punctuated by
the sound of endless gunfire. Marty drove whilst Loftie
sat with James in the back, their heads resting against
the window, their eyes expressionless as they passed
through grey, featureless shanties.

Piers had followed his son back into the cloister and found him moments later kneeling by the side of a bed, sobbing uncontrollably. A beautiful young woman lay dead under the covers. Kneeling down, Piers had put his arms around James and whispered gently.

'There is nothing we can do for her now son. We need to go. Think of your mother and Eleanor!'

With James still weeping and holding on to his father's shoulder and rucksack they had moved stealthily out of the cloister and crossed over to where Marty had been covering them. Loftie was still engaged in a chaotic fire-fight just outside the gate providing enough of a diversion for the Cooper-Browns to sneak along the wall and run for the cliffside. Jogging now in front of Piers, James had made it over, sliding down the muddy scree into the thick undergrowth below. But his father had not been so fortunate. A tango had climbed back into the tower and taking control of the Gatling gun, spotted the fleeing pair and opened fire, cutting Piers to pieces as he ran across the short stretch of wasteland at the edge of the *barranco*. Marty meanwhile had gone to retrieve Matthew Waterman from the kitchen when he encountered three more tangos. With his M16 out of bullets, he pulled out his remaining grenade and threw it at the advancing trio. The explosion blew him off his feet but killed the last guards in the building. He located the kitchen, pulled Matthew to his feet and employing a fireman's lift hauled his friend onto his back. With only his Glock to defend himself and bent double he made his way out of *San Blas* towards the wood pile where he found Loftie lying on his back, reloading his assault rifle.

'Go, go!' Loftie screamed at Marty. 'I will cover you!'

McGregor was kneeling once again and firing at the guard in the bell tower. The first few shots missed, ricocheting off the stone buttresses but then a bullet caught the sentry in the neck and he went down. Leaving his sniper rifle, Loftie ran for the cliff edge and threw himself over, where he rolled down the scree into a thicket. He heard shouting behind him, some horses neighing and the clatter of hooves on cobbles.

'*Andres*, take four men and search the woods,' shouted *Joaquin*. 'I will head down the track. There is nowhere for them to go!'

Loftie slid down the scree and mud to the overhanging boulder where the four men had taken shelter less than an hour before. Below, snaking their way through the trees, he could just make out Marty, Matthew and James 200 yards away. They were about a mile from the waterfall. Loftie dumped his rucksack, taking only his car keys, SOG knife, M16, his last grenade and his Glock, he ran down through broken trees and boulders to join them.

'I can't carry Matthew for much longer,' said Marty breathing heavily when Loftie had caught up with him. He was sweating profusely and was red in the face. 'He is still unconscious and weighs a fucking ton.' Loftie looked at James and saw an emaciated, gangly youth with a mop of shoulder length blonde hair and scraggly beard. He noticed the hideous scar on his forehead. He was filthy and covered in blood.

'Piers is dead,' Loftie whispered into Marty's ear. 'Don't tell the boy yet,' he said before turning to James.

'I am Loftie,' he said introducing himself. 'We will talk later. For now, we are all fighting for our lives and you have got to play your part.' He handed James his Glock.

'Ever used one of these before?' he asked the shocked young man. James confessed that he had not.

'Just aim and fire,' Loftie instructed. 'Now, come on we need to get up that waterfall.' He and Marty grabbed Matthew between them and dragged him down the slope behind them. The going was steep and slimy and they slipped constantly. The sun was almost up and behind them they could hear men speaking in Spanish. They could now see the fall below them and the deafening waters of the river as it cascaded down the hillside.

'There is no way we will get Matthew up there!' said Marty to Loftie shouting above the noise of the thundering torrent. 'We will have to scramble further down river and find an alternative crossing.'

'You take James,' said Loftie nodding in the young man's direction. 'I'll deal with these goons that are following us. Leave Matthew with me!'

Loftie hauled Matthew's inert body behind the roots of a fallen tree and crouched down beside him. He reloaded the M16, pulled his one remaining grenade from his pocket, putting it on the ground in front of him, stuck his knife into the tree trunk and waited. Thirty seconds later, a solitary tango came into view above him. Loftie breathed in and out steadily, waited for the man to pass him and then, holding his SOG knife by its serrated blade, between his thumb and first finger, he aimed the handle at the back of the man's head and threw the knife, flicking his wrist forward at the last moment. The SOG arched silently through the air and found its mark in the back of the man's neck penetrating through his throat where the blade emerged on the other side just below his Adam's apple. Silently Loftie retrieved his bloody knife and retreated to the fallen tree and moments later, three more men appeared, stepping down the muddy slope cautiously, cursing to themselves. Once again, hidden behind the tangled roots of the tree, Loftie waited. He picked up the grenade, withdrew the pin and threw it at the men just as they were passing. The huge explosion blocked out their agonising screams as shrapnel, clods of earth and shrubbery flew through the air. Lying dead on the sodden ground surrounded by debris, his right leg blown off and half his head missing, was *Andres Calderon*, one of Cesar's right hand men, still dressed in a suit.

Loftie picked up his M16, sheathed his knife and bent down to check Matthew's pulse. There was none. His face was deathly white and a thin trickle of blood and a clear fluid were running out of his right ear. He was dead. The trauma caused by the blow from the rifle butt had resulted in a massive brain haemorrhage from which the former commando never recovered.

'Shit!' Loftie cursed to himself and sighed deeply. He took his friend's side arm, grenades and knife from his utility belt and then rolled Matthew's body down the steep side of the precipice and into the swollen river below and watched for a moment as the current swallowed it up.

The Scotsman from Glasgow eventually caught up with Marty and James a mile above *Santo Tomas de los Platanos*. They were soaking wet, covered in mud and exhausted. The three survivors circumnavigated the still, sleeping town via some fields of maize and found the jeeps parked behind the fruit truck where they had left them. Marty took the wheel and Loftie and James piled into the back as they sped away from the nightmare scene of carnage and mayhem.

'Did you come across any other tangos?' Loftie asked Marty wearily when they were out on the open highway and James had fallen asleep, slumped against the car door.

'One,' answered Marty with no emotion in his voice. 'James killed him.'

'Do you want to tell me what happened?'

'After crossing the river, we stumbled on another track and took it southwards. James was lagging behind; the poor guy was like a zombie, as if he was sleep walking. From nowhere I heard the sound of hoofs coming down the path above us, so I pushed James off the trail and down a steep embankment where we lay in the brush. The rider came into view. He was alone. He stopped and dismounted and tethered his horse to a tree and took out his shotgun from its saddle sleeve and stood there for a while silently, his gun over his shoulder. He removed a packet of cigarettes from his shirt pocket and lit up. And then he did a curious thing. Cupping his hands together he shouted. "*Gringo*, I know you are out there and I will find you and when I do, you will die like your father and that *indigena* bitch you loved so much," and he began laughing. It was as if he knew we were there; could smell us even.

Something stirred in James. I thought he was unconscious for a moment and then his eyes were wide open and he was alert as if a highly charged electric current was passing through him. He looked deranged; his eyes were bloodshot and full of hatred. He stood up and taking the Glock you had given him from his pocket, he frantically climbed the steep bank and started shooting and screaming at the man. He must have fired six shots, one after the other almost at point blank range, first into the tango's face and then into the horse. When he turned around and dropped the gun he was drenched in blood. He looked just like Piers!'

0001 DAYS

CHAPTER 37

On 1 January 1994, when the NAFTA free trade agreement became effective, Sub-commander Marcos led an army of Mayan farmers into eastern Chiapas, to protest against the Mexican federal government's mistreatment of the nation's indigenous people.

✝

Just as Marty, Loftie and James hit the road again after stopping at the service station, Virginia and Linda were sitting in *Sambournes* in *San Angel* and had just ordered cafe *Americanos*, when Robert's frantic call came through.

'Virginia where are you?' he said urgently.

'I am having coffee with Linda Schultz; we are still waiting for Piers. Why? Has something happened?'

'Virginia, listen to me carefully, whoever you are with!'

'Robert, you are scaring me now!'

'Listen!' Robert said again impatiently. 'You and Piers are in great danger. You must get yourself to the British embassy as soon as possible and stay there. Do you have an embassy driver?'

'Yes, I do, he is waiting outside. But tell me what's happening!'

'There's no time, Virginia. Please do as I say and get yourself to the embassy now! I've got to go,' and he hung up abruptly.

Fifteen minutes before Robert called Virginia, Edward Hutchinson phoned him from the Foreign Office. Virginia had left the Swinton's number with him before leaving for Mexico in case she needed to be contacted.

'Mr Swinton,' Hutchinson had said gravely, introducing himself. 'We believe the Cooper-Browns are in danger. I have just got off the phone with *Alejandro Mondragon*, the Mexican Interior Minister, who informed me that your contact at Dakota Holdings, a *Senor Tato Labastida,* is in fact a mole acting on behalf of the *Veracruz* drug Cartel. A recent intelligence report suggests that *Labastida* is planning to hijack the ransom drop and has contracted assassins to kill the Cooper-Browns. As we speak, the British Embassy and members of Mexico's Special Forces are trying to locate Piers and Virginia to get them to a safe house – most probably the embassy itself. They did not find them at the hotel and the embassy driver entrusted to escort the Cooper-Browns around the city is missing and not answering his mobile. Can you contact them and tell them to make their way immediately to the British embassy?'

'We have got to go,' said Virginia to Linda quietly. 'That was Robert, my brother in law. The British Embassy has said we are in danger, we have got to go there now!' she said rising from her seat and picking up her coat and handbag. Linda registered the pale, shocked expression on Virginia's face and got up and followed her. They paid for the coffees and made their way to the parking lot where their driver said he would wait. He was nowhere to be seen.

'We will get a taxi,' said Linda firmly, grabbing Virginia by the arm, as she flagged down a green and white Volkswagen Beetle making its way towards the taxi rank. They got in and Linda asked to be taken to the British Embassy.

'I don't know exactly where it is, but it's bound to be where all the other embassies are,' she told the driver in Spanish.

'*Si Senora*, I know exactly where it is. It's in *Reforma*,' and he sped away from the curb and into the heavy morning traffic.

At half past one in the afternoon, Marty parked the battered Jeep Cherokee in the underground lot beneath the Hotel *Santa Maria* and the three men went in search of Virginia.

'She is not here *Senores*,' the hotel receptionist informed them. 'They went out this morning.'

'They?' asked Marty in surprise.

'Yes, *Senora* Brown was with a friend, an American lady called Mrs Schultz, they said they were meeting their husbands here later and would be back at around four o'clock in the afternoon.'

Marty smiled wryly. 'Linda: my wife has found me!' he said to Loftie chuckling. 'Our troubles are not over yet then,' Loftie replied.

'I am Marty Schultz, Linda Schultz' husband,' Marty said producing his passport from his pocket. 'Are there any messages for me?'

The receptionist looked in a file and produced a note on which Linda's clear cursive handwriting was visible. *'Change of plan Hubby!'* was how it began. *'How were the horse ranches in Montana? Get lost along the way?'* it went on sarcastically. *'I thought I would keep poor Virginia company since that bastard husband of her's left her all alone to deal with everything! Are you two out of your fucking minds? Marty, you are no longer a GI Joe for Christ sake! You are a rancher married to me; remember? We will deal with this situation later. For the time being Virginia is my concern. I have taken her shopping to get her mind off things. We will be back around 4!'* and the note ended.

'Oh, *Senor* Schultz, here is another message for you, from a Mr Swinton. He called about half an hour ago,' the receptionist added.

Marty looked perplexed. He did not know any Swintons. He unfolded the paper and read the note.

'Thank you,' he replied putting it in his pocket. 'They are at the embassy,' he said turning to Loftie and James. 'Safe and sound. They will brief us about what's been going on when we get there.'

Virginia and Linda were met at the Embassy's reception by Sir Humphrey Phillipson, the British Ambassador and were taken to an empty conference room where they were briefed by Colonel Edmund Fortescue, the Military Attaché.

'We received the intelligence just in time,' he said reassuringly. 'The Mexican Secret Police have been surveilling *Labastida* and his associates for some weeks now. Of course this business with your husband, Mrs Cooper-Brown, will create one hell of a hornets' nest for us to deal with. His name was flagged up when he passed through immigration. He and his companions were spotted again by some off-duty policemen at a remote roadhouse on the way to *Santo Tomas* and the Mexican Secret Police were alerted. Mondragon is sympathetic but the opposition PAN party are asking all kinds of questions as to how foreigners could come onto Mexican soil and launch a thing like this. We are expecting something of diplomatic fallout to ensue.'

An hour later, they were joined by Marty, James and Loftie. It was a bitter sweet reunion. James spotted his mother through the plate glass doors of the conference room and couldn't stop himself from running forward, pulling the heavy door open and clutching her in a huge hug. There were tears streaming down his face.

'Oh Darling!' she said weeping, 'you are back again, you are alive and well!' and they hugged again refusing to let go. And then Virginia said 'So where's Dad?' She was smiling with relief, her cheeks wet with tears as she held on to her son.

James could not bring himself to say the words. There was a pregnant silence. 'Marty? Loftie?' Virginia said, the smile turning to a horrified frown. 'Where's Piers; and Matthew?'

'They are dead Virginia,' Marty said flatly. 'I am so sorry. They died saving James' life. They died saving us all,' he added.

OOOO DAYS

CHAPTER 38

✝

Loftie and Marty flagged down a taxi and asked to be taken to *Coyoacan*. When the driver, a rotund man with thinning hair and a goatee, realised that Marty spoke Spanish he tried to engage him in a conversation about martial arts films.

'*Senor*, do you like Bruce Lee?' he asked looking at the American through his rear mirror.

'I love Bruce Lee,' he continued, 'but I think the big *gringo* Steven Seagal is even better. Pow-pow,' uttered the driver as he punched the air with a karate chop, taking his hands off the steering wheel for an instant and narrowly missing a head on collision with a cement truck.

'That French guy, Jean Claude Van-Damme, they say he is a *pinche maricon*,' he went on.

Loftie and Marty ignored him and sat in silence, their private thoughts caught up in recent, tragic events. More than anything they felt angry.

'Marty, do you think men like us will ever see heaven after the things we have done?' Loftie said quietly. Marty looked at him in surprise. There was much he admired about Loftie and over the course of the last two weeks he had developed a real fondness for the gritty Scotsman. But never in a million years had he stopped to consider that his companion might have any spiritual inclinations. For his own part he justified the life he had chosen and his actions by convincing himself that he had been fighting a greater evil. As a child, growing up in a religious community outside Bakersfield, he had admired warriors like King David, Joshua and Gideon but it had been Saul of Tarsus, a man of violence and hatred, whose life had been dramatically turned around, that had most impressed him as an adult.

'Loftie, call me patronising, but I didn't think you thought that deeply,' he said laughing. 'But to answer your question, yes I do. It is not so much our actions that will determine whether we get to heaven or not. It's our faith and accepting who we are and what God has done for us. We have to believe that even men like *Cesar* and *Madrigal* can be saved by grace at the very last moment; between the stirrup and the ground as it were. Otherwise we are all fucked!' and the two men were quiet again.

They asked to be dropped off in *Coyoacan's* central plaza. It was 10 o'clock at night on August 29th 2003 and the stall holders were beginning to pack up their wares and head home.

It was Robert Swinton who had provided them with *Labastida's* address. After the meeting at the embassy,

Linda, James and Virginia had been taken to a safe house in *Vireyes*. Shortly afterwards, Robert had called her. She was still in shock and had asked Linda to take the call.

'I feel so guilty,' Robert said. 'I had no idea *Labastida* was corrupt.'

'Mr Swinton, you did everything you could in good faith to help Virginia and I am sure, that despite what has happened, she will be forever grateful. But your role in this affair is now over. My husband will need to have *Labastida's* address and contact details.'

Calle San Pedro was located down a cobbled street to the right of *Coyoacan's* huge baroque church. Here there were spacious mansions hidden behind old stone walls covered in ivy and large imposing gates with intercoms. They found number 25 easily enough, towards the end of the street off a sweeping cul-de-sac. Inside the 15 foot wrought iron gate, they could see a small cabin where a guard in a black peak cap and uniform sat, his back to them looking at a TV monitor. The two men noticed the CCTV cameras on the gate and along the walls and presumed there were more inside. *Labastida's* house was set back 200 yards behind a fountain. It was a huge, red brick building, ostentatious rather than elegant, with large windows and imposing columns framing the front door.

Marty pressed the button on the intercom whilst Loftie concealed himself by the side of the wall.

Presently the guard stepped out of the hut and walked towards the gate.

'How can I help you *Senor*?' he asked.

Marty explained that he was an American tourist and was looking for the former residence of Leon Trotsky.

'*Senor*,' replied the guard, 'It will be closed now!'

'I realise that,' said Marty smiling, 'but I wanted to come back tomorrow to see it and wondered if you could point me in the right direction,' and he stuck his hand through the gate with the map.

'Of course *Senor*,' answered the man stepping closer to the gate. When he was a foot away, Loftie moved from the side of the wall and pointed his Glock and silencer at the man's head.

'Do exactly what we tell you to do,' said Marty firmly, 'and you will not get hurt. Put your left hand on your head and take the keys in your right hand and unlock the gate. Keep your eyes on me at all times.'

The guard was clearly terrified and did what he had been instructed to do. By now, Marty had put away the map and he too was armed with a black Glock. Once inside the grounds, they closed the gate and ordered the man into the hut where they bound his hands and feet before lashing him to his chair with thick black duct tape.

'Is Mr *Labastida* at home?' Marty asked him. The guard nodded. 'Who else is in the house?'

'There is just the cook and *Senor Labastida*. The *Senora* went out to a party. She will not be back until late.'

'What about dogs? Are there any dogs around?'

'No *Senor*, Mr *Labastida* does not like dogs.'

'Thank you,' replied Marty before gagging him with more tape and locking him in a utility cupboard and disabling the cameras. 'Let's do this!' he said turning to Loftie. 'We need to be out of here in 10 minutes.'

They drew down the blinds over the windows and locked the door behind them and made their way up through the gardens to the back of the house. Here they found a large kidney shaped pool basking in delicate lighting, surrounded by sun loungers and a large round glass table and heavy metal chairs. Expansive French windows looked into a spacious living room with four cream coloured sofas. There were oil paintings on the wall, a huge flat screen television and a butler's tray with glasses and crystal decanters. A man was sitting on one of the sofas, his right arm draped casually over the back, watching basketball on the cinema sized screen. Loftie and Marty could hear the commentator's muffled voice.

It was all over in seconds rather than minutes. Whilst Loftie covered him, Marty picked up one of the heavy chairs and swinging it in an arc, threw it straight at the French windows which shattered on impact. *Labastida* was on his feet in an instant, mouth open, staring at the two men across the sofa as they stepped over the broken glass and into the rom. He was wide eyed like a rabbit paralysed in a car's headlights. There was silence for a moment. And then Loftie spoke coldly.

'Are you *Tato Labastida*? yes or no?' he said menacingly.

'Yes I am,' replied the man as he began to wet himself.

'Because of your actions and those of evil men like you, my closest friend is dead. Not only that, you planned to kill his wife and son and steal the ransom money. You messed with the wrong men and now you are going to hell!'

Loftie walked slowly towards the terrified banker and shot him twice in the head sending him reeling backwards over the mahogany coffee table where he lay slumped on the floor.

Three minutes later they released the guard.

'You will need to find another job,' Marty said to him. 'Listen carefully because I am only going to say this once!' The guarded nodded. 'You will sit here for five minutes and do nothing,' Marty warned him. 'If we hear any police sirens in that time, we will come back and kill you, your family and your friends. Is that clear?' The guard nodded again.

They tucked their weapons back into their belts, closed the gate behind them and moments later flagged down a green taxi back to the safe house.

***

On the 7th of July, 2004, a year to the day from when he had been taken, James returned to Mexico. He stayed for one night in the Hotel Montecarlo where the management refused his payment.

'It is a pleasure to see you back again in Mexico, *Senor.* We are truly sorry for what happened to you and your family,' the concierge said to him as he handed him his key.

The following morning, rising early, he caught the bus from the city's southern terminal to *Oaxaca* where he spent two days revisiting old haunts. He returned to the internet cafe opposite the post office to email his mother back home in England. He was told by the cafe's owner that the pretty Californian girl he had chatted to 12 months before, no longer worked there.

Early in the morning on his fourth day in the State of *Oaxaca,* he found himself climbing the track up to *San Blas* from the small village of *Santo Tomas.* The village was quiet; the *fiesta* season had not begun yet. A young woman sweeping outside her house informed James that the old monastery had been boarded up and lay partly in ruins following a massive aerial assault on the area by Mexican Special Forces the year before.

'They cleaned out this part of the *Sierra,*' she said flicking at a leaf. She reminded James of *Carmela.* She had the same long black hair, wide animated eyes, high cheek bones and simple white dress.

'They killed and arrested dozens of men involved in the marijuana trade,' she went on. 'Ranches were razed to the ground and whole hillsides went up in flames. It is safe once again to walk in the *Sierra, guerro,*' she said smiling. 'If you are lucky you will see the butterflies. This year they have returned to the *oyamel* forests. My people call them the bringers of light and peace.'

James thanked her and began up the steep trail, a light daypack on his back. He stopped frequently in the morning sun to marvel at the view of rolling mountains and the thin line of the blue Pacific beyond and to take photographs. He passed the spot where he had shot the cowboy, but was surprised that he felt nothing. Memories came flooding back and tears ran down his face as reached the forbidding ruin after his four hour walk. The walls were black where fire had taken its toll. The fountain was empty and lay in a crushed heap of masonry. The entrance to the courtyard and cloisters was blocked and barricaded but through the slats he spotted the cell where he had been held, its roof now caved in. As he looked in, he recalled that terrible night which had begun so optimistically with the *fiesta*. He remembered how *Carmela* had confessed to being in love with him and felt a deep sadness and longing in his gut. He recalled the way he had held her tightly and how he had wanted that brief moment in time to last forever. He thought of his friend and companion *Pepe* and of the wonderful times they has spent together, cooped up in his cell. He could almost hear *Pepe's* infectious laugh and the sound of *Juan Gabriel's* voice coming out of the decrepit cassette player, singing *'Por todo tiempo'*. Weeds and poppies grew among the ruins and part of the tower had collapsed.

He walked around the building and finding a grassy bank, sat looking out over the hazy *Sierra Madre*. He heard a woodpecker banging against a tree trunk and the call of a kestrel. Placing his rucksack on the ground he sat for a while in silence and then he opened his bag and removed four small, simple wreaths of orange marigolds that a florist had made up for him in *Oaxaca*. One was for his godfather, Matthew Waterman: one was for *Pepe* who had saved his life, one was for his father, Lieutenant Colonel Piers Cooper-Brown and the last one was for *Carmela*. As the warm breeze picked up, he stood, said a quiet prayer and threw each wreath into the wind. As he turned to head back down to the village, an orange and black butterfly landed delicately on his hand, its paper thin wings twitching almost imperceptibly. 'The bringer of light and peace!' he said to himself and smiled.

Post Script

Virginia Cooper-Brown

On returning to Mosscombe, Virginia sold the family home and bought a small house in Reading, to be closer to her elderly mother.

Loftie McGregor

Loftie moved back to the Gorbals district of Glasgow where he opened a pub. He maintained regular contact with Marty Schultz, Virginia and James Cooper-Brown.

Marty Schultz

Marty and Linda sold their Californian horse ranch and spent two years travelling around the world in a Volkswagen camper van.

Lorenza Martinez

After Madrigal's death, Lorenza moved to Texas where she met and married a wealthy oil prospector.

Alondra Martinez

Alondra, Madrigal's eldest daughter, joined the PAN party. Political commentators predict that she will one day be Mexico's first female president.

Mike Espinetti

Mike continues to handle agents south of the U.S border. He has a picture of Monica Gonzalez on his desk in his Mexico City office.

Feliciano Hernandez

The ageing artist continues to paint. He also regularly lectures youth groups on the subject of Mexico's drug problem. He is an ardent campaigner for the legalisation of marijuana.

Federico Jimenez

The head of the *Veracruz* Cartel was gunned down by members of the Elite Corps as he was leaving his tropical retreat, three days after the raid on San Blas.

Charlotte Priestley

James and Charlotte met up for a coffee a month after James returned to the U.K. Charlotte asked James if he was interested in resuming their relationship. He declined. Charlotte moved out to New York shortly afterwards working for an advertising agency.

Lieutenant Piers Cooper-Brown

The Mexican government and the British Embassy arranged for Piers' body to be returned to England. He was buried in the church cemetery in Mosscombe

Pepe & Carmela

Pepe and Carmela were buried in a mass grave along with 82 other bodies retrieved from San Blas

The Elite Corps

The Elite Corps continues to combat drug related crime in Mexico

James Cooper-Brown

James turned down his place at Cambridge to study for a PHD and moved out to Oaxaca working for a Christian NGO.

El Fin

ACKNOWLEDGEMENTS

✠

Thank you to everyone who read the manuscript before it was published and advised me on how it could be improved.

A special thankyou goes to former U.S Navy Seals, Mitch and Chas, who gave me invaluable information and advice on the kind of ordnance, weaponry, resources and equipment used by commandos during operations.

REFERENCES

✤

Each Chapter begins with a statistic relating to some aspect of contemporary Mexican life relevant to the narrative.

*INEGI: Mexico's National Geographical Institute: produces maps etc

1: Wikipedia

2: Wikipedia: Timeline of the Mexican drug war

3: www.huffingtonpost.com/.../**mexico**-**guns**-arturo-sarukhan-us-**weapon**

4: en.wikipedia.org/wiki/Illegal_**drug_trade**

5: en.wikipedia.org/wiki/**Mexican_Drug**_War

7: www.depauliaonline.com/.../mexican-drug-cartels-this-is-our-war-too...

8: www.depauliaonline.com/.../mexican-**drug**-cartels-this-is-our-**war**-too...

9: www.huffingtonpost.com/.../missing-**immigrants**-mexico_n_200548...

10: en.wikipedia.org/wiki/**Mexican**_Drug_War

11: www.dolarian.com/.../body_july_2009_-_sept_2009. ht... - United States

13: select.cs.cmu.edu/code/graphlab/datasets/wikipedia/ wikipedia.../w3

14: en.wikipedia.org/wiki/**Mexican_Drug_**War

15: en.wikipedia.org/wiki/List_of_journalists_killed_ in_the_Mexican_Dr

16: askville.amazon.com › Miscellaneous › Popular News

17: en.wikipedia.org/wiki/**Mexican_**Drug_War

18: en.wikipedia.org/wiki/**Mexican_**Drug_War

19: en.wikipedia.org/wiki/**Mexican_**Drug_War

20: www.huffingtonpost.com/.../**mexican-drug-**violence-spi_n_...

22: www.globalpost.com/dispatches/.../no-reduction-mexico-**kidnappings**

23: www.huffingtonpost.com/2012/.../**mexico**-drug-war_n_2205415.ht...

24: local.sman3sda.sch.id/download/index.php?dir... of-**Mexico**...

25: economistsview.typepad.com/economistsview/ regulation/

27: usatoday30.usatoday.com/**new**s/world/story/2012... **mexico-bodies/**.../...

29: www.guardian.co.uk › News › World news › Mexico

30: blog.addictionhelpservices.com/category/binge-drinking/page/11/

31: en.wikipedia.org/wiki/**Mexican_**Drug_War

32: en.wikipedia.org/wiki/**Indigenous_peoples_**of_**Mexico**

33: www.planeta.com/ecotravel/**mexico**/mex**mountain**.
html

35: en.wikipedia.org/wiki/**Mexican**_Drug_War

36: en.wikipedia.org/wiki/Lacandon_Jungle

37: www.tumblr.com/tagged/zapatista-**army**-of-
national-liberation

GLOSSARY

✝

Alacran	Scorpion
Amigo	Friend
Apurate	Hurry up!
Barranco	Cliff/gorge
Barrio	Neighbourhood
Bienvenidos	Welcome
Caballos	Horses
Cafe de olla	Traditional Mexican coffee flavoured with spices
Calle	Street
Campesinos	Peasants
Cantina	Traditional Mexican bar
Casa de huespedes	Hotel
Centavo	A Mexican coin/100th of a peso
Charo	Mexican cowboys
Chicharon	Pork crackling
Chingaderos	Fucking idiots
Clinica	Clinic/surgery
Compadre	A close relative/friend
Comprende	Do you understand?
Corona	Crown

Coronel	Colonel
Curandero	Witch doctor
Coyotes	Prairie dog, jackal
Delincuente	Delinquent
Enchilada	A corn tortilla rolled around a filling
Fiesta	Party/traditional celebration
Fiesta de los muertos	Day of the Dead A traditional Mexican fiesta
Girasol	Sunflower
Huevos	Eggs
Hacienda	Large estate/farm/former plantation
Huipil	An embroidered, loose fitting garment commonly worn by Mexican indigenous people
Indigena	A native of Mexico
Jefe	Boss/chief
Gringo	Slang term for an American
Guerros	Blonde foreigners
Lancha	Motor boat
La Nacion	The nation/country
Los Ninos	The Children
Mal de ojo	Evil eye
Malinche	A Nahua woman who became Hernan Cortes' mistress/slang term for a traitor

Mariachi	Traditional Mexican musicians, originally from the state of Jalisco
Mendigos	Beggars
Mescal	Alcoholic beverage made from the Maguey cacti
Mucho gusto	You are welcome/with pleasure My pleasure
Oro	Gold
Paraiso	Paradise
Pendejo	Asshole/idiot
Pension	Small hotel
Peso	Mexican currency
Pinata	A hollow effigy made from clay or papier mache, filled with sweets
Pinche maricon	A derogatory term for a homosexual
Policia	Police
Plomo	lead
Pronto	Soon
Pueblito	Small town/village
Puta	Prostitute
Puton	Male prostitute
Ranchero	Ranch/country
Ranchito	Small farm/ranch/smallholding
Rio	River

Salsa	Sauce/Latin American dance
Serape	A long, blanket/shawl Often brightly coloured
Sevillana	Traditional, festive dance from Seville, Spain
Sierra	Mountains
Sol	Sun
Sombrero	Traditional Mexican straw hat
Sopa de fideo	Pasta soup
Tamales	A traditional dish made from corn dough wrapped around meat or chicken
Tipos	Types
Tortillas	Traditional Mexican flat bread made from maize
Vamonos Cabron	Come on, let's go!
Zapatistas	A rebel group named after Emiliano Zapata during the Mexican Revolution
Zocalo	Town square

Made in the USA
Charleston, SC
16 May 2013